I0726871

WORKBOOK PRESS LLC
187 E Warm Springs Rd,
Suite B285, Las Vegas, NV 89119, USA

Website: https://workbookpress.com/
Hotline: 1-888-818-4856
Email: admin@workbookpress.com

Ordering Information:
Quantity sales. Special discounts are available on quantity purchases by corporations, associations, and others. For details, contact the publisher at the address above.

ISBN-13:   978-1-960752-16-1 (Paperback Version)
                978-1-960752-17-8 (Digital Version)

REV. DATE: 02/21/2023

Cargo of Shorts

101 Short Stories for the Casual Reader

Michael Ignatius

To Agnieszka, Andrzej, and Marcin,

my three children from Poland.

The august achievements in your young lives are truly

admirable and more than an inspiration to me.

TABLE OF CONTENTS

Introduction

This work is simply a collection of a hundred and one short stories. They are meant to appeal to the casual reader. What is the "Casual Reader" you may ask? A valid question. Believe it or not, there are at least twenty types of readers classified in the literary world. None of them are called "Casual" explicitly. We are forging new territory here. So, what are those categories? Without going into too many details, here is the list, a brief synopsis, in no particular order from number one to twenty. They just always happen to fall out this way:

First there is the "Literary Snob" who only reads the classics. You get it.

The second is the habitual "Book Clubber." Just reads the books the club is reading. Again, you get the point.

Third is the "Partial Reader." The name speaks for itself. Never finishes a book.

Next is the "Series Junky." Getting more involved now. This is the reader who not only finishes every book she or he lays hands on, she or he can't even stand the thought of reading a standalone book.

Then there is "The Polygamist Reader." This type of reader doesn't discriminate. They will read everything and anything, regardless of genre or author. Somebody along the way taught them to do this and said it would make them smart.

Sixth on our list is the "The Reread Specialist." Once they fall in love with a book or a series, it will take a lot to get them to move on and try something else. Rather than trying a new book or author, they will just reread the same thing over and over. Hard to imagine.

That is followed by "The Physical Book Loyalist." These book lovers are addicted to the smell of old books, to the rustling sound of pages turned, and feel like nothing can ever replace the classical book, regardless of the benefits that come from modern technology, like e-books.

"The Digital Reader" is next. Like with anything else, the exact opposite of the physical book loyalist does exist. The digital reader has a completely different approach to reading than the aforementioned type. They like cheap books and can somehow read them on a tablet screen.

Then comes "The Spoiler Lover." Even though it's hard to imagine that there actually are people who do this, spoiler lovers have existed for decades. They are a special group of readers who prefer to find out how the book ends before reading it all.

Next comes "The Movie Adaptation Lover." No matter how enthusiastic these readers are, there is a big wave of opposition, as most readers will agree that the movies never do books justice and rarely rise to expectations.

Believe it or not, we are up to number eleven … which is, "The Nonfiction Lover." For some, the reading needs to be grounded in actual reality. The nonfiction lover will have a great time reading historical books or other factual materials most other readers would find boring or uninteresting.

Of course, they are followed by their direct opposite at number twelve, which is the "The Fiction Fanatic." On the other end of the scale, are those readers who want their books to take them to different universes and see their reading as an escape from reality. They appreciate an author's imagination and like to recreate in their minds the worlds they read about. Many introverts here.

Then there are "The Young Adults Lovers." Most adults nowadays lead hectic and often overwhelming lives. For some, the greatest escape is reading books that are destined for young adults. It is as if they are reverting back to much less complicated and interesting times.

A staple among the group is "The Emotional Reader." Whether it's appreciation for a good love story, a sense of accomplishment whenever the hero in a book manages to achieve his or her goals, or the overwhelming sadness of a tragic event from a drama novel, the emotional reader will resonate and will feel everything with a higher intensity than the average reader would. These are very popular.

They are followed by "The Fad Reader." Riding the wave of hype created around a book is something the fad reader thrives on. This kind of reader will read anything and everything other people read, simply because she or he wants to be a part of the hype.

Of course, there is always "The College Reader." While we don't encourage this habit, the college reader had to be mentioned in our list simply because of the large number of people who end up being one. There is a lot to read in college.

They are followed by "The Neurotic Reader." One of the most difficult types of readers, the neurotic reader, has a rule for every aspect of reading and will not stray from the course under any circumstances.

Then there is me. "The Writer-Reader." This kind of reader will take nothing at face value and will critique every aspect of a book she or he is reading. They will put themselves into the author's shoes and will state an opinion to anyone who is willing to listen. They love to predict where the plot will go.

Nearing the end of the list is "The Note Taker." While for most of us, reading is a relaxing way of passing the time, others take it a lot more seriously and want more than just to enjoy a book as entertainment. These people are the ones who want to learn everything that can be learned from a book and will make the best of their time spent reading it. They often write down or highlight all of the information they find interesting. You've seen these books. Half the pages are yellow.

Finally, at the list's end, there is the "The Vacation Reader." Many people love reading on holidays. No matter what the season. Seeing someone by the pool with a cocktail in one hand and a book in the other is not uncommon. However, the vacation reader only reads on holidays though.

So, as you can see, there is no known definition of "The Casual

Reader." That is because that type of reader, and hopefully you find yourself in this category, encompasses any and all of the above. Not formally, so as not to be cornered into a box, but at least generally speaking.

This book is entitled, *Cargo of Shorts: 101 Short Stories for the Casual Reader*. It is a collection of mostly short short stories (sometimes called flash fiction), and some not too short stories. All are especially suited for the casual reader as the subtitle suggests. So, sit back, relax and enjoy. Just turn the page.

Chapter 1

Ben's Battle

Ben accepted his mission out of love for his country. Parachuting behind enemy lines at night, he would blow up a strategic bridge, which would severely limit the enemy's ability to move about and close in on the allies. It would mark a turning point in the war. He would then escape to safety by hiking three miles as fast as he could to an awaiting jeep.

He had just planted the explosives on the support system of the bridge when he realized he was completely surrounded by the enemy who were quickly closing in. His plan of escaping into safety had now vanished. In order to accomplish his mission, he would have to detonate the bomb now! This meant, he would not only destroy the bridge, he would lose his life as well.

Could he do it? He wasn't sure. His stomach was tied in knots. His entire body throbbed. This would be the final decision he would make in his life. His entire life flashed before him in an instant. Again, he asked himself, saying aloud, "Could he do it? Would he do it?"

He made up his mind. He then gently placed his thumb on the switch. That's when he heard his mother's voice piercing the air, "Benny—it's time to come inside—dinner's ready."

Chapter 2

An Early Run

It's 5:30 am. The perfect time to put on those running shoes and go out for a jog while my family snoozes away. Those lazy bums!

Nothing beats warming up your body and getting into the rhythm of a good pace. My feet pound the pavement to the beat of the latest shuffled song in my earbuds. Peacefulness. Serenity all around me interrupted only by the trees rustling. My mind is still but for the low sound of the structured melody in my head. The sun yawns and begins to slowly flood the path before me with light. The rays are faint, probably because of the clouds, but the trees, houses, and bushes all stand at attention in our friendly neighborhood.

And the birds … wait … where are the birds? They're usually out by now.

I hear a faint pop as I pluck my earbuds out, and stop, standing there in silence.

No, no chirping, no singing, am I too early? Not even the flapping of wings … No, wait.

I look up at the clouds and see them for the flock of birds that they really are. The beating of their wings that I have mistaken for the rustling of trees.

Odd. Strange. Unusual. I should head back.

My phone's emergency alert goes off.

I start running back home.

Our town's sirens begin to sound.

Run!

Chapter 3

Alfred's Late to Work

Being hard-of-hearing Alfred didn't hear his alarm so he was already running late. No time for breakfast. He tried the door but it wouldn't budge.

Alfred yanked again on the doorknob, "Dang it!" He feared he would be late for work, and now he couldn't get the blasted door open. He recalled that one summer it had swelled with the humidity, sometimes lodging itself in its frame. Still, how hard should it be to open a door? He gave it a kick, pulled again with his admittedly scrawny arms, but it stayed stuck tight.

Alfred then went into the bedroom, ignoring Isabel who ignored him while she watched "The Price is Right" on the TV, not hearing a thing. Heading toward the room's only window, he judged that he could probably climb out if he pulled a chair over to stand on. First, he tried lifting the bottom lip of the window. Wouldn't budge. He banged on the frame a couple of times, tried again. "Dang it!" Alfred barked.

Next, he tried the window in Steward's room. Steward, a snoring lump beneath the covers, didn't move, and neither did the window.

On a mission now, Alfred marched down the hallway and turned right, the patio door in his sights. He pulled the handle left and smiled triumphantly. The shrilling of the alarm didn't phase him as he made a bee-line for the car, feeling around in his pocket for his keys. "Dang it!" Where had he put them? Hopefully, he didn't leave his keys locked inside the house.

As he came around the side of the house, the front door opened and Rita's slow, twangy voice called out, "Hey y'all, Alfred's escaped again!" Rita approached the old man and gently grasped his elbow, smiling affectionately as she coaxed him through the entrance of Old Saybrook Memory Care.

"Come on Alfred, let's go back inside and have a nice strong cup of coffee. I think it will be fine if you wait to go to work until tomorrow."

"Eh?" he said.

Chapter 4

Gunshots

He was about to fall asleep, his mind drifting in that place between consciousness and unconsciousness, when suddenly five loud cracks rang out. Gunshots!

Immediately fear gripped him as he snapped to, completely awake. He went to the open window where the sound had come from and looked down from the second floor to the street below and saw a man running with what looked like a gun in his hand. Instinctively, he ducked down as the man ran past. He then slowly raised his head above the window enough to see the man with the gun now running up the street.

Then there was another loud crack, just like the first ones, followed by two more consecutive shots that rang out in the night. This time it was from another source—a second man, chasing the first, with an obviously drawn gun in his hand. He stopped, almost directly below the window and fired another shot at the first gunman. Then the second gunman looked up toward the window where he was standing now, just frozen in fear. Their eyes met. The second man was starting to raise his arm with the gun as sirens were sounding nearby. Then he suddenly put the gun away and took off running.

Within seconds there were police cars swarming everywhere along the street just outside the window. The man observing it all from his bedroom was still stymied in fear but slowly became aware that the immediate danger had passed. The cops were here.

Feeling compelled to help in some way, he quickly dressed and headed for the door and stairs leading down to the street to tell the police what he had witnessed. As he stepped through the door leading to the street, a policeman yelled, "Stop! Stay right where you are and don't move! Keep your hands where I can see them!"

A second officer came over, gun drawn, and asked, "What were you doing?"

"I saw the whole thing from my bedroom window upstairs," was his muttering reply. "I was just coming down to tell you about it."

It was going to be a long night. Or was he just dreaming?

Chapter 5

Minding His Own Business

Jake was minding his own business, walking on the sidewalk in downtown Niantic, Connecticut, a quaint little beach town with lots of local joints to visit. Suddenly, a red Mustang screeched to a stop on the curb beside him and a big man jumped out of the passenger side. He was obviously angry and looked threatening as he dashed toward Jake. At a loss as to what was happening, Jake simply asked, "Can I help you?"

"You bet your ass you can help me! You thought you'd get off easy? Well, I'm here to tell you, you have no idea what's in store for you! I ought to take you out right here and now, but I promised Vinny I wouldn't. I'm just the messenger, tough guy!"

"What? What are you talking about?" inquired Jake.

"You know damn well! You sucker-punched my boss Vinny last night at the Night Owl club. Sent him to the hospital with a broken nose. Now he's coming after you!"

"I think you're mistaken," said Jake. "I was at home watching the game with my wife last night."

"Your wife? You mean widow. That's what she's gonna be when Vinny is through with you!" With that, the unknown man shoved an envelope in Jakes face. "Read it and weep, you bastard!"

Cautiously, Jake took the envelope away from his face and opened it up. Inside was a note. He unfolded the note and read it. It simply said: "By this time tomorrow you or somebody you love will be missing a body part. You messed up my nose, now I will mess you up even worse."

After a moment, Jake caught his breath and stammered as he spoke. "I swear to you it wasn't me. I never go to bars and you can even come to my house and ask my wife, she'll prove it."

Just then a police car pulled up with lights flashing. The two officers inside simultaneously exited their respective doors.

"What's going on here?" asked the driving officer, his hand positioned atop his gun.

Jake immediately spoke up. "Officer, this man thinks I'm somebody else."

Just then Jake noticed the other cop. It was Lawrence, his wife's brother.

Chapter 6

Near Death Light

Jerry was just driving along in his convertible on Route 11, a narrow, wooded road, to pick up his daughter from the school play rehearsal, when suddenly, out of nowhere the oncoming car crossed over the road into his lane at full speed and hit him head-on. Jerry's car spun around and tumbled over, and in spite of wearing a seatbelt, he was thrown from the car into the woods that lined the road.

Then it happened.

Almost as if it were a dream, he rose from where he had fallen and started to look around. He could see nothing but the forest that was ahead of him. In the distance was a bright light, whiter than white, with the trees framing it on either side. He felt compelled to get up and walk toward the light as he took small steps. The light seemed to be growing even brighter and coming closer as the trees continued to box it in. There was nothing else, other than complete darkness on either side of the trees.

Then suddenly, he heard a voice within him start to speak. "You now have a choice," the voice, almost like a loud whisper said. Yet he didn't actually hear the voice with his ears as he felt it inside him. The light between the trees still shined so bright that he couldn't see anything else. The voice spoke to him again. "It is time for you to go now. Walk into the light and face your life's destiny."

Frightened now, Jerry stopped and just stood there staring into the light. Then he spoke out loud. "What? Where am I? What happened?"

The voice answered him in his heart, the depth of his being. Without any words, he had the feeling that he was dying right there in the forest, in front of the light. It just kept beckoning him to come closer. He was about to take another step when it happened.

Just then Jerry felt a strong, sharp shock in his chest. The pain caused him to fall over and roll onto his back gripping his chest. Right there in the darkness.

When he opened his eyes, he saw the EMT hovering over him. "He's back!" the medic shouted. "He's alive!"

Chapter 7

Polka Fest

The annual polka fest was in full swing. All the ladies were adorned in their colorful dresses complete with flowered crowns in their hair. The men all seemed to have lumber-jack looking outfits with lots of red plaid showing and the twelve-piece polka band was decked out in identical red coats with white shirts. It was a colossal scene of the Polish people and their friends enjoying the festivities.

Of course, all the traditional foods were also available under the big circus-like tent that housed the stage, dance floor, and tables. There was a huge buffet of kielbasa, golumpki, pierogis, kapusta, and all the usual traditional trimmings. The focus point was the dance floor, which was oversized and situated in the center of the tent featuring numerous couples dancing the polka in round-about fashion.

Suddenly, out of nowhere came a strong gust of wind out of the western side of the parking lot where the tent was pitched. The tent's sides began to flop away as the whole enclosure started to shake vigorously in the sudden wind. The band played on as if nothing was happening. The dancers seemed to be oblivious to the wind that was gyrating the tent as they just continued to hop and bounce to the lively music. Then came another huge gust of wind. This one twice as fierce as the previous one such that it actually lifted the tent a few feet up into the air with a mighty shake. Luckily, it was secured by the ropes outside, deeply staked into the ground, so that even though the tent lifted a bit, it stayed securely in place.

The band just played on. The dancers swayed almost in rhythm to the bellowing tent. Nobody seemed to care that it looked as though it was about to fall in. The crowd at the spiked punch bowl filled their drinks and just enjoyed the sudden show of nature's force on their merrymaking.

Finally, it happened. On the third humungous gust of wind, greater than the previous two combined, the tent was unleashed from the supporting rope and poles and took off straight up into the air. The band played on. The dancers danced. What was in that punch?

Chapter 8

Forgetfulness

"Oh, no!" I say to myself, once I leave the shopping mall heading to the parking lot. "Where's my car?" Confusion set in a few years ago, but recently it's gotten much worse. Before my mind went blank, I could remember the general direction of where the car was parked. But now, I seem to wander around the foggy sea of cars hoping that one of them is mine.

I feel a lot of anxiety, wondering if I even have a car in the first place. Sometimes I forget the car's color and make. Was it white or red? Did I have a Mazda, or was it a Toyota? The past and present all get jumbled up in my mind. Don't ask me what day it is or who is the president because I'll just shrug my shoulders.

Why did I go to the mall in the first place? There's nothing that I wanted to buy. I'm not carrying any bags. It's like I was dropped in this mall by a bunch of space aliens. I wish there was someone to help me, perhaps a security officer could drive me around the parking lot until I find my car. Then I could get warm and not shake and shiver so much.

I look down at my shoes. I'm not wearing any socks again … oh, there it is! Hmmm. It's a white Mazda hatchback. Did I have a hatchback? I look inside. Yup! That's mine. There's the little bugs bunny figurine on the dashboard that my wife bought for me. The seat covers have holes on the driver's side. Yup, that's it. I try to open the car door but it doesn't budge. I reach into my pocket for the keys. Holy smokes! I must have lost my keys. Or did I leave them at home?

A kind man with a "Quiet Meadows" windbreaker taps me on the shoulder. He takes my arm in his and leads me to a big white van with seniors inside. He slides open the door like a gentleman, puts a stool down and helps me up into the van. He seems to know my name. He seems to know where I live.

"Who are you?" I ask.

Chapter 9

Gun to the Head

He held the gun up to my head. "Please don't shoot!" Was the only reaction that snapped out of my lips. How could I have been so stupid to get myself into this position in the first place? I thought it would be really cool, that's how. I thought it would be exciting to go and see what the protest was all about. Seeing the angry faces on the mob of protesters as I walked deeper into the crowd should have been enough to turn me away. I knew that because I felt it inside. My gut told me. And my brain reasoned as much as well. Yet, curiosity got the best of me. It always has. It's a character flaw of mine. The local businesses had already taken precautions by boarding up their windows and doors. That should have been enough to warn me not to go.

Throwing caution to the wind, I entered the crowd to see if I could get to the front of where everyone was facing. To see exactly what was being protested. As I made my way, the people started looking sketchier and sketchier. Some had baseball bats, others had bottles and bricks. Suddenly, it was too late and I was caught in the middle with nowhere to go. That's when a bald-headed man came right up to me and pulled out the gun. I just froze in that instant. "Don't shoot," is all I could muster to say.

"Yeah, why not? Who are you and what are you doing here?" was his response.

"Do you know who I am?" I asked him, trying to keep the terror I was feeling at bay.

"No, I don't. And why should I care?"

"Because I'm here for you. I was sent into this crowd to find you."

"What are you talking about? Freak!" was his response.

At this point I didn't know what else to say, so I just told him the truth. "I'm here for you and all of your friends as well as the people you are protesting against."

"What da ya mean by that?" he asked. The gun was slightly lowering now.

"I'm merely doing my job," I explained. "You see, I'm a Catholic priest and I'm here to serve all God's people, you especially."

Chapter 10

Second Time Around

This was the second wedding for both of us. My fiancé and I are both widowed and we "found" each other at a church social event one fine Sunday after Mass eight months ago. Let's just say we really hit it off. And at our age, both of us in our late-sixties, we didn't take long to discover that we always wanted to be together either. So, after just four short months of courtship, or dating, or whatever you want to call it, we were engaged.

Now we're getting married next Saturday on the beach, since we both love the beach. Again, being older, we like vintage stuff so we both decided to buy used and rather old outfits for the wedding instead of wasting money on new. I found a three-piece charcoal gray suit at Brother Benno's thrift store which was almost my size roughly, close enough not to notice that it sagged on me a little. The best part was it only cost me twelve bucks! My fiancé did likewise, finding a used dress at a consignment place for half of the normal price. It looked practically brand new. What was it? Worn once? The point is, we will look circa 1980s in our respective garments, just like we did when both of us were married for the first time.

What's really amazing though, is what I found in the inside pocket of the suit's vest. It was a piece of paper with writing on it. "What could this be?" I wondered aloud as I unfolded it. That's when I saw that it was a hand-written wedding message. It contained the actual words of the groom's vows to the bride! It was so beautiful that I decided to use them as my own since I had been struggling over finding the right words to convey my feelings to my new bride. Being older and experienced and all, I found the words on the paper to be almost heaven-sent. They stated exactly how I felt about her. They even seemed to describe her to a tee.

When I got home from the thrift store and showed the suit that I had found to my fiancé, she said to me, "You know, that suit looks almost identical to the one my deceased husband wore at our wedding forty years ago."

21

Chapter 11

Sly Waitress

Jane, the waitress, asked, "Is there anything else I can get for you?"

"We'll just take the check for now, thanks," came his reply speaking for the couple.

"I'll get that for you right away."

As Jane left the check on the table, she noticed he was paying with a credit card. Perfect! After waiting a minute, she took the card and check and headed for the wait station. Quickly, and without anyone noticing, she took out her cell phone and snapped a picture of the card, both front and back, then dropped her cell phone into her apron's front pocket as if it never happened. She then ran the card through the point-of-sale machine and took the receipts and the card back to the gentleman who had given it to her for payment.

After a few minutes, he signed the receipt and included a penned-in tip for $5.00 added to the balance of $36.50 already on the bill. Then the couple got up and nonchalantly went out of the restaurant, none the wiser to what Jane had done.

A few hours later, at the end of her shift, Jane left the restaurant and once safely inside her car, pulled out her cell phone and went immediately into the picture app. There were the photos of not just the one credit card, but also of ten others that she had managed to take during her entire eight-hour shift.

Nervously, and shaking, out of both fear of getting caught and adrenaline, she began tagging each photo in her texting app. She then sent the entire batch of photos off to the number on the paper she had been given by the man in the long coat who came up to her as she was leaving the restaurant. Once the "whoosh" sounded on her phone, signifying all the pictures were sent, she breathed a sigh of relief. Her role in the scheme was over.

Now all the images of the cards of the suspects had been sent to headquarters. Perhaps now, finally, the FBI would be able to link the cards to the crime family they had been investigating for months.

Jane relished her career as an FBI undercover agent but it was the days like this that were especially satisfying. Perhaps she was one step closer now to making lieutenant.

Chapter 12

Boat Launch

As we drove up to the boat launch in the early morning sun, the white globe shining in the low horizon like a beacon welcoming the new day ahead, the feeling of anticipation within me started to rise with it to a fevered pitch. My father, who was the one driving, pulled the car around to the incline that reached the water's edge. With the boat trailer attached on back of our Plymouth station wagon, he began to back it down until the trailer was partially submerged and then stopped. Almost like programmed robots, my brother and I jumped out of our seats on either side of the back and began walking slowly alongside as my dad continued to ease the trailer with our eighteen-foot Boston Whaler fishing boat atop into the welcoming sea. The sound of the waves crashing against the nearby rocks that lined the launch area echoed like a call from heaven as the seagulls perched on the dock poles were squawking in concert with them.

I was the oldest, so it was my job to secure the main tie from the trailer and using the attached crank in front, to loosen the pull. That allowed the boat to gently slide off the trailer into the splashing ebb tide. This was the tricky part. Once the boat was afloat on its own, I had to hold the harness attached to the bow, and reaching over the port side of our little boat, guide it off the trailer beneath, and fully into the water on its own. My brother did the same move on the starboard side until our small craft, which was nicknamed "Mom's Bliss," was free of any obstruction from the trailer and fully seaworthy. Then it was up to me to signal dad to begin driving the car, now boatless, with the trailer attached, slowly out of the water. The trick here was to not get your feet run over by the trailer's tires as it pulled away.

Once Dad had cleared out to go park, my brother and I tugged on our respective harnesses to bring the bow just to the water's edge in front of us. It nestled into the soft sand a bit as the waves continued to crash in gently. Just ahead was another great day of memories to be made while fishing with my dad and my kid brother. A fun day for us and a blissful one for Mom who, with all of us gone fishing, finally had the whole house to herself.

Chapter 13

Big Boy Broken Bone

The emergency room waiting area was obviously overcrowded when she arrived and so she made a quick decision to evaluate the boy's broken arm right there in the lobby.

"It hurts real bad," he cried.

"You're going to be alright, but I need you to be really brave for a moment and let me hold your arm," the ER doctor said. As she took ahold of his thin little arm she asked, "What's your name?"

"Justin," he sheepishly replied, "Justin Case." She almost laughed, but quickly caught herself and switched into professional mode.

"I'm Doctor Colangelo. But you could call me Doctor Laura. Okay?"

"Yes ma'am, I mean Doctor Laura. Please help me, it hurts real bad!"

"That's because it's broken. You've got a broken arm. See how it's twisted the wrong way?"

"Yes. Can you make it feel better?"

"In order to do that, I'm going to need to hold on to your arm with both my hands."

"Okay?"

"Then I'm going to count to three and on three, I'm going to twist your arm back to the way it's supposed to be. Can you be a real brave big boy for me?"

The boy replied, "I don't know. I've never had anything like this happen to me before."

"I promise you. It will feel much better once I set your arm straight again," Doctor Laura responded. Then, "Nurse, get an air splint."

"Where do you want to do this, doctor? All the examination rooms are filled," came the nurse.

"We're going to do it right here, right now. Justin, are you ready to be a big boy for me?"

"Yes Doctor Laura, I can be brave," he responded.

"Okay here we go. I'm going to grab your arm with both my hands now." With that, she firmly held the boy's arm on either side of the disjointed break. Then she said, "Remember, I'm going to count to three then pull your arm back. Are you ready?"

With tears in his eyes, Justin nodded and replied, "Yes, Doctor Laura."

She counted, "one, two," and suddenly pulled his arm in opposite directions as it snapped back into place.

Justin didn't even scream as he was waiting to hear her say "three."

Suddenly he smiled and said, "You were right Doctor Laura, it feels much better now."

"You were right too. You've been a brave big boy."

Chapter 14

Last Call Bus

It was closing time, the "last call," as the saying goes. Tom was at the Main Pub in downtown Manchester, a popular "watering hole," as the saying goes. He was admittedly feeling a warm buzz from the six drafts he managed to down over the past two hours. He thought it was probably time to go home but wanted "just one more for the road," as the saying goes.

After a quick trip to the men's room and chugging down that last beer, he was now ready to leave. "Feeling it," as the saying goes. He had no problem or hesitation with the fact that he was "tying one on," as the saying goes, because he wouldn't be driving. Instead, he would catch the eighty-eight-bus, on the corner, which would go right to Pratt Street at the end of the line. Only a block away from where he lived. It was such a convenience to have a "designated driver," as the saying goes, albeit the bus driver.

Feeling really groggy now, Tom tried to focus on the marquee of the approaching bus. He saw, or so he thought he saw, the number eighty-eight on the front display. Actually, it was an eighty-six. But due to his "impaired state," as the saying goes, he thought it was the eighty-eight so he hopped on board. He then promptly went to the back seat and proceeded to "pass out," as the saying goes. He figured he need not worry about catching a nap since the driver would wake him at the end of the line.

Finally, the driver did, in fact, wake Tom up and told him to get off the bus and that it was "the end of the line," as the saying goes.

Tom then walked about outside, completely lost, as he was unfamiliar with the eight-six's end of the line part of town. What to do now? A song suddenly rang in his mind as he thought, "Well, how did I get here? This is not my beautiful house. This is not my beautiful wife," as the saying goes.

After a few more moments of thought, Tom then took out his cell phone and dialed the local area code followed by "444-4444." It was a number he remembered seeing on the side of a yellow cab. "The rest is history," as the saying goes.

Chapter 15

Dad in the Study

After greeting my mother-in-law with the customary hug, having come into their house through the kitchen door as usual, I noticed that she looked distressed. "What gives?" I asked her.

"Go see Dad. He's in the study," she responded.

I went down the hall to the study where my father-in-law was staring out the window, watching the rain come down.

"Dad?" I asked.

"Oh, Larry. Come in. We need to talk. Please close the door," he said in a foreboding voice.

"What gives?" I said again. This time to my father-in-law. He got right to the point. One thing I really like about him is he doesn't beat around the bush.

"You know, you've been gone a lot this month with your job's demands on your time and all and, well, it's having a negative effect on the family."

"Did my wife, your daughter, put you up to this? Because I wouldn't put it past her, with all her complaining about the same thing lately," I queried.

"No. It wasn't her, it's solely me. I've just noticed when you two were first married you spent a lot of time together and—she, you both, were obviously really happy. Now she just seems to be glum all the time and I surmise that it's because you're hardly ever around."

I responded to my father-in-law's assessment. "Look, Dad. I've got a whole lot more on my plate now. Work just isn't like it was when we were first married. Please don't think that I'm ignoring her or you all for that matter, but I'm not so much on my own anymore. I have a whole team to think about now. There's a ton more responsibility and I can't just walk away when I feel like it."

"I know," said my father-in-law. "And I get it. But you need to consider your wife's, my daughter's, point of view." You are in charge of scheduling your own meetings, aren't you? Can't you figure out a way to schedule her into your busy day. Hell, you're gone from sunup till past sundown nearly every day, weekends included."

"So, what would you have me do? Quit?"

"I can't answer that son, but you have to decide if being the Chief of Police is worth it to you and your family."

It wasn't worth it to me. I'd go back to being just a detective.

Chapter 16

San Diego Stagecoach

The San Diego via Rio Grande stagecoach east left Old Town station at 10:00 every morning. It would be a four-day ride all the way to El Paso following the southern route. We were told to arrive by 9:00 at the latest in order to load up the coach with our suitcases and other belongings while the horses received their last meal before the journey. Fuel for the four horse-powered engine. The mix of hay and oats was a special blend, I was told, in order to give the beasts of burden the energy and strength they needed. They would be hauling us eight passengers riding inside the coach, along with the two engineers, topside, a long way.

After dropping our luggage off at the station and purchasing our tickets, we still had an hour to kill so why not hit the saloon for a quick drink or two to lessen the agony of the long ride ahead? It would perhaps even help dispose us to get some shut-eye during the trip.

Finally, it was time to board and the lead engineer read off his list of precautions for us passengers. First, there was the usual warning to use the restroom right before boarding since there would be no stops until we reached our first station in four hours. It made me wish I hadn't had that second beer at the saloon. Next, he told us to keep within the compartment and warned of various safety issues, all of which seemed completely obvious to me. Interesting though, was the warning to be on the lookout for bandits as there had been several hold-ups over the past month. We were told to make sure we had no valuables on our persons as the bandits would just usually take cash, watches and jewelry and such, not bothering with the luggage.

Now they tell us! Had I known, I would have packed my watch inside my trunk, so it could be hidden safely inside. It was worth over a thousand dollars, a bonified heirloom made in Switzerland, having belonged to my grandfather originally.

Oh well, perhaps we'll have an uneventful ride and during one of our three overnight stops along the way, I could secure my watch in my suitcase then. So instead, I tied it around my ankle, inside my boot. I thought it would be safe there. Even stagecoach bandits wouldn't be so brazen, as to take our shoes.

Chapter 17

Neighborly Fires

Miranda opened her bedroom window one fine autumn morning and caught a whiff of leaves burning. It was that pesky neighbor, Mr. Caffro again. He had already raked several small piles of leaves in his backyard which was adjacent to Miranda's backyard. She could see him out of her window bending over to light yet another pile of leaves. In a strange way, the smell of leaves burning in the cool, crisp air was somewhat welcome and appealing to her.

But that was typical Mr. Caffro, up early on a Saturday morning, it was only 7:30, raking his leaves into several neat little piles to set aflame. Miranda knew it was no use complaining to him or to the town authorities as it was perfectly legal to do what he was doing, provided you had gotten a burning permit from the fire commissioner's office. She also knew that the elderly neighbor, who was pushing ninety, was nothing if not thorough in his preparation for the task at hand. It was just his way. He would have a permit, alright, and probably had it on his person just in case anyone should question what he was doing.

It was then that Miranda noticed that he did not stop raking the leaves at his property boarder but had also raked up all the leaves in her backyard as well. In fact, she saw several piles in line with his, as he approached the first one in her backyard. She watched intently as he walked over with what looked like a red gallon gas can and poured some of the golden liquid on the first pile of leaves in her own yard! Then he went on to the next pile, also in her yard, and repeated the act of dousing the leaves with gas. She couldn't believe what she saw next, as he took out some matches and proceeded to set both piles of leaves in her yard aflame.

Surely you couldn't get a burning permit that covered both your yard and your neighbor's. Could you? No, Mr. Caffro probably used that charm of his on the lady fire commissioner to get a permit for burning in her yard as well. Or so Miranda thought.

No use making a fuss. Her yard was raked up and the leave piles were being disposed of. She decided to go downstairs to the kitchen and make her neighbor a nice apple pie to thank him.

Chapter 18

Daughter's Recital

I remember her dance recital like it was yesterday. It's a memory that resides in that special place, the one exclusively reserved in the heart. Cherished. It was in the Manchester High School Auditorium. We parents had been sitting there since an hour before it started, just to be sure to get a good seat. Everyone is sharing the same experience and it's not what you think. We parents are firmly ensconced there, and the show is like three hours long and it's so damn boring and you're just waiting. Waiting for the two minutes that your own kid is on stage.

And I remember my daughter Dyana's cotton-candy or lollypop sugar plumb dance was maybe the eighth or ninth act out of, what, twenty-five, maybe thirty. Suddenly, she comes on and my wife and I start nudging each other. I remember smiling then, you know, and I'm looking at my daughter, and for a few moments, you feel such a pure joy.

It's like a light in my chest starts beaming and I'm looking at Dyana and her little face is all scrunched up because, you know her—even then, Dyana was Dyana! She didn't want anything to go wrong. Every step of the dance is exact and precise. I mean, there's no rhythm or expression, but Dyana makes no mistakes. And I'm looking at this little wonder and I'm almost bursting.

And you're sitting there and you have tears in your eyes and you think about the wonder of this moment, and then—and this is the amazing thing—you look around the auditorium, at all the other parents, and realize that every one of them feels exactly the same way about their own kid. I mean, that's so obvious and simple and yet something about it overwhelms me. I can't believe this tremendous feeling, this wave of love, doesn't belong to us alone, that what we're experiencing isn't unique. And that just made it seem somehow greater.

I remember just watching the other parents in the auditorium. There were the wet eyes and the smiles on faces illuminated by the glow from the lights on the stage. You see wives reach for the hand of their husbands with no words exchanged. Eyes glued forward. And I remember being just awed. Like—I don't know—like I couldn't believe one room, this simple school auditorium, could be so full of pure love and not just take off from the ground.

Chapter 19

Montserrat Summit Proof

I broke the number one rule when it comes to mountain climbing and hiking. I went alone. No buddy system to rely on. Just me. Montserrat was just too majestic as it loomed before me. It is a multi-peaked mountain range near Barcelona, in Catalonia, Spain. It is part of the Catalan Pre-Coastal Range. I was alone but I simply had to climb it and I had only the one day to do so. It was early morning when I started and figured it would take me half the day to reach the summit, then the other half of the day to return to the base before darkness set in.

The trail was well worn and had seen its share of climbers. It wound around the mountain through valleys, hills and dales while making a gradual ascent to the top. A beautiful walk. The journey took me a little over six hours to reach the summit and when I did, I was glad that I took the risk to go it alone. As I sat looking at scene below before me, I remember thinking that this was proof that God existed. I felt a closeness to the Almighty that I had never felt before. Looking down on the world below stretching out for miles, as far as the eye could see, gave me such a profound appreciation for how small I really was and a sense of joy that I had the privilege to behold the magnificent view.

If only I could get a picture of me atop Montserrat. A selfie wouldn't do it justice. I had my camera so I snapped 360-degree shots of the astounding view below but other than that, there was no proof that I was at the top. Then, low and behold, just as I had the thought it would be nice if there was someone else there—if only to take a picture of me—he suddenly appeared. Another solo climber had just come through the brush on the trail leading to the rocky summit. We greeted each other with first a smile and then some conversation where we related how much we enjoyed the hike up the mountain solo. Then we agreed to take each other's picture at the top. It was the proof that I had hoped to have.

After the picture, we parted our ways and went on to make the dissent back to base following different paths. To this day I don't know if he was really just another climber who happened to be there when I needed or perhaps, just maybe, since we were up so high, he was actually an angel.

Chapter 20

Carrier Landings

He had spent the better part of the past two weeks preparing his speech. The conference had him slated in the keynote position due mostly to his success as a business man and past reputation as a Navy fighter pilot. Having him give the main speech was a choice made by the organization, of which he was a member, that he reluctantly agreed to do.

She had been incredibly supportive of his upcoming role, by offering a listening ear, helping him brainstorm a suitable topic, even suggesting what suit and tie to wear. With there being over three thousand attendees at the convention present for the keynote address, he was sure to leave an impression. But what impression? That was the question he had gnawing at him in the back of his mind.

As he whittled down his story of the highlights of his drinking life that he was to relate—the story of his whole life really, some parts were shocking to say the least. Like the part when he would recall his drunken behavior in college, particularly with the rugby team at the bar parties that followed every game and some of the antics that would ensue as a result of their drunkenness. He knew that the point of his speech was to show that a life of living with the bottle was to be shunned, so he had to be careful not to glorify his former drunken behavior too much. After all, the whole point of his story was to show that the program works if you work it and not to revel in the shenanigans of the past.

He would, however, include one example of tomfoolery which was how he and his fellow officer buddies would play "carrier landing" in the Navy officers' club. The game involved chugging a mug of beer with a shot of whiskey dropped inside it, like a depth charge, then running up to the pool table with arms outstretched like a jet, capped off by splaying one's body across the table. Just like landing on an aircraft carrier. Then, of course, another beer would be downed while making his way back to the line of officers patiently waiting for their turn to "land," repeating the process. The one with the most coherent landings, that is, without falling over the side of the table onto the floor, would win.

But that was just one anecdote that he would tell. The point of his speech was, after all, how drinking was a disease and not something to glory over. He had to walk that thin line between being interesting and making that point.

She doubted he could pull it off. Even though he lived a rather benign existence now, he enjoyed talking about the hijinks of his drinking past way too much.

Chapter 21

Grace Greater Than Sin

After the service ended, my friend (who I had brought with me to church for the first time), and I got to talking about the message of the day that the pastor had preached about. I had just explained to him how much God loved him and that God wanted to have a personal relationship, echoing the message.

"But I've done some really bad things in my life. Surely God wouldn't want a relationship with me. I'm not worthy," he stated.

"No one is worthy," I replied. "Those bad things that have been done are called sin. God is always willing to forgive us of those sins if we are truly serious about wanting them to be forgiven, and we desire not to do them again."

"No, you don't understand. I've done some really bad things," he responded.

"Have you ever committed murder?" I asked.

"Well, no I haven't," he replied.

"Do you realize that over a third of the Bible is written by former murderers or by men who were accessories to murder?" I asked.

"You've got to be kidding. Really?"

"Really!" I continued, "God can use anybody who is willing to be used by him."

I went on to tell him, "There is an observation that I and others have made that is a constant message of hope for those who think they have fallen too far for grace to grab them. I am often amazed at the fact that so much of the Bible was written by people associated with murderers. Remember this the next time your sin looks bigger than grace:

"Moses wrote five books, called the Pentateuch. After looking in all directions to make sure no one was watching, Moses killed the Egyptian and hid the body in the sand. The whole incident is even recorded in Exodus, chapter two.

"David wrote most of the Psalms. In a letter he wrote to Joab, David instructed him to, 'Station Uriah on the front lines where the battle is fiercest, then pull back so he will be killed.' That passage is in second Samuel, chapters fourteen through fifteen.

"Paul wrote thirteen letters in the New Testament. In them he stated, 'You know what I was like—how I violently persecuted God's church. I did my best to destroy it even by murder.' Paul makes this remark in several of his letters."

My friend smiled at me as I went on to conclude, "I don't care what you've done. Jesus doesn't care what you've done. Grace is greater than all our sin. Don't abuse it, but be changed by it."

Chapter 22

Writer's Block

There is nothing like getting into "the zone" when I write. Even though I go into it with a somewhat developed idea or plot line, much of what I write just comes to me from an "unknown source" that evades my conscious comprehension as I am in the process. This doesn't come without a few bad habits, however. It would seem that just the thrill of achieving "the zone" would be motivation enough, but alas, it's not. At times I have solid ideas and an impeccable plot line in mind but I find myself procrastinating over actually doing the writing. That's one bad habit.

Another is poor timing. That is, the use of time in my day, sitting down to actually write. Lately, this has only been for only a few short hours after dinner. I would like to improve that to a much longer stretch. Maybe even the normal working hours of a day. It just seems too difficult to do for some reason.

Then there are those authors that I like and wish to emulate in some ways. They not only inspire me with their talent in what they write, but also in how they write as well.

Take Lee Child for example, who can conjure up a thriller with non-stop action and has created a hero that spans over dozens of novels, Jack Reacher. Child has nailed it. Who wouldn't want to be Jack?

Then there is another of my favorites, John Sandford. He has also created a series of related novels with the same word in each title, based on not only a single character but several—all with well-developed attributes where the reader, me, feels like I know them as real human beings.

Of course, as far as writing details go, there is Tom Clancy. He can spend fourteen pages in a Jack Ryan novel describing how to break down and rebuild an M-16 rifle in the dark while providing a short history on the development of rifles over the past century. Truly gifted.

But as far as style goes, I rely on Neal Stephenson who has authored numerous voluminous science fiction thrillers—including trilogies, and whose mind is beyond this or any number of geometric planes, including those that seem to reach the stratosphere in range and scope and far exceeds, even the most brilliant thoughts of human mental capacity, using a unique technique of almost litigating commas, punctuation, alliteration, and an adjective-adverbial assault, that even a genius like Einstein would appreciate, as he brings numerous sentiments into his well-encapsulated compounded compound sentences that go on and on and seem to never end, without repeating a single noun or verb just like this one.

Guess I'm ready to write now.

Chapter 23

College Recommendation

Mr. Cunningham, the social studies teacher, was a favorite among the Mercy High School students. His good nature was a reflection of his true heart-felt concern for each of his students. He simply wanted to see all of them succeed, not just in passing his class with a good grade, but also to excel in life. He had two teenagers of his own, daughters, so he could especially relate to his students by incorporating many of their trillings into his own expressions. In other words, to use a more antiquated term, he was hip. He used it to his advantage in not only conveying the content of his various classes but also to establish a congenial rapport with his students of the all-girls school.

Since he taught a senior class, he was also often asked to write college recommendations for his soon-to-graduate students. One pupil in particular, Laurie Gainor was his pride and joy, though he kept that to himself and would never reveal a preference for her to other students or faculty staff in any way. But Laurie was different. She reminded him of his own older daughter, who was also a student at the school, in many ways. Laurie not only showed a certain high level of enthusiasm for social studies, she also often proved her interest by consistently acing tests and going the extra mile in completing homework assignments. In class, as far as participation went, her hand was always up.

So, it did not seem foreign at all to Mr. Cunningham when Laurie approached him after class one day to ask him if he would write her a college recommendation to go along with her applications. Of course, he wanted to do it. If anyone deserved a college recommendation from him it was Laurie. Yet the consummate teacher in him had to put yet one more test to her before he would acquiesce.

"I'll gladly write you a recommendation if you'll do one thing more for me," he alluded.

The proposal stunned her. She felt a lump in her heart. What did he want? In the end, she reasoned it couldn't hurt but to ask him.

"What is it?" she asked sheepishly.

"First you have to promise to do it," he returned. She was feeling even more apprehensive now but she really wanted that recommendation. Finally, she gave in to his demand.

"Okay. Whatever you ask," she replied.

Mr. Cunningham smiled. He had her now. Right where he wanted her.

He said, "I want you to read Genesis, the first book in the Bible, and write me a five-hundred-word book report on how it relates to your life."

Chapter 24

Lonesome Heart

Put a stamp on that note … not letter … and mail it to a lonesome heart. If only she could read my mind, she would know that a note from her is all I desire. It's been almost two years since I last saw her. The three months we were together again passed much too quickly. Yes, we both agreed to just cut it off. She more than me. Especially before it got any more serious than it already did. Fat chance! Why is it we both agree to sabotage our feelings just when they are getting real? Perhaps it is to avoid complacency which surely would follow. It always does. So, what do we do?

We try to stay in that exciting zone of a budding relationship. Take it slow while occasionally sprinting along the way. If it weren't for our past, how different it would be now. Spending two years together during college only to break up and go our separate ways. Then to suddenly meet again after thirty plus years!

I can still feel my stomach churn when I remember that first date after so much time had passed between us. That romantic, supposedly plutonic dinner together at the Mediterranean restaurant. Sitting there in the darkened corner booth. You with your baked Dijon salmon, me with my Xinomavro duck. Cheers to us with a glass of Pinot Noir. I can't recall the taste of the food as I can the candlelight glistening in your green eyes as you looked at me. Our first time together after so many years, just to attempt to rekindle the newness we both felt so long ago.

The times together became more numerous over the next few weeks until, at last, we were a daily issue again. Even simple things like shopping for groceries, sharing a meal at your house, helping you in your garden and going to church together became thrilling to me. My heart skipping a beat with every step I took beside you.

But you drew the line between us. I couldn't hold your hand. It was too intimate you told me. Not yet. It was too soon and that you weren't ready.

Then you suddenly retreated. Stopped returning texts and wouldn't answer my calls. Puzzled, I didn't know what to do. What had I done? After long, hard consideration I realized it was nothing I said or did. It was you. You feared it would happen to us again. You awakened me to that possibility. So, I reluctantly agreed. Out of consideration for you and your feelings. We should stop it. Again.

So now, instead, I go to the mailbox each day hoping. And each day I'm disappointed because you can't read my mind.

Chapter 25

Building Contractor

"Hello, Mr. Brown? This is Jay, from Jay and Em Builders. How are you today? … That's great, glad to hear things are going so well. Listen Mr. Brown, … Oh, okay thanks. So, Jim, the reason I'm calling was to just check in and see if you've had a chance to look over that bid that I sent you last week and … Uh huh, yeah. Well, yeah, I expected you would seek a few other bids on that job. Do you mind if I ask you who you put it out to?" asked Jay of Jay and Em Builders.

"I'd rather not," replied Jim Brown, the homeowner. "I'm kind of using that as my leverage with you, but I will tell you that I'm looking at three quotes right now."

"I totally respect that, mister, er ah, Jim. It's just that I've been in business with my wife Emma for over twenty-five years now and we've seen a lot of contractors and builders come and go if you know what I mean."

"Yes. I appreciate that, but this is a big step for us, my wife and I. We've never hired a contractor before. But with the baby coming and all, we've decided to add on to our little cape house as you well know."

"Yes, I do. I've been over the plans we discussed with a fine-toothed comb and I can assure you that the bid I gave you is the absolute best price you're going to get," returned Jay.

Jim responded, "Well, to be totally upfront and honest, yours wasn't the lowest price we received, there was one lower by a considerable sum."

"I assure you Mr. Brown, er uh Jim, the price I gave you is the best you could expect if you keep quality in the equation. I could quote you a lower price too, but that means the quality of materials would suffer."

Jim retorted, "I appreciate that Jay, and to be completely frank, I'd like to go with you, in spite of the higher price, but it's the missis that needs convincing more than me. You see, the lower quote was almost ten-thousand dollars less than yours."

"Wow! That's a lot less," Jay responded. "I can't imagine how anyone could do the job for that much less unless …"

"Yes?"

"Unless the labor cost was really low. I don't want to make any accusations here, but there must be some fundamental way that other much lower bid of yours is possible. Again, my experience tells me that he's got to have a much, much lower labor cost. And there is only one way that he can be doing that."

"I hear you, Jay."

Chapter 26

Powder Conditions

The snow had started out by falling slowly which indicated it would be coming down for a long time and would likely get much worse than the lazy, tiny flakes that were gracefully whirling and filling the late morning sky indicated. In other words, it would pile up significantly. Slowly and surely. By mid-afternoon and only two hours of snowfall, there was already eight inches on the packed surface and the sky had gone from blue with tiny white dots to white with tiny blue ones. It kept steadily coming down throughout the afternoon as the couple looked out of their chalet high atop Mount Mansfield in the Green Mountains of Vermont at the Smuggler's Notch ski resort.

What a perfect scenario, what a perfect place to be during a perfect storm.

The falling snow finally let up at about 3:00 in the afternoon. Since their chalet was near the summit, and just a few hundred yards from the chairlift that supported the seven trails that led to the bottom, it would be ideal for a late afternoon run in pure powder—the best kind of circumstances. Jerry and Jamie waited another half hour and saw the chairlift begin to move. It meant that the trails were open. Quickly they both donned their ski-suits and got their gear together. The couple then went outside into the cold, crisp, clean air that still had a few straggling flakes blowing about in the light wind. On the surface was as swath of almost two feet of new fallen snow. Perfect!

After tightening the straps on their ski-boots the two snapped into their skis, pulled their visors down, and began the long, five-mile run down along the intermediate trail on Smuggler's Madonna Mountain. Knee-deep in the snow, they cruised along. Bouncing over the moguls with soft landings, the skiing surface wasn't too fast and wasn't too slow, but just right. As he cruised along, Jerry thought of what it would be like being back in Boston just now. Since it was a Monday, he would be heading home from the office, snarled in traffic due to the hazardous conditions, bumper to bumper, skidding about. Not here. Not on his yearly February vacation full of skiing and fun with his wife. Instead, he was gliding along effortlessly with Jamie right behind him following his furrowed path in the gloriously white, frosty trail. The two were enjoying the unique experience of having the mountain entirely to themselves.

Suddenly, Jerry stopped right at the edge of the notch which offered a spectacular view of the valley below as Jamie pulled up right beside him.

"What are you thinking about?" she asked.

"How we are doing in rush hour," he stated with a smirk.

"We're doing just fine," she added, "now kiss me."

Chapter 27

French Experiment

One educational experiment undertaken back in 1966 was for educators and various primary school systems to try teaching a foreign language to fourth graders. Back then, teaching a foreign language in grade school was considered novel. There was also a measuring system put in place to monitor the progression of learning a new language at such a young age—most students being between eight and ten years old.

In addition, the "experiment" offered students and parents the choice between French and Spanish, both considered to be the other "worldly" languages at the time, aside from English, of course. I personally was part of the experiment. Having always been taken by how beautiful the French language sounded, with all its unique sounds (not to mention that I loved the crêpes my mom always made for us), it was an easy decision for me. I would choose French over Spanish. A decision, that when I look back on it today, I probably made in childish haste instead of practicality. Oh well. I also opted for Latin over Spanish in high school. So today, living in southern Texas, I find myself surrounded by people who can speak Spanish and nobody who speaks French or Latin. Except for the old days, in church. The Latin came in handy back then.

So, anyway, I opted to take French. I can still vividly remember the class of about thirty of us learning to write and speak what was called conversational French from Madame, as she liked to be called. Mrs. Bessette was her real name. I don't remember what her first name was or if she even had one. I can still vividly recall familiar phrases such as, "Where is the library?" being "Où est la bibliothèque?" and "What time is it?" translated to "Quelle heure est-il?" If someone asked me, "Comment vous-appelez vous?" I could respond that "My name is Michael" by saying "Mon nom est Michel." That is the feminine version if Michael, which is my actual name, the only version there is in French. Then there was "un, deux, trois, quatre, …" I knew all the numbers. Enough to get by at least. Aside from what I have just illustrated, I can't remember anything else in French.

The whole class experiment was a rewarding one for me for two reasons. The first was, I achieved the highest grade in the class at the time, a ninety-nine. Only one point off a perfect score. Mrs. Bessette said she never had a single student score so highly in all the years she taught French to younger pupils. The second reason the class was so rewarding was because of Mrs. Bessette. To this day, I have never had a hotter looking teacher!

Chapter 28

Jack and Sally

Jack really loved this time of day. He finished washing up after another long day working at the business—a garden center nursery. The business he proudly owned and had built from scratch. He poured himself his daily ritual Manhattan, took the evening newspaper out to the enclosed back porch, and went up to his favorite easy chair. He sat down, took a long sip and started to read his favorite section—the comics. It was another productive day at work in the can and a chance to relax while his wife Sally was preparing the dinner for the two of them in the adjacent kitchen. Jack had been in business thirty-five years now and the last ten of them were spent exactly like today. He was comfortable with his completely conventional lifestyle to say the least.

Suddenly, the phone rang. "Sally! Could you get that?" Jack yelled to his wife.

"I can't. I'm busy with supper. You get it."

"Fine."

Jack got up out of his comfy chair and hobbled over to the wall phone. "I don't know why you couldn't answer it. You're right here," he said to his wife as he neared the continuously ringing communication device.

"My hands are full of flour," said Sally as she raised them up for Jack to see. She was coating the chicken thighs with egg and flour before frying the combo. Begrudgingly, Jack picked up the receiver and put the phone to his ear.

"Hello. Who is it?" he grumbled.

"It's me, Dad," came the reply, "I need your help."

"Oh, hi Tina. What kind of help? Wait. Do you think you can call me back in about an hour? Mom and I were just about to sit down and eat supper."

"Dad, don't get upset, but I'm at the hospital."

Suddenly, fear gripped Jack as he inquired, "What? What's wrong? Why are you there?"

"It's your grandson, Luke. He broke his leg at football practice. I'm in emergency with him now. Don't worry, he's okay."

"What do you want me to do?"

"Can you come down here? We're at Saint Francis," came Tina's response.

"Why do you need me to come down there if everything's okay?" Jack asked.

"I don't have my car. I rode in the ambulance with Luke when they came for him at practice. We need a ride back to the high school so I can get my car," Tina explained. "Oh, and one more thing. Don't tell Mom. We already had a big fight over me letting Luke play football, since he's so skinny. I don't want to deal with her right now. She'll just say 'I told you so' and go on and on."

"So … what should I tell her?"

"Tell me what?" Sally suddenly asked in a very annoyed tone of voice.

Chapter 29

Doggy Gone

I knew I shouldn't have chased that rabbit. It was a bad idea to start with. I don't know why. I just couldn't seem to control myself. I'm a dog after all. They call it instinct. My nice family let me walk in the woods for a minute without a leash to do my duty as we did every stop along the way on our summer vacation. I was just happy they decided to bring me along this time instead of forcing me to go to that stupid doggie daycare place for the week.

So, there I was, minding my own business just doing my business, when hop, hop, hop. That stupid rabbit crossed right in front of me. For a moment, we just froze staring at each other. Then he took off into the woods and naturally, I followed after him. We were darting left and right sprinting on until suddenly I realized I didn't know where I was. I walked around for hours and tried to find my family but everywhere there was just woods. Finally, it was getting dark so I decided to get some rest and continue searching at first light. So, I nestled myself up against the trunk of a tree and nodded off.

Night turned to day and after some long walking, I found my way out of the woods to the opening at the roadside rest stop that looked familiar. But my family was gone. Long gone.

Now, we dogs usually have a great sense of direction, and I was convinced I could find my way back home by following Route 66 in the opposite way that we had come. It was the right road, because we were on it for most of the time before I got lost. I knew the road's name because I had my head out the window and tongue flapping in the breeze as we drove and I kept seeing the Route 66 signs. Thing was, we were already eight hours away from home when we stopped and I chased the rabbit. So, I decided the best plan of action was to follow the road back to sights that were familiar and hopefully, I could find my family again.

What happened was, that trip took me over a year to make. There were all sorts of detours, including finding another really nice family that took me in, fed me, and cared for me. I still remember the little girl asking, "Can we keep him, Mom?" That was when I decided to hit the road again.

I hitched a few rides along the way and finally made it back to familiar territory. It was my old neighborhood! After another hour of walking up and down the street, I found my old house. I was so sure. There it was! I went up to the door and started to bark. I wondered if they would remember me.

Chapter 30

A Golf Tail

I could tell it was going to be a tough day after my first strike with the club. I sliced my drive nearly a hundred yards off the fairway, almost in the adjacent eighteenth hole's rough. Had the ball gone straight, I would have been in line for par on the first hole at Pebble Beach. Call it over excitement, the jitters, or what have you, I was just thrilled to be playing golf with three of my best buddies on one of the most prestigious courses in the world.

Normally, I'm a pretty good golfer. I shoot in the mid to high seventies, that is, if I'm on one of the blue-collar courses that I usually frequent. But the thrill of being on a "big league" course had me more than flustered. It was all thanks to my buddy Johnny O, whose father was a big-time U.S. attorney to OPEC, that we scored a reservation to play on the otherwise "elites only" course. Thankfully, Johnny O's dad also paid for the round for the four of us, which totaled somewhere north of eight hundred dollars as I recall.

So here was my chance. Easily regarded by my three other golf buddies to be the best golfer among us, I was ready to school them on the finer points of the game. But if you know anything about golf, you know that the game can get you at any time. Of all the times to be gotten! I ended up hitting the ball all over the course sideways that day and was missing three-foot puts by four feet! In the end, mercifully, I shot a ninety-nine. At least I didn't break a hundred. It was a total disaster. I had the highest score of the foursome. Talk about lemons!

The one redeeming moment of the day came on the seventh hole when we had to hit around a group of sea lions that decided to beach themselves along the edge of the picturesque green which butts up to the Pacific Ocean. Naturally, my shot landed in the midst of them and I had to wander in between four or five sea lions to take a chip shot up to the green. It miraculously landed just a foot away from the hole and

I putted in for one of my best holes of the day, two over par.

The whole shot was captured by my buddy Rick, who characteristically brought along his 35-millimeter Nikon camera and took a beautiful picture of me, club in hand, among the sea lions.

That event took place over thirty years ago. Needless to say, everyone has forgotten my disastrous score of ninety-nine but with the aid of Rick's on-the-spot photography, I've become infamous as the golfer who putted with the sea lions at Pebble Beach.

Chapter 31

Atlantic Cliff Conversation

The view from the top of the cliff spans as far as the eye can see. To the right is the Atlantic Ocean, clear-blue with waves towering over a hundred feet high. It is the highest surf in the world. Straight ahead, below the cliff, is winding beach spanning over ten kilometers, or nearly seven miles. To the left is a picturesque mountainside accented with colorful orange-roofed bone-white flats and small villas. A long road snakes its way at the base separating the pristine beach sand from the town proper and all its unique shops and charming restaurants. If anyplace could be deemed a paradise in Portugal, then Nazaré would fit that description. Standing at that point on the top of the cliff made one feel exuberant, appreciative, and small.

Positioned right there, in the midst of such grand beauty, the couple was starting to argue with each other.

"I can't believe you read my text messages," he stated.

"I can't believe you are texting her at all," came her return.

"You sure do know how to bring conflict into an otherwise amazing vacation," he retorted.

"Well, you're the one who brought her along on your iPhone. What else are you keeping from me on that thing?"

"You are bringing this up here? Of all places! I mean, didn't we look forward to this trip for months? Just look around you. This place is magnificent," he countered.

"I'm sorry, but I can't get into the atmosphere of this place knowing what I know about you going behind my back and texting her!"

"Me going behind your back? Who is the one that invaded my privacy by reading my text messages in the first place? Huh, Missy?!"

"Don't you call me that, it's demeaning! Besides, why didn't you tell me you've been texting her instead of sneaking around on your phone?"

"It doesn't mean anything. We're just friends. Look at those waves. Am I enjoying that view, which is awesome by the way, with you or with her?" he pleaded.

"Who knows? Perhaps you would rather she be here with you instead of me."

"Don't say that. It's not true. Look. It, she, means nothing to me. We're friends is all, and not besties by a long shot. That's a place only reserved for you," he petitioned.

"How do I believe you?"

"Because I brought you here to this, one of the most enchanting places in the world, to this exact spot, for a reason. That's how."

"Oh, and what would that be?"

He figured that now was as good a time as ever. As he got down on one knee, he reached into his back pocket, took out the small box and opened it before her. There it was. A breathtakingly beautiful diamond ring, capturing the rays of the sun in all its splendor, shimmering in front of the stunning cliff before them.

Chapter 32

Letter From Dad

Dear Family,

As the main provider of your livelihood, that is, the guy who works over fifty hours a week and comes up with the cash to pay the mortgage on the house, for the heat to warm it, and electricity to power it, as well as supply the means to put food on the table, I have one simple request.

Before I get into that, let me assure you that I am not asking for your cooperation as much as I am, in a sense, demanding it. I won't be specific right now as to what my retaliation will be if you don't comply with my demands, but be advised that it won't be pleasant for anyone.

Now my specific gripe is probably with just one of you, or perhaps others, but since I am not sure who is to blame, I'm not going to speculate. Instead, if what I am about to describe fits your MO, then be warned. We are a family after all, and need to be supportive of each other, "one for all and all for one" as the adage goes. So, I humbly request that whomever is responsible, kindly cease and desist from the behavior immediately. Again, you know who you are, so I'm not going to name names although, I probably could do so accurately.

All that being said, please pay close attention to the following: Could the person in this family who is the one that is using up all the ice in the ice tray and then putting it back in the freezer empty please stop this behavior and instead make a new batch of ice before putting the tray back? We all love cold drinks. And I have gone into the freezer to put some ice in my glass of Diet Coke on numerous occasions only to find that the tray is empty. This is now gotten to the point where it is occurring day after day. So, there I am; always the only one making a new batch of ice. Apparently, nobody else is, since the tray in the freezer is always completely empty when I go to get some.

Therefore, I am asking you all, who are distinguished members of this family, yes, all seven of you—including myself, that you kindly fill the tray when you see it nearing empty and certainly fill it with water if you use up the last cubes. If you cannot find your way to accommodate my simple request, I will be forced to take more drastic action such as banning the use of ice for this family entirely. We don't want to go there. None of us do.

Thank you in advance for your support and willingness to adhere to my simple suggestion. Let's all try to keep this family on ice.

Sincerely,

Your Provider and Father

Chapter 33

Being Sous Chef

I had only been on the job for two weeks, yet I could tell there was going to be a big problem. Lloyd was the head chef or rather the executive chef (as we call them in the biz), my new boss. I had just been hired to be the sous chef, second in command of the kitchen and everything that takes place in preparing the meals. We were a scratch kitchen, which meant we prepared everything ourselves rather than buy any ready-made foods. The restaurant's owner, named Keith, who also acted as the general manager, thought highly of Lloyd and decided to move him up from sous chef to the executive position rather than hire from outside when the last executive chef suddenly quit. In other words, I now had the job that Lloyd held just two weeks ago before I was hired.

Thing was, Lloyd tended to micromanage everyone. Not really the job of the executive chef. The exec's job is to be the boss and lead by example, ensure that the back of the house (as we call it in the biz) runs smoothly. Keith the owner-manager has responsibility for the front, where the food is actually served. I had tried for two weeks to subtly hint to Lloyd to lay off the other cooks and not micromanage the kitchen, to focus on the bigger role he had such as determining the menu, how the meals are prepared, and expediting orders. Managing the cooks and the prep-work is the job of the sous chef as is seeing to it that the executive chef's directions are followed. In other words, Lloyd wasn't doing his new job as executive chef, he was still actually doing his old job as sous chef which was my job now.

Over the course of the two weeks since the change, the friction between us became palpable. Lloyd had even gone to Keith to complain that I wasn't doing my job when actually he wasn't doing his. Thing is, I really do like being a chef and on Lloyd's day off, the kitchen ran smoothly under my sole direction. I even thought to myself that maybe I should be the executive chef. But unfortunately, Lloyd continued to bad-mouth me to Keith. What should I do? Should I stay or should I go? These were the questions I came to ask myself. Something had to be done.

Finally, I went to Keith and told him everything that was going on. He told me he knew all about it and that he had met with Lloyd to determine how to hire a new executive chef two weeks ago, before I came on, and this was the plan they came up with. He was wondering how long it would take for me to realize it and come to him. Just then Lloyd came in with a big smile on his face.

"Welcome aboard boss," he said.

Chapter 34

New Lifestyle in Nature

My name is Sven. Sven Müller, that's with a "u" and two dots over it. I live in the mountains adjacent to the Swiss Alps, sometimes called the little alps region. I've only been here for just over a year now as I used to live in Stockholm. I was a banker, as there are very many banks in Switzerland. There are also many bankers like I used to be. I worked for over thirty years at a desk and lived in an apartment downtown. I was your typical Swiss city-guy. A master at the metropolitan way of life. Then I left it all behind and came here.

Since I was a very good banker, I was also very good at saving money. I used some of the money I saved and bought this mountain lodge-like home. It's quite different than the city. First of all, the nearest town to me is thirty kilometers away and it is small with only a general store, a gas station, and of course, a bank. You have to go another eighty kilometers beyond it, to reach a reasonably sized city. I also don't have a car anymore. I couldn't afford to have one and buy the cabin which is my new home now. Did I say I am sixty-two years old and think of myself as retired? That may be so, but just trying to keep up with day-to-day needs is a rigorous fulltime job.

You see there is a lake nearby where I live and a thick forest all around me. So, for food I hunt and fish a lot. When I do go to town for supplies, I hike or take my dog and a sled to carry provisions back. Usually, I go every ten days or so. I chop wood for the two fireplaces and woodstove that provides heat and that I use to cook. Fortunately, I do have electricity and indoor plumbing so life's not really that rough. I must say that getting up every morning to the beautiful mountain surroundings that are just outside my windows beats waking up in a skyscraper jungle like I did for so many years before.

But the best part of my new lifestyle is the sound—or lack of it. The silence is wonderful and broken only by a nearby running stream or the birds chirping, or the occasional wolf howls at night. I probably work physically harder—more than I have in my entire life—now that I'm "retired." I have a case full of books that I haven't read yet that I am eager to delve into. Then there's the occasional friend or distant neighbor that stops by to keep me company from time to time. And, of course, my trusty dog, Smittie, is always there to be my daily companion.

As someone who has worked with money his entire life, trust me when I say, I wouldn't trade this lifestyle for all the money in the world. I am at peace at last. Take that to the bank.

Chapter 35

Matter of Perspective

With the Christmas holidays upon us and people planning visits and all, if anyone should ask how I'm doing or "Where is he now?" You would be accurate in saying the following:

"Oh, he's living in a very exclusive (and expensive) gated community located in the heart of the magnificently scenic northeast corner foothills of Connecticut affectionately known as the 'Quiet Corner.'

"It's quite a complex really, with many amenities. There is a complete dining facility that serves breakfast, lunch, and dinner every day of the week offering a variety of foods with basic nutrition in mind. There is also a common community hall for social gatherings such as playing chess, checkers, cards, and other board games with staff members always present to be sure everyone is safe. There is an on-site medical clinic with a full-time nursing staff and doctors on-call. A physical fitness center is also available with basketball, handball, volleyball and a weight room. It even has exercise matts. If you prefer some fresh air, there is a fenced-in, fully enclosed outside walking area with a set schedule of times of access, including security personnel to be sure that it too is always safe. Perhaps one of the best features is the laundry service. You simply leave your laundry bag at your door and it is picked up dirty and delivered clean for you the very same day.

"As far as social activities go, there's bingo every Thursday night, a common TV viewing area complete with movie and sports nights. And best of all, it has a state-of-the-art security system in place for everyone's safety with expertly trained aegis personnel, second to none, that are on-site 24/7, 365 days a year in all corners of the place.

"Perhaps one often overlooked benefit of living here is the professional services that are readily available. You need only to sign up for visits from counselors, psychologists and social workers who are fully trained and equipped to handle any intangible needs that might arise.

"Oh yeah, and there is a weekly food and basic needs service that will deliver a whole list of various items and goods that can be pre-ordered right to your door.

"You wonder what a place like this might cost? Actually, the State of Connecticut recently released an independent study that was based on all the support services included in a single residence package. It came to $62,159 per unit per year. So, for a fair comparison, you can figure that computes to a rent of $5,180 per month and is all inclusive! Compared to many other "over 55" communities popping up around the state, it's actually quite a deal when you consider it is far less than the cost of a retirement home facility and some of those other communities that don't offer as many included services. It's really quite the place—so unique in so many ways!"

So, that's what you should tell them. Don't mention the fact that what I have just most accurately described is life at the Brooklyn Correctional Institution that has an inmate population of 346.

Chapter 36

Grizzley River Run Rapids

I want to see my family again, who all drowned while we tried fleeing Syria in a small boat. It was during our effort to get to Turkey and eventually the United States. The Mediterranean Sea is very choppy off the northwest coast of Syria and our small boat simply couldn't take the journey. But I have found a way to see my family again, now that I have made it to California in the United States.

I go to Disneyland where they have a ride called Grizzly River Run, a waterfall ride which travels around the water and through some rapids for a while before ending at a calm landing. It is just like the sea off Syria and Turkey.

I save up my money from working in a shop as an illegal immigrant and when I go to this water ride, my heart starts racing as I am in the circular boat that goes down the rapids. I started having flashbacks due to PTSD, and during an episode, I am there again with my family. My wife is there, my teenaged daughter is there and so is my baby boy. Everything is good at first, but when the ride gets bumpy and starts going faster, I see my family drowning. I start screaming but when I come around to reality, I observe all the other people on the ride just staring at me.

Then I am back at the shop, a job I am very grateful for. Because of it, I have food, clean water, and other necessities in my small studio which I didn't always have back in Syria. My wife and I had no choice but to flee the terrorists and other criminal organizations that were destroying everything. We would surely have been killed. The war was raging and there seemed to be a never-ending of it all.

It's funny how we humans don't see ourselves as animals but when things become scarce, we become animals so quickly. Animal instinct kicks in. I've concluded that being human is only possible in times of peace and freedom. And so, I save my money at the shop, not for retirement, but to go to Disneyland again and ride the Grizzly River Run water ride, so I can see my family.

The last time I went there I got banned. The reason I got banned from Disneyland was because when I went on the Grizzly River Run water ride, I started to see my family again, all around me. I could actually feel them. When the ride got faster, I started grabbing hold of them, my family, but they still went into the water. When I came back to reality, I found out that I was grabbing hold of actual people on the ride and I was screaming and shouting. The security guards kicked me out and now I must find another theme park with a similar water ride so that I could make my way to see my family again.

Chapter 37

Chapel of Bones

Christian Carvalho was on his way home traveling from Saville, Spain to Lisbon, Portugal in a cross-country bus ride. His next seat passenger, a Portuguese youth, had asked Christian if he had ever been to the interesting and somewhat ancient town of Evora. A place that they were approaching on the bus. Christian, also being Portuguese and living just outside of Lisbon most of his life, was rather embarrassed that he had not. The youth would go on to suggest that Christian should take a break from his journey and check out the town since they would be going right through it and stopping there. He mentioned that not only the ruins of ancient Roman pillars still stood inside the city walls, but also beautiful churches and relics from follow up historical periods adorned the city.

Then, with a mysterious smile, he told Christian not to miss out on seeing a smaller chapel known to the locals as "Capela dos Ossos" without elaborating on any further details of the place. Christian followed his advice, deciding to take a day's break to visit Evora's historic ruins. Being Portuguese, he knew that "Capela dos Ossos" translated into "Chapel of the Bones." Upon entering the city and walking its perimeter, he did in fact see the Roman ruins of the temple of Diana along with other artifacts from the period dating back to the first century. Upon finishing his exploration and reaching the south end of the city, he came upon the Church of Saint Francis, which was where the foreboding Chapel of the Bones was located.

Christian headed toward the parent church. At the end of his visit there, he was directed to the attached smaller chapel whose entrance door bore the sign that translated loosely into "We whose bones are here await yours." Upon entering, he realized by observation that the entire inner hall was decorated and constructed with original human skulls and bones. Historically, the place was built by Franciscan monks in the sixteenth century preaching the essence of "Momento mori" metaphorically meaning, "Remember you have to die." In building the chapel, the monks wanted to inspire followers into contemplating life's transient nature.

It has been estimated that the over five-thousand skeletons that were utilized in completing the interior came from the graves of monks in nearby cemeteries, many of which were martyred and hastily buried in mass graves. While walking inside the chapel toward the altar, he came upon a display board. The words on it would change his whole outlook on life.

In the dim light he was able to read only a section: "Where are you going in such a hurry traveler? Pause … Do not proceed. You have no greater concern than this one: that on which you focus your sight. Recall how many have passed from this world. Reflect on your similar end. There is good reason to reflect. If only all did the same. Ponder, you so influenced by fate. Among the many concerns of the world, so little do you reflect on death. If by chance you glance at this place. Stop … for the sake of your journey. The longer you pause, the further on your journey you will be."

Chapter 38

Pandemic Time

To me, a major lesson I learned during the pandemic of 2020 was how valuable time was. A pandemic, like the Covid-19 one that had gripped the world back then, causes two things to happen regarding time. The first being, what I normally could spend time doing, could no longer be done due to the massive shut down. And secondly, with that, comes a gain in time to do new things that there was never the time to do before.

Over the time of the pandemic, like most of us, my life's normal activities had been altered due to the paradigm shift that occurred from "time used" to "time available." I found myself walking in circles, so to speak (although, sometimes quite literally) trying to figure out what to do now that I had to "stay in place." That led to taking up activities that I didn't normally have any time for before. One in particular was life-changing for me. It was simply to go grocery shopping.

For example, due to public closures, there was no more going out to a restaurant to eat for me. Which I did on an almost daily basis. Instead, I had to stay inside. So, I learned how to cook amazing dishes for myself. It's fascinating how many recipes are out there, available at your finger-tips, online. I would maybe be joined by a friend or two on occasion—if caught fraternizing, we could just lie about being from the same household—but mostly it was the skill of cooking for one that I had perfected. In relation to that, I found that going shopping became the highlight of my day and that I really enjoyed doing it. I would get just enough provisions for my daily meal. Fortunately, I live within a short walking distance of two major grocery stores, one of them being El Super, with lots of Mexican fare, and the other being a Vons, which has just about anything you could imagine. It's where I found tuna steak for a tantalizing recipe I stumbled upon while surfing the internet. I also live really close to a smaller corner market if I found myself needing something in a hurry, which was rare in the days of the pandemic.

Two side effects that I realized by having a daily pilgrimage to buy my meals was that it was a lot less expensive than eating out every day and that it was easy to gain weight. To combat the later, I took to walking about four miles every day, sans a mask, which was allowed. It felt good to just get out and breathe the fresh air. Going the extra distance every day also opened up new places for me to explore. Again, time was of the essence. I never had the time to do these things before, but with the "restrictions" of the pandemic, I did now. Or perhaps I always did have the time and the pandemic just taught me how to use it more wisely. So, what will happen now that the pandemic is over? Only time will tell.

Chapter 39

Hear the Sermon

"Let one who has ears to hear, hear."

As soon as he started, I knew it was going to be bad. The old priest began his sermon with a faltering voice, and proceeded to tell an obscure story that made no sense to me at all. I was quickly lost and bored. This was not my usual church. I was traveling and just decided to drop in for the Saturday vigil Mass so I could sleep-in the next morning. But I knew right away that the sermon was going to be one of the worst ever. The priest seemed unprepared, vague, and detached.

So, I tuned him out and started fuming inside my head. Suddenly I realized I had become more incensed than the incense burning at the altar. There I sat stupefied, practically gnashing my teeth. If I was in the back pew, I would have snuck out. At long last, he ended his sermon. For the rest of the service, my mind was elsewhere.

After Mass, I walked to my car in the parking lot. No longer able to contain my protest, I complained out loud to the man walking next to me, "What did you think of that sermon?" He walked in silence beside me for a moment, lost in thought. Finally, he gave a gentle reply.

"That was one of the most beautiful sermons I have ever heard."

I was stunned and looked at him expecting to see a sarcastic grin on his face. To my astonishment, I saw that he was weeping. His face was tear-stained, his eyes glistened in the twilight. Suddenly embarrassed, I asked what he meant.

He thought for a moment and responded with a smile, "I've spent most of my life estranged from God, going my own way. Last year I found him, or rather, he found me and now I find him speaking to me in wonderful ways. Like that sermon we just heard. It was all about waking up and listening and hearing God in a new light. That described my life, the love I've found."

In face of his testimony, I was speechless. I shook his hand sheepishly and thanked him. "He may not speak to me but he speaks to thee," I thought.

As I drove home, I marveled at how God could use such a dull and ordinary priest to speak in such an extraordinary way to one of his faithful beloveds. What is meaningless for me to hear, and a cross for me to bear, may be fruitful words of life to a person sitting near to me. Now, I am a more humble, and appreciative listener. Ever since that experience, years ago, I cannot hear a boring sermon without imagining that someone, somewhere out there in the pews might be wiping a tear from their eye and smiling. They may be hearing the voice of God speaking directly into their heart, with healing words raining down like a spring shower on a dry and thirsty desert.

Chapter 40

Grandma's Legacy

My paternal grandmother had passed on a month earlier. I, being the eldest grandson and thereby her designated next of kin, due to the tragic accident that took my father's life eight years ago, was tasked with sorting out her estate. While I was going through her dresser, I found three items that were apparently hidden in her stocking drawer. One was a ring with a large stone that was brilliant enough to be a diamond and was rather antique looking. The second item was a small cross that looked to be home-made and whittled, perhaps by her husband, my grandpa, as it also had a date carved into it that I recognized as their wedding date of November 10, 1936.

The third object was most intriguing. It was disk-shaped, wooden, with concentric circles on the surface—eight in total, signifying it was once part of a tree that was eight years old. It was a half inch thick, about two inches in diameter with a cream-colored center and brown spotted bark along the edge. It had one anomaly; an even darker brown spot. Perhaps the nucleus of a branch begun four years prior to being cut according to its location among the concentric circles. It also had shaven marks where saw teeth likely passed through it. Basically, it was a slice of a young tree.

I was curious as to why this sawed-off disk strip from a birch tree was coupled with the two other, obviously valuable treasured items, neatly tucked away in her sock drawer—her personal hiding space. I had to figure out where it came from and why it was there.

The mystery continued to rack my brain for the next two weeks until I was back at her house yet again to sort her belongings out. This time I had to determine what would be sold at a tag sale and what would eventually go to family members. As I was digging through her hope chest, I came across a photo album. This would definitely go to a family member, perhaps I would even keep it for myself. As I started thumbing through the album, I came upon a picture of the wooden disk!

Excitedly, I took the photo out and noticed it had an inscription on the back which read, "Henry's Eagle Scout Project". Next to it was a date which read: 9/1/53. I immediately recalled that my father had earned his Eagle Scout badge his senior year of high school by building a hut-like shelter at the small town's one athletic field. The shelter was made of woven birch limbs and used to house various and sundry supplies for sporting events, such as the bases for the baseball field.

The story of the little hut had become family lore since it is still there to this day. Nailed to it is a plaque stating my father's name, the year it was built, and the fact that it was an Eagle Scout project dedicated "To My Mom."

Chapter 41

Dollar For Your Thoughts

Gee I smelled great! Nothing like that fresh ink smell. Kind of like a new car smell, only better! That's how my week started. I was put into a tight stack, a hundred of us in total, who were all just exactly like me, except for the small green numbers.

Then a band was put around us. After that, we were stuck into a metal box and took a ride in the fortified truck where the guards have guns even, apparently so we won't be stolen. A while later, we ended up at the bank. I guess we all start out this way. Treated like some sort of political big shots. After being freed from the box and a small stay in a big metal chamber in the basement of the bank, we were taken out, carried upstairs and stuffed in a drawer where eventually the band was ripped off of my ninety-nine buddies and me. That's when my life took a turn for the worse.

I was thumbed out of the drawer and handed by a woman who quickly stuffed me in an envelope with a hole in the middle front so the picture of George could show through. I was in there along with a few of my buddies, nine others I think, when she handed us to another woman on the other side of the counter. Then, together in the envelope, we all went into her purse. She eventually took just me out of the envelope and handed me to a kid with sticky fingers. He immediately crumpled me up, almost using me as a napkin, and stuffed me into the front pocket of his pants. It was warm in there but the new ink smell was now fading fast.

After a while in the pocket with some other flat metal disks, he suddenly grabbed me out and started to flatten me. He handed me, along with two of the bigger flat metal disks, to some chubby guy who placed an ice cream cone in the kid's hand where I had just been. The guy put me in a wooden drawer that had many others who looked somewhat like me, except that they were really wrinkly and some of them were very old looking. One even had scotch tape holding some torn edges together.

The rest of my story saw me taken out of the drawer by the guy and handed out, along with two others, to another person. This time it was some lady who immediately crumpled me up, jamming me into a small purse with a bunch of flat metal disks that were already in there. From there she took me out, flattening me and I was put through a device that was connected to a bus and ended up in a large bin with others just like me yet again. At the end of that night, we were all taken out and put through a different machine that made us all stand neatly in line with each other. Another band was put around us. By "us" I mean all one-hundred of us.

Then we were placed in a metal box and the box eventually went into that fortified truck with the guys who had guns and it was off to the bank again. From there everything was sort of a repeat of before, going into the draw, taken out, stuffed in an envelope and passed around again. It was at that point that I determined, there was no way around it. Life was going to be strange.

Chapter 42

Morning in the Village

In the tiny village of Aljustral, near Fátima in Portugal, the new day begins just like every other day. It starts with the sound of the roosters in the pen heralding the sun about to rise. I don't actually know what time it is, since there is only one clock in the little house where I live with my parents, my two brothers and two sisters and it is in the main room, up behind the woodstove. My brothers and I share one of the three tiny bedrooms together and they wake up along with me to the same rooster-alarm.

After rising, we all know almost instinctively what we are supposed to do, as each one of us has a morning chore. My oldest brother turns on the one light in the room as we get dressed. It is time to take our turns going outside to the outhouse. Being the youngest boy, I have to wait until my two brothers are finished. After that, it's to the kitchen to use the single sink in the house to wash up. We now have a hand-pump of running water inside, something my father and uncle just recently connected last summer. Being that the year is 1921, it's a real convenience for us now.

My first chore is to feed the chickens, which I do like clockwork. Then it will be time to take the sheep out of their pen and herd them to the pasture that my parents own, about a half a mile away from our tiny house. My two younger sisters will accompany me along with our fifteen sheep. They both are waiting anxiously at the pen's gate, one of them has a picnic basket containing some bread, cheese, and olives which Mom prepared and we will have for breakfast once we get the sheep to the pasture. As we lead the sheep, we take up our usual positions, me at the front, my littlest sister to the right and my older sister to the left. Both my brothers, who are older than the three of us, no longer tend the sheep as that is left to us younger kids. They now take care of the cows and garden and chop the wood for the stove that heats our home and cooks our food.

As we make our way along the rock-lined pathway to the open pasture, the sun is just starting to come up and there is a nice film of dew on the grass of the field. That's why we come early every morning since the dew makes the pasture food for the sheep that much better being wet. As we sit down to uncover our picnic basket and enjoy our breakfast together, my older sister leads us in grace. "Bless us, our Lord, and these thy gifts which we receive from thy bounty, through Christ our Lord."

As we eat our breakfast, I look forward to three hours from now when I will get to be at school and see all my friends again. I'm really happy and appreciate that I have it so good seeing as I'm just a kid.

Chapter 43

Alice Left Alone

All Alice wanted was to be left alone. When she was a child, her parents were constantly telling her what to do and making what she considered to be unreasonable demands. To make matters worse, her older brother would join in. It became unbearable and she hated it. She just wanted to be left alone.

She looked forward to the first day of school, as she believed her life would change. She was quickly disappointed when she discovered that her teachers were just as demanding as her parents. Alice wondered if there would ever be a time in her life when she would be left alone.

One day she came to the conclusion that in order to reach her life goal of being left alone she would have to leave school and move away from her family. She knew that this plan would involve marriage. She met a young man who eventually proposed to her and she accepted. Shortly after her wedding day, Alice realized she had made a big mistake. Her husband was even more demanding than her parents and teachers. She needed her space and to be left alone.

She thought that a job would be the answer to her problem, giving her a temporary reprieve from her husband. Her boss was a tyrant. He constantly berated her, demanding of her far more than what she was capable of doing. Alice wished he would just leave her be and let her get her work done. Why was he always on her case? She just wanted to be left alone.

Her husband was able to talk her into quitting her job and starting a family. Yes, she thought, I'll finally be left alone. She had no idea how demanding a baby could be, but she quickly learned. Do not get the wrong idea. Alice loved her baby boy. She just couldn't stand all the new demands being placed on her. She experienced dark times through those years but somehow managed to survive.

In the twilight years of her life, Alice had lost her husband, parents, and brother to death. She agreed with her son that she would move into Sunset Meadows Assisted Living Care Home on the condition that she would have a private room. Her son complied, and though it was more expensive, she got her own room.

Alice sat in the room facing the window allowing the sunshine to warm her wrinkled face. She was thinking it took eighty-seven years to reach her goal of being alone. At last! All of a sudden, an orderly burst into the room yelling, "Hey Alice! You need to hurry up. You have your medication to take and you …"

Alice interrupted him as decades of frustration that had welled up inside her suddenly erupted out of her mouth directly targeting the unassuming orderly. Stunned, he quickly left the room.

Not even a minute later, Alice began clutching her chest, feeling extreme pain, as she slumped to the floor, unable to move. She looked around the room. No one was there. Her emergency button was well out of reach. Her final thought was that the best thing to happen to her was also the worst. Alice was finally … left alone.

Chapter 44

Recruitment Dinner

The recruitment dinner was buffet-style with an abundance of food. The V.F.W. hall was set up with the chow line and four dining tables, forming a circle of sorts, so that everyone sitting down to eat could see everyone else. Leading the event was Master Sergeant Phelps who had the distinct honor of welcoming the eight new recruit prospects. He had been instructed by the captain to include all four of the recruitment sergeants who were responsible for getting two recruits apiece to sign up. So, including Phelps, there were five sergeants and eight new recruits who sat at the tables. Two of the sergeants Phelps liked and two he didn't much care for. Luckily, being the master sergeant, he out ranked them all.

On the left of Phelps were Gunnery Sergeant Watson and Staff Sergeant Burns who Phelps had known for some time and had all become good buddies. On his right were two buck sergeants, McKinney and Russo that Phelps didn't much care for since they were so green. Those two had never seen combat but somehow in spite of their inexperience and through the perfunctory Marine bureaucracy, landed the cushy job of recruiters.

Phelps turned first to address his buddy Watson, in front of the others, in order to get the conversation over dinner going. "Hey Gunnery Sergeant Watson, remember that time in Fallujah when we ran out of water for showers at the bivouac and the whole platoon hadn't washed in over two weeks?"

Sergeant Watson laughed out loud and followed, "Yeah, I remember we were rubbing sand under our armpits instead of using water!" The two started laughing heartedly together while the new recruits just snickered. Phelps and Watson were winning them over.

Then he turned to McKinny, one of the two buck sergeants and said, "And how about you Sergeant McKinny? Get any paper cuts lately from all that paperwork you've been doing?" McKinny didn't respond but was notably embarrassed as his cheeks turned red. This time the new recruits just looked at each other.

Phelps then turned back to Staff Sergeant Burns, his other buddy. "So, Staff Sergeant Burns, remember that time were in the helo in Afghanistan and we were running out of gas and had to put down outside the wire?"

Burns responded, "Yeah Sarge, you looked like you were gonna lose it with the stupid Army puke pilot!" The two roared in laughter and the new recruits joined in this time.

Finally, Phelps addressed the other green sergeant, Russo. "Hey Sergeant Russo, you been making any pizza and spaghetti lately? That's the closest you've come to seeing any blood red!" Sheepishly, Russo just shook his head "no" as the new recruits giggled like school girls.

Then Master Sergeant Phelps spoke up loudly. "You new recruits! How dare you laugh at my jokes at the expense of a superior! All four of these sergeants out rank you or will out rank you and are due your upmost respect—as am I! You are therefore to remain silent through the rest of the diner, while we share our stories. Now, all of you, move away from the table and drop and give me twenty!"

Chapter 45

Paths Crossing

The river divided them, but their paths crossed each morning on the bridge that linked east to west. Tramping to his office in the financial district, it was her yellow scarf that first snagged his attention. Hurrying home from folding clothes at the laundromat, she noticed his mop of hair untamed by the comb peeking out of the chest pocket in his gray suit. In a city choked with traffic, they both found it quicker, and much more pleasant, to walk.

In searing sun, in wind or rain, or on dry or humid days, they pounded the pavement on their separate journeys. They would both cut through various alleyways and parks. On the bridge, the breeze sweeping up from the rushing water below refreshed them in the summer heat. The open view unbounded their thoughts as they walked.

They began to look for each other, progressing through nods of acknowledgement to a crisp "Good Morning!" and a jolly "Fine Day!" when the weather deserved it. In her colorful outfits, he imagined her a fashion student; she envisioned him a scientist juggling concepts unfathomable to the ordinary mind.

One morning, he pointed out the sun gilding the weathervane atop the nearby church on the wayside, without breaking his stride. On another, she showed him the stork perched on the window ledge of a derelict building, as if resting on a La Jolla cliff. They shared a raised-eyebrow moment when a jogger barged past them, tinny music leaking from the cans on his ears. And they giggled when a sudden gust of wind grabbed her skirt like Marilyn Munroe's.

He could have told her that his grandfather had designed the bridge. She could have told him that her father helped construct the walkways they used. But they both had more pressing matters to address. If they could just summon the courage.

The morning that he determined to finally ask her out, she didn't appear. He dawdled, strained his eyes for a glimpse of yellow, until, at the risk of being late, he had to race the last hundred yards to work. He didn't see her the next day either. Or the next. Perhaps their friendship wasn't meant to be.

All the previous week she tried to tell him. Her new job would entail an entirely different commute. But although she practiced before the mirror in her one-room studio, the words had stalled in her throat. Why would a professor care about her promotion to barista in the city shopping mall? Would he even notice she'd gone?

He kept hoping to see her up until the day of the party. But why would a fashionista care about seeing a boring accountant? Once, in a restaurant, he thought he recognized the waitress serving another table. Once, in the market square, she thought she saw him queueing with a child for an ice cream cone.

Although both had made homes in the city, they never spoke again. But whenever either of them happened to cross the bridge at rush hour, alone, they felt a surge of well-being. His soft and yellow like her scarf; hers gray and toothy, like his pocket comb.

Chapter 46

Splinter Sprinter

I always was rather fast as a sprinter. I first noticed this gift participating in the hundred-meter dash in track during high school and my ability to move quickly carried over into other team sports as well. In football, I was always flanked outside the line as a wide receiver, able to run fast behind the defense and get open for a pass from the quarterback. In soccer, I always played mid-field, again, a position that required much sprinting either attacking the goal on offense or getting back quickly to play defense. And in baseball, I was always a threat once I hit the basepath. Stealing bases became my forte. I couldn't knock the ball out of the park very often because my upper body didn't have the brute-force strength to do so, but as long as I could connect with the pitch, my legs would get me onboard the bases.

I became acutely aware of just how valuable my legs were during one particular game of baseball in high school. It was a home game and it was in the bottom of the seventh, the last inning. The score was tied five to five. I had reached first base on a line drive to right field and with only one out, was ready to go on a hit-and-run play called by the third base coach. My teammate did his job at the plate and managed to connect on a hit to deep center field. I took off on the pitch and was already rounding second when the centerfielder finally reached the ball that had bounced in. The third base coach was waving his arms signaling me into third, full steam ahead. Then suddenly he started to wave his arms down and across his body toward home plate. That meant only one thing. He wanted me to keep going around third and into home. There would be a play at the plate.

As I neared homebase, I could see the throw from the second baseman who was relaying it out of the corner of my eye, coming in toward the catcher. I slid hard feet-first into home plate, and as I did, my left heel's cleat caught the lip of the plate and there was a loud snap. My leg broke at the left shin—a compound tibial shaft fracture—bone through the skin. At least I was safe at the plate.

The team's doctor was watching in the bleachers and ran down to administer the proper first aid. He set my leg right there at home plate as I was still lying on the ground. Then he remarked that I had an incredibly high threshold of pain since I didn't even yell out in agony. Instead, I just quietly sat there. I remember that it just felt weird, like a dream, until he set my bone back inside my shin where it belonged.

I can still feel the effect of that break over the many years since, especially when there is a storm approaching. Something about the barometric pressure, I guess. And I still revel in the fact that my sprinting speed had allowed me to score the winning run that day, broken leg and all.

Chapter 47

Taken Away

He is easily approachable. An open, gregarious chap that usually has a smile on his face. His worldview is simple. That is, to look for opportunities to enhance the daily life experience with whatever comes his way. He has a deep faith and it is reflected almost immediately upon meeting him for the first time. If not directly, then by his welcoming demeanor—one that puts every person at ease no matter where they have come from. There is not a judgmental or prejudice bone in his body, though he is quick to rely on good judgment. He is a person you would like to call on or have as a friend.

Now he is sitting in the back of a police car. Not as a willing passenger, but under arrest. The pain from the handcuffs cutting into his wrists, secured behind his back, only increases as he struggles to move them away from his body. They only cut in deeper. It was impossible to get comfortable. The cuffs were simply on way too tight. He is starting to get annoyed. No, that's putting it mildly. He is getting pissed! He didn't do anything wrong but the two cops simply won't listen.

Only moments earlier, he was at his friend Lola's door knocking and wondering what had happened to her. That's when the cops spotted him and came at him fast.

"What are you doing here?" one demanded.

"I've come to help Lola. She called me. Where is she?" came his rapid response.

"This is private property and you're trespassing!" bellowed the other cop.

"She called me. She was having an episode. Where is she? What have you done with her?"

Just then he glanced toward the road and noticed the cop car with

Lola in the back. Her shoulders were drawn behind since her hands were cuffed. She looked straight at him with a terrified look on her face as the blue and red strobe lights blared on, accenting her features in the night. Their momentary glance was suddenly interrupted.

"Hands behind your back sir!" came the first cop. "We're taking you in for trespassing. This is a restricted facility!"

He was aware that it was a restricted facility. It was a residence for people with mental illnesses. But he and Lola were close friends and he'd been here to her place a number of times before.

"What happened to Lola? Why is she in that police car?" he inquired.

"That's none of your business! You are coming with us downtown. You have the right to remain silent …"

Then the cuffs clicked on behind his back. "Wait! Wait, I've done nothing wrong. She called me and asked me to come over and help her. She was having an episode I tell you!"

"She had an episode alright," came the second cop. "Get in the car! You're going with us."

"Wait. What's going to happen to me?" he pleaded.

The two cops stayed silent at that point and handled him over to their cruiser, stuffing him in the back.

Now he could only look out his window and see Lola sitting in the back of the other police car again. She just stared at him with deadpan eyes as the blue and red lights strobed enough for him to see the sullen look on her face. In spite of all his good intentions, there was nothing that he could do for her.

Chapter 48

Desert Breakdown

The couple was fuming while riding along Route 16, a secondary road through the desert. They had stopped for gas a few minutes earlier after having an hour-long arguing session prior to the break. Now that they were on the road again, they picked right up with the bickering. They argued over almost everything. It was a wonder they were still together as a couple.

As they were driving along, they passed a sign that warned it was another sixty miles until the next town. Nothing but the desert on either side of the road but plenty of time for more heated discussion between them. About thirty-five minutes into their trek, the woman, Bonnie, who was the passenger, noticed a car pulled over and motioned to the driver, her so-called boyfriend Claude, that they should stop. She thought that they should make sure the car's driver was okay because there wasn't anyone sitting in the driver's seat. She wanted to be certain that they weren't out of gas or something worse, since it was a long way to walk to town in the middle of the desert stretch.

Claude at first objected but then obliged by slowing down to a crawl. When they got next to the car, they could see that it was a Ferrari Daytona convertible and it sounded as if the engine was running. It purred. They couldn't see anyone inside, so Claude stopped in front of the car. The couple got out and went up to the seemingly abandoned vehicle. They looked in all directions and couldn't see the driver anywhere. Yet the car was still running.

"What a strange situation," Bonnie stated.

"The car is still motoring with the keys in the ignition," Claude added.

"What should we do?" she asked.

"That's a loaded question," Claude responded.

Bonnie continued, "Well, obviously something's very wrong here. There's no one in sight and the engine is running."

Claude leaned into the driver's side and said, "There's about a half a tank of gas left, surely enough to make it to the next town."

"Maybe we should drive it," Bonnie stated.

"Don't think that's a good idea. The owner probably got kidnapped or something, I mean, an expensive car like this and all. Maybe we should just call 9-1-1."

"Can't," Bonnie said, "No bars. I already thought of that. I still think we should drive it into the next town and turn it in to the police so it doesn't get stolen out here in the middle of nowhere."

"It will look like we're stealing it if we drive off in it," said Claude. He continued, "let's just get in our car and leave things alone."

"You know I'm not like that!" Bonnie exclaimed. "We've got to do something!"

"Fine then," he said, "You drive it. If you get arrested, I don't know you!" They were arguing again.

With that, Bonnie got in behind the wheel of the Ferrari and pushed the accelerator while in neutral, to rev up the engine. It was as if she was growling at him. She then peeled out, screeching onto the pavement.

She was almost out of sight by the time Claude got back behind the wheel of his car and turned around to go back from where they had come. He thought to himself saying aloud, "Good riddance!"

Chapter 49

Sickle Cell Diary

The first entry in his diary was about the day we met and he mentioned me to be a sweet girl with a determined attitude. He was the complete opposite of me, innocent and childish. The next entry in his diary was on his birthday when I took him to a pet store like he asked, and got him a beagle. His face lit up and he was so cute when he first saw the dog. He gave me one of the sweetest smiles I can ever recall. He didn't leave the dog alone for a second that day and I remember his mother was furious that he got a dog without her permission. She started scolding me and telling me that I was spoiling him.

The next entry was something that I never expected to see and which was intended for me. I was shocked to see that he had hidden something that important from me. He was suffering from Sickle Cell Anemia and was first diagnosed with this in the first grade. He wrote that it was mostly like a living hell for him until he met me because he never had a single friend since his schooling began.

He said, "My schooling was in correspondences and lately I was shifted to emergency wards for blood transfusions almost every day. After my schooling, my condition started to stabilize and I had hope for life. On my birthday night, I had to be rushed to the hospital because I had a severe seizure and it brought uncontrollable pain to the left side of my body. My mom told me that my vitals were dropping, the doctors lost hope, and asked my parents to lose hope. Then, the next day, I started getting better with stable vitals and the doctors said that my chance of survival was about three weeks.

"This crushed me from within because I had just three weeks to spend with you. I thought of telling you about my condition but I didn't want to see pity, and more importantly, I didn't want you to cry like everyone else. Every day after that was great. They were the best three weeks I could imagine because you fulfilled my wishes without even knowing I was going to die soon. You got me a dog. You took me on a long drive, you let me eat ice cream till I couldn't eat another bite, you took me to a fair and made me ride the Ferris wheel. I know these wishes seemed to be childish, yet you fulfilled all of them leaving me just one last wish.

"My last wish is, that I want you to live your life the way it was before and not cry over my grave every time you remember me. You should forget me and move on because I know how it feels to be stuck up with one thought in your head and being unable to continue with your life. Don't worry because once I'm in heaven, I'll make sure I watch every move of yours and if I see you crying another tear for me, I'll start haunting you. So, live your life and promise me you are going to fulfill this ONE LAST WISH of mine."

Chapter 50

Ice Storm

The weather in New England is always unpredictable. How's that saying go? If you want to know the weather forecast—just look outside. Point is, it can change on a dime. I'll never forget one weather episode that occurred in my life while living in New England, and growing up in Connecticut. It was the winter of 1973, right before Christmas. In fact, it was the week before Christmas. It wasn't a "normal" event like a snowstorm, though that's how it started out. No, we had an ice storm which hit us out of nowhere. Nobody expected it. There was no preparation beforehand.

I was only a junior in high school at the time and the events of that week left a lasting impression upon me. You see, the storm started as rain but the cold air immediately turned the rain to ice. It caused all the trees and powerlines to become completely encased and frozen as it stuck like glue to the surfaces of whatever the rain touched. Everything had a thick ice coating. This caused considerable added weight to the lines and trees especially. That in turn caused tree limbs and powerlines to break off and fall under the weight caused by the ice, resulting in a massive power outage throughout the state and region. This wasn't one of those temporary power outages that only last a few hours or so. This one lasted over a week.

So, there we were in winter conditions with no power resulting in no heat or electricity due to the outage that blanketed everywhere. There was no going over to the next town or county. The result was the same throughout the state. A total blackout.

Fortunately, our family had just finished an addition to our house that included a new, huge family room with an oversized, floor to ceiling, fieldstone fireplace designed specifically for heating the room. Needless to say, we were fortunate. Even though we couldn't use the oil burner that needed electricity to fire up and circulate the air, we could at least keep warm in that spacious room from the heat generated by the fireplace. Luckily, my father insisted that I chop wood for it the previous weekend and I had stored the wood inside the garage. It was safe and dry from the outside icy environment.

I'll never forget all the adjustments our family made that Christmas. We stayed in that fireplace-heated room for everything. We all slept on the carpeted floor, gathered in front of the fire to play games and pass the time, and we even cooked our meals over the flames. Nothing like a December hot dog roast, complete with melted marshmallows, in your family room. Fortunately, we had a well-stocked canning cellar so food wasn't an issue for us. Yet throughout all the trials and challenges we faced that week, the Christmas tree stood proudly decorated in the corner. Only the lights were gloomy, unable to be lit.

The glow of our faces reflecting the flickering flames of the fire seemed to make that Christmas one to be forever a fond memory in spite of the turbulent weather conditions. Our "Little House on the Prairie" Christmas of 1973 was in fact the best Christmas I remember, even though Santa never came that year.

Chapter 51

P.11 Fighter Down

The sky was slashed with trails of smoke as I limped away in a wounded PZL P.11 fighter plane, the lone survivor of an air battle that all but decimated the final remnants of the Polish Air Force. It was a struggle to maintain the airspeed necessary just to keep flying. On either side of me, my wings were torn and punctured by bullets fired from the three, far superior German Messerschmitt Bf 109s, as well as from a few over-zealous Polish gunners on the ground.

In addition to this, my fighter's engine made sputtering noises that would be disconcerting to any pilot, courteously alerting me that it was on its last leg. With this in mind, I searched for a suitable place to land which, fortunately for me, was not hard to find as the Polish countryside below had many open fields for landing in.

I didn't so much set my plane down as I dropped it into the field. Since most of my P.11's control surfaces had been shot away, the precise adjustments required to execute a proper landing were close to impossible to actually carry out.

The ground beneath me, appearing from the air to be hard and compacted earth, almost immediately gave way under the weight of my machine. For it was actually soft and freshly tilled. The violent sounds of wrenching and twisting metal followed shortly thereafter before the nose of my aircraft dug itself firmly into the ground with a sharp jerk. The propellor, still spinning, flung about heaps of grass and dirt before finally coming to an abrupt halt.

I then freed myself out of my harness making a short leap out of my aircraft onto the ground. I shook myself a bit, wiggling my toes and fingers, patted myself up and down my body inspecting for any serious injury. Although I was no doctor, I determined that I was unharmed—sore but not broken.

Next, I checked my sidearm, a Tokarev TT-33, and I counted seven rounds. I wouldn't be winning any gunfights anytime soon but it could aid in a hasty getaway. Around me lay nothing but open farm fields with a wooded area on the perimeter that looked to be about a mile out to the north. My map made no mention of any town nearby but I was eager to get away from the crash site and find a place to hide while I figured out my plan of action.

It was sunny. It was peaceful. Any sign indicating that a dogfight had transpired had already long since left the sky. From that field, the invasion of Poland seemed like nothing more than a horrible dream. Or maybe, I thought, I was dead and just didn't know it yet. However, the sound of gunfire cracking in the distance reminded me that the war was very much a real thing and not very far away.

As I neared the edge of the wood-line, I looked back on the field one last time where I was only able to just make out the wreckage of my downed P.11. It was a sordid sight and I felt almost as though I was leaving behind a wounded comrade. Weighed down heavily by melancholy, I proceeded into the wood-line, hoping to disappear from it all.

Chapter 52

Demanding Boss

Bradley McFerson was running late. Again. It was the third time this week that he would be late for the luncheon meeting with his boss, Albert Finch. And, on top of that, it was only Thursday. So, a week's worth of scheduled lunch meetings and Bradley was already running late for the third out of four times.

Unfortunatly for him, Albert was your stereotypical demanding boss type. Very boisterous and demeaning toward his underlings, expecting them to do what they were told and keep their mouths shut. Bradley realized this as he had been chastised by him numerous times for not only being late this week, but also for the many other shortcomings he possessed that didn't meet Albert's unreasonably high expectations.

Why was Bradley running late? This time it would be because of Jenny. Oh yes, Jenny. She was the group's pooled secretary that Bradley and three other associates shared to help them offload the ton of paperwork that seemed to never end. It was all par for the course as a second-year paralegal at the well-established, prestigious law firm. Paperwork was the name of the game. More paperwork meant more billable hours.

Jenny had something other than her obvious good looks and efficient working style going for her. She seemed more interested in Bradley than the average bear. It had gotten so that he would invent reasons to stop by her desk just to be close to her and get a sniff of the rose-scented perfume that she always wore. It would make his heart jump. This time, as he passed her desk, he was in a rush to meet his boss Albert for lunch. That's when she suddenly flagged him down.

"I've got a problem with my printer. Can you help me, Bradley? Please?" Her coquettish query, accenting the words "you" and "me." Bradley couldn't resist. It was a chance to be her knight in shining armor. So, he stopped at her desk. He had a crush on her for months now, but never had the nerve to ask her out. He wasn't even sure if it was even allowed, with office fraternizing policies and all.

"Let me take a look-see at it," he said with his southern Texas accent. Jenny just beamed at the thought of his help.

"I sure would appreciate it," she added. So, Bradley stopped and helped Jenny with her printer. It was really more to be within inches of her and her intoxicating scent of roses. Albert would just have to wait. Again. Bradley said to himself, "It will probably get me fired. Or at least docked in pay when I show up late again." But he couldn't help himself. His heart was pounding in his chest as he tended to Jenny's printer. Just the proximity of her being so near, practically leaning into him was making him melt.

Finally, he had the printer adjusted to where Bradley thought it would work. "Try it now Jenny, dear," he ventured as he closed the lid.

She selected the print icon on the computer screen and paper started spewing forth.

"My hero!" she exclaimed. "I hope I didn't keep you from your lunch meeting."

"I'll be alright. I'll get some flowers for Albert or maybe, better yet, a bottle of Scotch and hopefully that will soften him up."

"More like get you fired on the spot!" Jenny added.

"That's okay. At least I'll be free for dinner with you. That is, if you're game."

Chapter 53

Rail Trail

It is one of my favorite spots to go to in the world. The nice thing is that I can go there every day if I want to. It's only two miles from my house and it only takes me an hour, round-trip. Not that it takes a long time to go the two miles by driving there, but by walking instead. Something I love to do. You see, down in back of my place there's some woods. And if you walk into the woods from my backyard and go about a hundred yards, you'll come upon some old railroad track ruins.

I live in my parents' old house, the place I grew up. In my youth, we used to hear the trains go by since the tracks were so close. You could almost set your clocks by them. Seven in the morning, noontime, three o'clock, five in the evening, and eight o'clock at night, they would go by everyday without fail. My neighborhood buddies and I used to go down there in spite of our parents warning us to stay away from the tracks. We would set empty cans on the tracks and stand in the abutting woods waiting for a train to come. We'd watch as the trains would crush the cans flat or split them in two. It was a blast for us and our parents never once caught us.

Now the trains no longer run on the tracks, of course, as the rails have been upended, the beds torn down and in their place is a smooth passageway called the "Rail Trail." The trail runs where the trains used to go, for several miles in either direction and that includes over some scenic bridges and through some small cavernous tunnels. When they built the new surface, they put a fine gravel down on top so that joggers, biking enthusiasts, or ambitious walkers like me, can make their way along the route with ease. There is not too much that betrays that it was once the main passageway through our little town which was strictly for the trains to travel on. Though there are still some remnants of the powerlines that ran the distance along the side of the tracks. Most of them are now either collapsed or just survive as barren, tall poles stuck in the ground. A few still retain their cross beams, but all of them that do remain standing are weathered away to a brownish gray color. If you are lucky, you might occasionally find a green glass transformer covering buried in the leaves below the poles.

Depending on the time of day that you are on the trail, early morning or late in the day, you can catch the sun beaming in through the trees brightly illuminating the path. Since the pathway traverses through the woods, there is also lots of game that can be occasionally be seen, from wild turkeys and rabbits to the disparate deer, all venturing near the pathway looking for dropped food. There are also mile markers at every quarter mile. The stakes in the ground enumerate the distance from one town to the next along the way giving the foot-bound interlopers a reading on their progress.

I have found the Rail Trail to be the perfect venue for appreciating nature, meditating, or just clearing one's mind. Taking a brisk, four-mile walk, going two miles out to the Vernon town line marker and the two miles back, is just right. It takes me about a half hour each way including several stops to just enjoy nature. Sometimes I even think up short stories as I'm walking. Even though the passing trains that you could set your clocks by are long since gone, it is something I try to do like clockwork every day.

Chapter 54

Light in the Night

It was getting late. Too late to be five miles out and away from basecamp. Alone. Twilight blanketed the narrow trail ahead and soon it would be too dark to see anything. On top of that, it was to be a moonless night according to the calendar. The distant stars, although majestic, wouldn't offer him much relief. And like a fool, he had forgotten his flashlight when he left at noon—conversely, the brightest time of the day. The thought of bringing it along just didn't enter his mind back then. His lack of preparation had led him to this moment. Only his stupidity was to blame. As if blaming anything, including himself, would make him feel better and offer any inkling of relief. Fear started to tighten its grip on him.

Then he thought of the effect that the sun setting below the horizon had had on him in the past. It was nothing but soothing and comforting. He appreciated the beautiful sunsets over the ocean, with the fiery ball glowing almost red as it touched the sea. It would dip below the horizon as the blackening sky approached, almost like a tenebrous, soft blanket covering the earth for the night. There were the brilliant streaks of clouds, like purple and pink whisps of cotton candy giving off one last burst of dazzling color against the rapidly darkening navy-blue firmament. He thought about the way that, as twilight blanketed the city, the lights in the buildings would come alive like scores of fireflies dancing in the night. All sorts of majestic images were conjured up in his mind at the mere thought of sunset. None of it brought fear. Instead, there often came a deep sense of appreciation of the glory of God's magnificent creation. Until now.

What he wouldn't give in this situation for just one of those city lights as the darkness crept in on him like a foreboding wave of doom and peril. He tried his best not to panic because he knew that would only make things worse.

Then there were the strange new sounds that the night was bringing, which seemed to just come out of nowhere. Or perhaps they were there all along, but as his vision was becoming limited, his hearing was perking up. It was as if the call of the night creatures all around him were invading the last of his comforting senses. It got so loud that it felt deafening. What he wouldn't give to be back at basecamp right now sitting by the fledgling campfire with a pot of coffee perking up on the coals and singing camp songs instead. Or to be comfortably sitting against a tree trunk, listening to a twangy harmonica taming the night noise while watching the lazy flames flicker to the dancing sound of the notes.

But no. His foolishness had stranded him out in the wilderness as the night settled in and took dominion over everything around him. He simply wasn't in control anymore. Nature now had the upper hand. He realized that he wouldn't be settling in this night. He realized just how small he really was in the face of the power of darkness. He would stay awake and anticipate, for eight long hours, the relief that would only come to him with dawn's early light.

Chapter 55

Lance and the Donkey

Lance grew up in a large village in France during the Middle Ages. When he was younger, he was one of those kids who was just a pain in the ... well, let's just say a donkey's behind. Since that's where this story is going. The problem only worsened as he grew older. He became not only a complete annoyance to everyone, but he was also constantly flirting with the justice system. Though he was guilty of several offenses, he always evaded jail by trickery, deception, a technicality, or a loophole. Lance took advantage of anything and everything he could get away with, even though he knew it was definitely wrong. He thought he was too clever for any watchmen, county sheriff, or judge. In fact, he considered it a badge of honor that he could outsmart any judge he went before. Remember, this was the Middle Ages, medieval times, and tactics in the legal system were not what they are today.

One evening Lance committed a crime which had the consequence of having him put away in a dungeon for a very, very long time. He was apprehended by the law and found himself face-to-face with a brand-new judge. "This will be a new challenge and should be fun," he said to himself.

The judge made it clear to Lance that a new way of determining guilt or innocence in a crime had recently been put into law and was now being enforced. The judge further explained to him that he would enter the room next to the judge's chamber. The room was completely dark and contained a donkey. Lance was to find the donkey and pull on its tail. If the donkey brayed, Lance would be found guilty. Should the donkey remain silent, he would be considered innocent and immediately released. Lance headed for the room as he conjured up in his mind how he would get out of this dilemma.

The door closed behind him as he realized what he had to do. Absolutely nothing. By not pulling the tail of the donkey would ensure no braying. He only had to wait a few moments there in the dark then he could reemerge in the next room with that stupid judge and be declared innocent. He could then go about his merry way and think about his next crime. He thought, "This is too easy." Lance walked back into the room with the judge patiently waiting for him, displaying a defiant smirk on his face.

"Did you do exactly as I instructed you to do?" asked the judge solemnly.

"Yes, your honor, I did everything you said," lied Lance.

"Lance, approach the bench and let me see both of your hands," demanded the judge.

Lance walked forward and wondered what the heck was going on. He then showed the judged his clean, well-manicured hands, holding them out defiantly.

"Lance," the judge declared, "I find you guilty as charged and hereby sentence you to life in prison!"

Lance was totally shocked and he had just barely opened his mouth to let the judge have it when the bailiff walked the donkey into the room passing right by Lance.

There it was. The explanation of it all. When the donkey turned, Lance could see the donkey's behind. It revealed everything. The entire tail of the donkey had been coated with soot and coal dust.

Chapter 56

Bravehearted

When the alarm in my mind went off at 5:30 am, I snapped to, sat up, ran my fingers through my hair, raised my arms over my head and stretched. Love that feeling every day. If there is a favorite minute of the day that I would choose to relive repeatedly it is this one.

After all the get-up-and-go routine activities like taking a shower, brushing my teeth, and all, I love to have that first cup of coffee. Black. I say first cup because it won't be the last of the day, or anywhere near it for me. I love coffee. Then, after getting dressed in my only pair of pants and shirt, I repack my pockets with the few things I own which I had put on the nightstand the evening before. I grab my two IDs, one an expired passport the other a library card, my portable toothbrush, a pocket knife, my only debit card and whatever cash I have left over from the last withdrawal, about a hundred bucks in twenties.

Next, I set out from wherever I slept the night before. Usually, it's a cheap motel, like this one but I have on occasion, more often than not, slept out under the stars. Provided it's warm. My destination? Nowhere in particular. I like to walk long distances, so transportation is never an issue. I could always grab a bus or hitch-hike, but that last option is getting much harder to do these days.

On this occasion, I am making my way from Denver to San Diego, via Los Angeles, where I am now. No particular reason for going to San Diego except that I've never been there before and I hear it is usually warm no matter what time of year it is. Today I am leaving Venice Beach and hitch-hiking down U.S. Route 101, also called the Coastal Highway. I hope to get a ride from an interesting driver. If that doesn't work out, I'll catch a bus. There seems to be a lot of them on this road. Plenty of time during the day to determine that. Of course, I'll stop for more coffee along the way.

One thing for sure, I'm about ready for a new change of clothes. I bought the ones I have on now, four days ago. So, it's about time to stop in at another hardware store and buy a new pair of pants, some socks, and a work shirt. My shoes are good quality and will probably last me another four hundred miles of walking at least. Tomorrow, I also plan to get a haircut and a shave from a good full-service barber, or maybe the next day, if I can't find one tomorrow.

I haven't been to a baseball game in forever. I read in the newspaper at the diner during dinner last night that the Dodgers will be in San Diego for the weekend. Apparently, that's some rivalry. If I make it to S.D. in time (before the weekend runs out), I'll go catch the game. One place I was told to check out, by the lady who gave me a ride yesterday, was someplace called La Jolla. She said it was on the way and very quaint. After crossing the Rocky Mountains and the desert, I could use a little "quaint" right about now.

So off I go. Another day of adventure and who knows what it will bring. My chosen retirement lifestyle. I'm just happy to be alive and physically able, thank God, to enjoy whatever is in store next. What was it that Mel Gibson shouted in that Braveheart movie?

Chapter 57

Two Firsts

There were two things that I had never done before and both were happening to me for the first time and at the same time. One was the fact that I was now married after living twenty-three years being single growing up from a very happy childhood into a responsible adult. Being a newlywed, a husband for only a few hours, I would be doing the second thing for the first time almost simultaneously. That was leaving the country. We were leaving the continental U.S. for the Cayman Islands. The fact that I was traveling "abroad" with my new bride Chrissy only made the entire trip that much more exciting. There is a first time for everything, and for us as a couple it was our first trip together being married—the honeymoon. For Chrissy, it was mainly a visceral experience since she had long since been a world traveler. But for me it was entirely novel, having never been outside the United States before.

I remember looking into her deep, aqua blue eyes as we were flying from Miami to the island in the small double prop plane and thinking, "Wow! I'm married to her!" Just seeing her shoulder length, soft, sandy blonde hair reflecting the sun from behind her creating a halo effect, as she had the window seat, was mesmerizing. I remember thinking, "I seemed to have married an angel." She just smiled at me and offered that oft used expression of hers, "Penny for your thoughts?"

To which I replied, as I always did, "They will cost you a dollar!"

As the plane reached Grand Cayman Island, we circled once around and I recall thinking that the pristine white sands that were on the boarder and contrasted so starkly with the turquoise water made the island look like a true pearl of paradise. I was not to be disappointed. My first trip abroad!

After we finally landed and deplaned, I made a gesture of kneeling down right there on the tarmac and kissing the ground. Well, not really.

My lips came to within an inch but not literally on the blacktop. Chrissy just laughed at me and my memory building antics as I assured her that I didn't actually kiss the dirt because we had lots to do with our lips together over the next week in the land of marital bliss.

Since the year was 1980, there wouldn't be any technological annoyances to deal with, such as mobile phones, as they weren't even a twinkle in Steve Jobs' eye yet. But it also meant that there were not any phones handy for taking pictures either. I simply needed to have a picture of my first visit to a foreign land. Being the good wife that she already was, Chrissy took my 35-millimeter camera and snapped a shot of me with my hands on the fuselage of our puddle jumper being sure to include my feet firmly planted in the soil of the first country outside of the United States I had ever visited.

Getting married and leaving the country for the first time were two big "firsts" that I experienced together at the same time. Little did I know or appreciate fully at the time, that they were only the beginning of innumerable "firsts" that were to follow in the life of Chrissy and I together as husband and wife.

Chapter 58

Surprise Phone Call

Sometimes you need to hear a story of deep appreciation and pride. Especially if it is just in time for Christmas. Somehow that time of year makes everything more noticeable when common events are so often taken for granted. So, when the phone rang last Monday morning at five o'clock in the morning, I was awakened to a sudden sense of fear and apprehension. I don't usually get calls that early. In fact, we have a rule that all my friends and family are aware of, that we take no calls except between nine in the morning and nine at night. This one was well outside that boundary.

Then I saw on the caller ID that it was my daughter, Agnieszka, who was calling me so early. My sense of trepidation only increased. She lives on the east coast and I live on the west, so it actually was eight o'clock her time when she called. Perhaps it wasn't an emergency after all. Maybe she just didn't stop to think about the time difference, or so I hoped.

With a groggy voice trying to speak clearly and seeing that it was her calling, before I answered the phone, a rush of worries came over me. I wondered why Aga would be calling me so early on a Monday morning. Maybe she had an accident on her way to work at the Amazon distribution center or something of that nature. But no, that couldn't be it, I thought to myself. She starts at eight, so she'd already be there. Funny how the mind can so rapidly consider different scenarios when something out of the ordinary, like a rogue phone call, triggers it. I was certain something was wrong so a sudden streak of apprehension overcame me as I answered the phone.

"Hello? Aga? What is it? Are you okay?"

Her response was, "I'm doing great!" And she sounded so excited I thought that maybe she won the lottery or something. She continued, "Papa! Papa! Guess what?"

I played along, realizing that this was no emergency as the tone of her voice was so jubilant. "Pray, please tell me. I can't guess. I'm still trying to figure out why you woke me up with a phone call at five o'clock in the morning."

"Well, sit down, because I have some big news," she warned me.

"What is it? Did you get a raise? More hours at work?"

"No, silly father of mine … I'm an aunt!"

Suddenly it hit me. Her brother Marcin and his wife Destiny were expecting a baby. They had told me they were expecting in December, and I just naturally assumed it was going to be at the end of the month, near Christmas. That's what my son had told me when we spoke online at Thanksgiving a week ago. Apparently, the baby had a mind of its own and came two weeks early.

"It's a boy!" Aga exclaimed. "He's seven pounds and three ounces. They're naming him Kayden. I'm texting you a picture right now."

"Where are you?" I asked.

"I'm at the hospital. I was Destiny's coach through the whole thing. It was amazing!"

"How is Mom doing?"

"She's tired. But doing great. It wasn't too long of a labor, only two hours. Check out the text I just sent you."

Just then my phone dinged—a text message. There he was! I had a one-minute-old picture of my new baby grandson!

Chapter 59

Cupid's Arrow

It is well known that Cupid's arrows have a certain power. That is, the person who is struck will suddenly and most certainly become a very loving and caring person. His arrows have the power to melt even the hardest of hearts. There's no limit to the love they can infuse.

Imagine how I felt when Cupid came to me and informed me that he was down to his last arrow. Even more astonishing was the fact that he wanted me to decide who to use the arrow on. He told me that I could choose anyone I wished, either real or fantasy. The only stipulation was it couldn't be anyone that I was already in love with. So, the first obvious choice of my wife or my kids was out of the picture.

The proposal sent my mind reeling. Who do I choose? I started by going through the list of people I knew and considering how they were as people. Perhaps a shot of love could change the target's life and that of the ones around them. So, I considered the list of candidates.

There was my stingy old aunt who seemed to never consider anyone but herself. I could only imagine how pleasant she would make all of our lives with a change of attitude. Then there was her husband, my Uncle Freddie. He was a constant complainer. It seemed as if nothing could ever be good enough for him. Maybe he'd be a good choice. The thought of everybody feeling encouraged by him was tantalizing. My own brother and I had been at odds for years now, estranged really. Perhaps an arrow of love could soften his heart enough for us to reconcile. It could at least change his disposition towards me.

Then there was that so-called neighbor of mine who had all the "DO NOT TRESSPASS" signs around his yard and that mean old Pitbull of his that barked at everything, especially at night when I was trying to sleep. Maybe I could change his attitude (and thereby his dog's) with an arrow and it would have a calming effect on everyone in the neighborhood around him. I imagined what it would be like to actually want to pet his dog.

I started to consider things on a grander scale. Perhaps there was a world leader who needed a good dose of love to change entire nations. The dictators in China or North Korea for instance. A love arrow would impact so many repressed people if either of them suddenly became lovers of others. But the problem is I'd need more than one arrow. One would change, but what about the other? Or, how about shooting some known terrorist? Again, it wouldn't solve the bigger problem that there were more than one of them in the world.

I kept on thinking who? Who would be the best person to strike with love? Cupid told me it could be real or it could be fantasy. I couldn't think of anyone in the world of fantasy, but suddenly I did think of someone that some people think is fantasy. But I know he isn't. I know he's real. Of course!

I knew suddenly in my heart of hearts who would be the best target for that last arrow. Perhaps it would even change the world. So, I decided. I asked Cupid to shoot him for me and for all mankind. Who was it, you ask? Satan!

Chapter 60

Trip to the Salon

He really didn't want to do this. He'd never been in a nail salon before. In fact, he always referred to them as "women's nail salons" for just that reason. They were not for men. But his wife had been getting on him for weeks now to have his "toes done" by a professional since his toenails were growing every which way and admittedly looked rather gross. So, he reluctantly agreed and went to the nail salon that his wife seemed to frequent every other week. She was always getting her fingernails done and more often than not, her toenails as well. Painted and all.

His agreement to get a pedicure came with a caveat. First, it had to be the cheapest priced option available and secondly, that there would be no coloring of nails. In the end, he resigned it was the best way to get his wife to stop nagging him about his unsightly toenails.

As he approached the entrance to his wife's favorite salon, he noticed there were a lot of cars parked out front. It would be a busy place. Sure enough, upon entering, he was overwhelmed by all the activity going on. There were rows of tables with, what do you call them? Beauticians? Manicurists? They were all sitting across from clients, busily sanding or painting the nails of limply held patron hands. Then he noticed to one side of the salon there were a row of chairs in front of tubs with women sitting in the chairs, their feet in the tubs, with pedicurists sitting before them working on their toes.

A second, much longer glance around the inside of the place confirmed that he was the only male in the establishment. He felt as if every pair of eyes were looking at him since the door had a strap of bells attached to it which rang every time someone entered. He just stood there, like a deer caught in the headlights, in front of the reception desk. Then there was the smell. The odor of nail polish and remover reminded him of the turpentine in his garage.

Finally, the woman behind the reception desk looked away from her cell phone long enough to ask him if she could help and, "You have appointment?" He told her that he did not have an appointment and that he had never been to a nail salon before. He further stated that he was interested in getting the cheapest pedicure that they had to offer. The woman, who appeared to be in charge, assured him that it would only cost thirty dollars. So, in the end, he agreed. Then, as if out of nowhere, another nail technician appeared and led him to one of the chairs with tubs in front. He simply followed orders from that point on.

He was told to remove his shoes and socks and that he did without so much as a fuss. Then the entire pedicure procedure took just under a half hour as he sat back and relaxed watching the silly foreign talent show program that was playing on the big screen attached to the back wall of the place.

When it was all over, he had to admit, his toes looked great (without polish, of course). He could see why women liked to have it done. He could even agree that his wife was right (although he would never admit it to her). Perhaps he would even come back next month. This was confirmed when he said to the manager as he paid, "See you next time."

Chapter 61

Midget Football Championship

It was the championship game. Our team was only in its second year of existence and we made it through the regular season without a single loss. We had easily won our division. And even though our midget football team was from a small town, which meant we had a limited number of players to draw from—most of us had to play both offense and defense—we were scrappy.

Now we faced the East Hartford Cardinals. City-boys who had with them city-boy attitudes that were obnoxious. Even their warm-up drills were intimidating. No worries. We wouldn't let that psych us out. After all, we were the Bolton Bulldogs and even though ours was a tiny town of mostly farmers, we were just like bulldogs. Tough.

For most of the championship game we held our own against a team that was much bigger than us in both in size and numbers. We managed to keep the Cardinals to only fourteen points. The trouble was, the game came down to the final forty-five seconds and we only had ten points. But we had the ball on the Cardinal's forty-yard line. There was still a chance for us to win, but it meant we needed a touchdown. Three more pass plays that went nowhere, another thirty seconds off the clock and we found ourselves looking at fourth and final down with still a long way to go. The coach then used our last time out to stop the clock with just fifteen seconds remaining. On the sideline, he gave us a quick pep talk and the trick play that we were to run.

Twenty-eight option pass was the call. I was the wide receiver. But on this play, I would line up close to the left tight end as if I was part of the line. The halfback, Paul, would get a pitch from the quarterback and start running opposite my side and appear to be running a sweep around the right side. He would then stop suddenly and pass to me downfield as I would hesitate for an instant and then take off running fast as I could toward the flag in the endzone. Hopefully, we would fool the Cardinal defense into thinking it was just a run around end.

The ball was snapped, the play ensued just as we had practiced so many times. But the safety back on the Cardinal defense was not fooled and neither was the middle linebacker as they both picked me up in coverage. Two against one. Paul stopped at the end of the line in the backfield and threw the pass anyway. It was our only chance, after all. He hurled it with everything he had, being forty yards away, and I saw it coming toward me as I was now running full-stride between the two defenders.

As I reached the goal line, I leaped up and caught the ball with my right hand, one handed, as the defensive backs crushed into me. Too late for them, as I went tumbling over the goal line. At the same time this was happening, the defenders had smashed into my free left hand with their helmets on either side of it. But I held onto the ball, with my right hand held up high, as I fell into the endzone. Touchdown!

We took the lead 16-14 with only two seconds left to play and went on to win the championship. I can't explain the exuberance I felt in that moment. The end result was that the two defenders had completely shattered my left hand in the collision. Multiple fractures. Yet in all the excitement, I felt no pain.

Chapter 62

Weekend at the Farm

It was the start of the Memorial Day weekend and Danny was excited that he would be spending it on the farm with his Polish grandmother (called Babcia) and her sister, his great aunt (called Coitka). Danny always liked being with the two elderly sisters because they tended to spoil him. Being only ten years old, the thought of running along the brook, going fishing, and playing with the animals on the forty-acre farm was extremely exciting to say the least. Little did he know what was really in store for him.

The Memorial Day weekend was the traditional weekend for planting certain crops for the coming growing season. Squash and zucchini, cucumbers and tomatoes, peppers and corn, all had to be planted over the weekend to ensure they would be ready for the summer harvest in July and August. At least that was the growing season in the town of Avon in northwestern Connecticut where the farm was located. Danny's Babcia was pushing ninety and his Coitka was already ninety-two, yet the two sisters were healthy and spry as they still lived and worked on the farm (with the help of younger family members) in spite of having no running water nor plumbing of any kind. For cooking and heat, a large woodstove was the only major appliance. An old-fashioned vintage Frigidaire was their source of refrigeration. It was over forty years old but still ran flawlessly.

The farmhouse was built in 1902 and so by 1967 it had seen a lot of wear and tear. Danny's great uncle (called Wujek) who had since died, and Coitka started the farm from scratch all those years ago. With the help of family and friends, they constructed the farmhouse and a big barn which housed the animals and hay. The farm grew the aforementioned crops along with other herbs and produce, as well as had a flock of a dozen sheep, three cows for milking, a couple dozen chickens, some ducks and rabbits, three cats that roamed the grounds and a Shetland sheepdog named Lucky. The farm was supported by a roadside stand where the crops were sold beginning in July along with fresh eggs and rabbit pelts available year-round.

What Danny didn't realize was that this particular Memorial Day weekend he would now be expected to help plant the seeds for the crops and tend the animals. It was no longer going to be a playground for him but rather a busy weekend of considerably hard work. He and his similarly aged younger cousins would be expected to work this and every weekend throughout the summer right up until the school year began in September. While this caused Danny to be sad that he would be missing out on sports on the weekends and playing with his buddies from school, it would be instilling a solid work-ethic—one that he would carry into the rest of his life.

All was not lost though, as Babcia and Coitka informed Danny he would be getting a reward for his hard work. That since he would be expected to be at the farm every weekend in the summer months, spending his time gathering in the crops when they were ready and milking the cows to supply the roadside stand, he would also be expected to work at the stand starting in July. And for that, they would give him half of the profits of all the money that they took in.

Suddenly, the thought of no baseball, swimming, and getting a tan at the beach on weekends wasn't so bad to the boy after all. Besides, he would still be able to get a little fishing in at the pond and stream that ran through the property while watering the sheep.

In the end, he would go on to make over three-thousand dollars that summer from his cut. An entrepreneur was born at age ten on the farm in Avon with Babcia and Coitka.

Chapter 63

Youth Conference Storm

The Franciscan University of Steubenville Youth Conference in July was the highlight of the Saint James Youth Group's summer. It was held on the university's grounds in Ohio which is located on the banks of the Ohio river just a short distance from Pittsburgh. We got there, covering the five hundred miles in just over nine hours, by travelling all day on Friday via bus from "the city of village charm" as it was known, Manchester, Connecticut, where Saint James Church is located, right on the corner of Main and Park streets. The long ride was half the fun. Thirty-five high school youth and four adult advisors along with me, the youth minister, shared the bus ride together getting psyched up listening to the upbeat worship music on boom boxes (that the conference was well-known for), and enjoying each other's company along the way.

Once there, we pitched our four ten-person tents in the grassy area just outside of the huge, double-canopied event tent that would house the nearly thousand youth from all over the country for the weekend of spirited fellowship. After leaving Saint James at six o'clock that morning, we arrived in Steubenville a little after three in the afternoon. Plenty of time to settle in, relax a little, get some supper before the main event started at six-thirty. The event tent had seats arranged in a semi-circle around the center stage. Friday evening was the big celebration night as several well-known Christian song artists and groups would perform their versions of worship and praise music—way upbeat. Our group had filed in and we took our place near the south edge of the tent facing stage left.

About half-way through the opening performance, just as the musical group was starting to lead us in worship songs, the sides of the tent began to flop in the wind from outside, rather violently. The gusts continued to pick up and the sky grew darker with thick clouds threatening above. In a matter of minutes, it was almost pitch black.

It seemed as if night had come suddenly because of the foreboding murky sky due to the weather front moving in fast. It was enough to frighten the conference director into evacuating the tent as he feared the worse. His experience of being at the campus, located so close to the river, was that the thunderstorms that came up every now and again could be devastating. He feared such a tempest was fast approaching.

So, quickly and quite orderly, everyone started leaving the tent and making their way outside, heading down the hill into the nearby dormitories of the college, our group include. There would be no sleeping under the stars tonight. Once everyone had made it safely into the five surrounding dorms, the storm did come. It wasn't a thunderstorm at all. It was a small tornado! Miraculously, everyone, and I mean every last person who was in the tent just moments prior, had made it safely into a dorm and was accounted for. We all ended up spending the night indoors, most of us sleeping huddled up on the floors. In spite of the tragic end to the evening's opening salvo of acts in the tent, there was an enthusiastic and positive response of singing and praying among the attendees, complete with breaking out the guitars and tambourines, throughout the night in the dorms. It really was quite festive.

The next morning, right at dawn, we all went out to see what had happened. The big tent was completely destroyed. Even the massive poles that held it up had been snapped in two and were sticking out of the ground like spears that were thrown by the mighty wind. All four of our sleeping tents were just gone. Nothing was left but the empty grass where we had pitched them. The tornado had swept it all away.

The concert that was to be may have been halted, but the spirits of all those who attended that particular conference rejoiced that not a single person was harmed in any way. Perhaps, after all, the angels had been there to protect and lead us, in spite of the weather that had threatened to dampen our spirits.

Chapter 64

Inspired Teacher

The restaurant was crowded for just being a Chili's on a Tuesday night. Already at the table, I nodded my consent when the hostess came over and told me that the other party who would be joining me for dinner had arrived. She told me that the man said he knew me but I wasn't sure that I knew him.

I thought back to when I was in the office. There was just a post-it note left on my desk at work that I had to go by. It simply stated that a gentleman would be joining me for dinner at Chili's at 6:30. It must be him, I thought. I assumed it was another home purchase prospect as I am in sales, now that I have officially retired from teaching junior high school after thirty-five years. For a retirement job, real estate seems to agree with me. I have had a lot of experience from buying my own four homes over the years and that certainly came into play in landing the new job. It had become a common routine for the office to send potential clients to me this way, that is, by simply leaving yellow post-it notes on my desk. The goal, of course, being that I was supposed to wine and dine the potential client for a bit and see if we could consummate a more substantial interest in working with us exclusively. That would lead to using our agency for the sale of the client's home and the commission that came with it.

The newcomer was middle aged, and seemed vaguely familiar, but I could not quite place him.

After the hostess showed him to my table and promised to send a server our way, we greeted each other. He was a bit more amorous than I would have expected. With a vigorously clutched shake of my hand and half-hug, he questioned me before I could get a word out edgewise.

"Do you remember me sir?" my new tablemate asked me.

I shook my head, looking closely at him from above my readers that I had been using to scan the menu.

"My name is Joseph. I was your student."

So that's why he looked familiar. I vaguely remembered him in that instant. "Glad to hear that. When?" I asked.

He told me.

"What do you do now?" I followed.

"I'm a teacher. And sir, it was you who inspired me to choose that career."

"Very interesting. How's that?"

He went on to tell me.

The incident happened years ago when he was a seventh-grade student. The school was patronized by mainly poor kids from the inner city. Hardly any of them came to school well dressed. Only the most important notes were taken, and those were exclusively in marble notebooks using number two pencils. That is except for one student, whose name was Allen. His uncle, who was some rich engineer someplace, gave him a real fancy fountain pen with four different color refills. Allen loved that pen and used it all the time. He was the only one with inked notes. And Joseph wanted that pen from the moment he saw it.

One day, when Allen wasn't looking, Joseph stole it from Allen's bag and hid it in his pants pocket. It didn't take much time for Allen to discover that his coveted pen was missing. That's when he came to complain to me, the teacher. I then came up with an idea to find out who the offender was.

All the students were told to stand up and close their eyes while I walked around the room and checked. It didn't take long. Soon I found the pen sticking partially out of Joseph's pocket. I took it out. To Joseph's surprise, I kept walking around the room as if I were still searching for it without making any announcement. "Now you all can open your eyes," I had said. "Allen, here is your pen." I handed it to him without another word.

There was no mention of who the thief was, though every student expected it. I could have exposed Joseph as the thief, taken him to the principal, shamed him in front of them all, but I had done nothing of the sort.

"That was the day I wanted to be a teacher like you. However, please don't tell me you don't remember me, sir. It was from my pocket that you found the pen," Joseph said.

I told him, "I remember the incident but not the culprit. I too, had closed my eyes while searching."

Of course, I had done nothing of the sort, but I had kept mum to give him a second chance.

Chapter 65

Rattling Sound

We had been making our trip cross-country in the trusty '74 Volvo wagon, stopping at all the important destinations. Starting in D.C., we were traveling the northern route via I-80 to the west coast with a bit of zig-zagging to be sure to catch all the hot spots along the way. There was Mount Rushmore, the Badlands of South Dakota, Yellowstone, Grand Teton… you get the idea.

Did I say we camped the whole way? Well, most of it. Yes indeed, good ol' KOA campsites that we had booked in advance with AAA before leaving. We even had one of those special ticket maps to guide us on our journey and keep us on schedule. TripTiks they were called. This was all back in the summer of 1978, almost a year after Elvis died. Fortunately, all the camp sites we stayed at were better than we anticipated. That is, until we reached the Grand Canyon.

After entering the park and following the winding road that leads in alongside the majestic canyon itself, we came upon a rather unique restaurant. It was a log cabin designed place with a fully stocked bar inside. Conveniently, it was also adjacent to the KOA site where we had a reservation to pitch our tent, which was roomy enough to house the three of us comfortably. We didn't bother to get anything to eat but my two buddies, John and Rick, and I, each imbibed on the ice-cold Coors that were running off the bar's tap.

We enjoyed ourselves immensely being in such a picturesque setting with our new beverage of choice—one we had come to love after trying it for the first time while passing through Colorado where Coors is brewed. We only stayed at the bar a little over an hour since it was late in the day and starting to get dark. We still needed to pitch our tent for sleeping through the night. Somehow, probably because we chugged so many of them, we managed to consume at least five or six beers apiece in that short while as we relished in our newfound environment. It was the Grand Canyon for Pete's sake! A reason to celebrate. After leaving the bar, we set out across the parking lot looking for our designated KOA campsite. In our condition, that is, much more than slightly buzzed, it took us a while of staggering around but we finally found it.

The campsite was nothing like we expected. It was small to say the least. We had barely enough room to put up the tent. It had a tiny stone fireplace and solid rock surrounded three of the four sides. The fourth side butted up against a cliff! A genuine fifty to eighty-foot drop right there on the back end of our camping site. A hazard that we really didn't need. Needless to say, it was not what we expected after staying at such wonderfully beautiful campsites thus far in the trip. That is, until this one. Also, in our current inebriated condition, it took us a while to get the tent put up and secured properly, given the constraints of the small site. It was well after dark by the time we finished.

The three of us were way past being exhausted and got right in the tent to go to sleep. We didn't even bother to build a fire. After about ten minutes of just lying there, we all easily drifted off to sleep. Or maybe we just passed out. Who knows? Then, what must have been two or so hours later, still feeling a bit tipsy, I was awakened to a clicking or rattling sound. Oh no! It just kept rattling and it was in the tent! I shook and woke up Rick and John and they too heard the noise.

What was it? It had to be a rattler—right there in our tent with us. It sounded as if it was coming from just next to Rick. We all then got up slowly, moved cautiously outside and listened intently as we heard the clicking noise continue non-stop. Finally, we got the nerve to take out our flashlights and look inside to see if we could spot where the noise was coming from.

There it was! Right next to Rick's sleeping bag. His wind-up clock was ticking away.

Chapter 66

Friday Visit to Babcia

It was a Friday afternoon, a little after four and was time for my weekly visit to see my grandmother. Babcia we called her, Polish for grandmother and a term of endearment. She had been in the assisted living facility/hospital for the past six months as her Alzheimer's or Dementia had gotten worse. Now she hardly ever left her bed, which was in a room she shared with another patient. Milly was her roommate's name, also a lady in her late eighties just like Babcia.

Whenever I went to see Babcia and Milly, I was always overcome with the smell of Lysol upon entering the wing of the facility where their room was. It was clean enough, for sure, but that familiar harsh scent was trying to cover up a much more putrid smell—that of urine. Then, upon entering Babcia and Milly's room, the odor of something else took over. It was the smell of baby powder. That was because my mother, Babcia's daughter, would cover her in the powder to keep Babcia dry. Since she visited her on an almost daily basis, she was always sporting a fresh coat of the stuff on her skin.

It was sad to see Babcia gradually forget who I was as I continued to visit each week. At first it was frustrating, but then I realized that it was just the reality of her disease. At least she was always receptive to my hugs and kisses. They always brought a big smile to her face. Then there was Milly.

One day I just decided that I would lean in and give her a hug and a peck on the forehead too. As I did, tears welled up in Milly's eyes. I realized the first time I did it that she probably had nobody who visited her and was simply starved for any sort of affection. From then on, every time I visited and greeted my Babcia with a hug and kiss, I greeted Milly the same way as well.

Aside from that, I would talk to the both of them, as if they were able to understand me. Perhaps they did or perhaps they did not. It didn't matter. They were both God's children as far as I was concerned and deserved to be treated with dignity and affectionate care. That's how I saw myself. Kind of like a weekly shot of caregiving to the both of them. It was the least I could do. I wondered if they ever even tried to communicate with each other as they seemed to just lay there and stare at the ceiling. Or if they were even aware there was another patient in the room for that matter.

Alas, finally, about the eighth month into her stay at the facility, my Babcia did pass away. It was in her sleep and it happened just before I got there on another Friday afternoon to see her. The nurse at the station informed me of her passing and that she had just been taken away about an hour earlier. I still went into her room, baby powder smell and all, to see how Milly was doing. She just laid there as usual, looking up and unaware of her surroundings. I leaned in to give her a hug and kiss and her eyes filled with tears again. I knew she could sense my presence. Or perhaps she was sad because she knew that my Babcia was gone.

I continued to go there every Friday to see Milly and visit some others in the wing as well. It just felt like it had become part of my weekly routine and it was the least I could do given that I'm perfectly healthy. About two months after Babcia passed on, Milly died. I just hope they both somehow knew how much they meant to me.

Chapter 67

Lighthouse Keeper

On a rock this forgotten, a lighthouse is needed. On a rock this forgotten, the lighthouse keeper is needed too. Though he feels unnecessary, neglected, taken for granted, and antiquated, the lighthouse is only as functional as he makes it. Having been alone for so long he has adjusted to life without any companionship. He leaves his front door open. The thin, old door banging about in the approaching storm; salty wind blowing straight off the sea and stirring the light objects in his room into open rebellion; unsecured papers lift up into the room and dip like birds, and the lighthouse keeper sits and plays his piano slowly, as if to calm things down. The rain is starting and blows in too. It mingles with the sea spray on the threshold, and taps on the windows.

The music he plays is hesitant and tinged with sadness and the lighthouse keeper looks almost as though he is asleep, but his fingers keep moving.

Outside, the waves build and combine, mash into each other and twist into foamy masses, or rear up over a submerged rock, and curl up into dampening waves that pop and boom along the rocks. No beam of light passes across the sea, because for the most part, ships have stopped coming this way. The lighthouse keeper stopped turning the light on months ago. This night, however, the lighthouse keeper looks out of his front door as he finishes playing a bar of music and the next note hangs in the air, desperately needing to be played, but it hangs; then stays unresolved. The lighthouse keeper stares, frozen.

Out there, pitching, leaning, rocking, a ship is struggling in the gray chaos. It is mostly shadow, but a single light on that ship shines through the sheets of slanting rain. Just for a moment the lighthouse keeper watches the light ride up and own, and watches it tip and disappear behind the high waves; then he jumps up and hurries up the spiraling staircase, puffing. It is harder than he remembers, and he leans heavily on the cold iron handrail as he climbs.

At the top he can see the ship better: it looks like it will survive the storm, but it is heading straight for the lighthouse, and the jagged rocks beneath. The ship is getting closer and closer and the lighthouse keeper swears at himself as he works; but soon the light starts up and a beam of light, getting brighter and brighter with each pass, punches through the rain and out towards the ship; and the ship sees, and makes a dramatic veering maneuver; dangerous in the heavy sea; but passes unscathed, now parallel to the shore, and soon disappears into the dark and the stormy weather.

The lighthouse keeper makes his way down the stairs, closes the front door, and collapses on his bed, suddenly exhausted. The storm carries on.

In the morning it is clear and sunny. The lighthouse keeper is up early, sitting on the bed and staring down at the space between his feet. Eventually he gets dressed and steps out his front door, leaving the door open again, this time drinking in the warm sunrise and lightly salted breeze blowing gently off the sea. He walks down the hill to a meager dock, sheltered amongst the rocks, where a small boat waits. Most of his belongings are in a heavy waterproof bag which he put on his boat a few days ago, and he awkwardly hefts the bag up onto his shoulder and carries it back up the hill. He walks in the front door and dumps the bag right in the middle of the room, sits down at the piano, and picks up where he left off the night before.

Outside, sea birds make their noises and small waves break against the rocks.

Chapter 68

Retired Life

Eyes snap open, another exciting day begins. Being retired. Check the clock. Sure enough, it's not quite 4:30 am. Just like countless days before, no use trying to go back to sleep. Need to get out of the warm bed now and have frozen feet … again, as they hit the cold tile floor. Looking at the alarm. It's set to go off at 5:00, no need for that now. Disengage. The next ten minutes? Always the same. Trip to the bathroom, face is washed, weight is checked, and finally a glance at the calendar. Already aware of the day's main event, nonetheless, it's checked again. Notice that it's day number 6821 as today's weight is jotted down beneath the number. 6821 days for what? Since the last time. That was over eighteen and a half years ago. A long time to remain clean and sober. Still, it's recorded every day.

Time to get dressed. The calendar indicates the main event of the day. The eye test at Scripps in La Jolla. Thrilling! Not. That's three busses and over two hours away. Got to be there by 8:00 so that means leave here by 5:30. Still almost an hour to kill. Do some reading. Too early for the crosswords. Have coffee, it's just instant. Never got around to buying a maker. Decide what to wear. Same as yesterday. Cargo shorts and a tee, with a short-sleeved shirt over it. Get dressed and wait, walking around in circles just looking at stuff in the studio apartment. It used to be a garage. Think that the owner did a good job with the conversion to a living space. Can't beat the rent. It's only $700 a month. For San Diego, that's cheap.

Time to go now. Lock the door. It's double locked with a metal storm screen because of the neighborhood. A bit rough. Now on to the bus stop. Short walk down 46th to University Avenue. Takes just five minutes.

The number 7 bus is right on time according to the check of the schedule made last night. Always is in the morning. Folks need to get to work. All abord, take a seat in the back. Time for dozing off with the earbuds on. Not music—talk radio—an addiction perhaps. Listening to talk because ideas are sweet! Finally get to Old Town, transfer to the 30 bus and ride it all the way to UTC. Over an hour on this one. Still one more bus to catch. The ride is thankfully uneventful. No crazies today. Pass the rush hour traffic while riding in the HOV lane. That's one advantage in taking the bus. Finally at UTC. Two busses down, one to go.

Arrived ten minutes early. That's okay. Better to be early than late. The 201 bus is the last ride. It takes the loop right to the front of Scripps. Once there, a bit of a walk across the esplanade. The morning air is refreshing. Cool, crisp and appreciated as later today is supposed to be a scorcher. Once inside the medical center, a check of the clock on the wall. Twenty minutes to spare as it's only 7:40. What? What's that? They'll take me early. Sweet!

Taking the eye test entails looking into a box at a beam of light for about thirty seconds with one eye closed. Now repeat the process with the other eye. The test is over. Wait two minutes for the results as they are printed off. Time is up. That lasted a whole five minutes. Take the manila envelope from the technician with the results inside. That's for the exam at the eye doctor's office. The event of the day tomorrow.

The eye test adventure is now complete. Time to make the return trip home. This has been the highlight of the day. It's all over now. Maybe get something to eat on the way back. Such is the life. Of retirement.

Chapter 69

Start Up

When Nathan walked through the door to their home at 2:00 on a Monday afternoon, his wife was stunned. "What are you doing home so early?" she asked.

"Do you believe in me?" he responded.

"What do you mean?"

"Sit down. I have something to discuss with you," he said.

Nathan went on to inform his wife, Kathy, that he had just lost his job as a senior systems analyst. The reason was that the company he worked for was being sold by his boss who was also the sole owner of the small a computer aided design firm. A much larger competitor was buying it off, mostly for the technology they recently developed and would not be needing the majority of the forty staff members who worked there. Nathan included. Effective immediately, they were all given one month's severance pay and promptly escorted out of the building.

"What will happen to us?" his wife asked. The couple just had their second child, still an infant, and moved into the bigger house that they had recently built for their growing family. A brand-new home that had a brand-new grande mortgage to go along with it. Since Nathan was paid quite handsomely, the life changes they had recently undergone were not so pressing, financially speaking. That is, until he just lost his job.

"There's the mortgage. It's twice what it was before we built this place. We still have the deductible at the hospital to pay for having the baby. What about all the other bills? The oil and electricity? Not to mention the cost of preschool for Adam. Will you be able to get another job soon?" The questions from his wife kept coming. She was frightened, it was obvious to Nathan. The two sat there in the kitchen and went on discussing all the expenses and considered the realistic options they had for over an hour.

Finally, Nathan said, "I want to go out on my own. I'm tired of working for someone else, of doing all the work only to have what happened today happen to us. Never again! If we go broke it will be because I didn't perform—for me. For us!" His wife finally let go of a few tears after remaining silent during his venting.

Sheepishly, she asked, "What will you do? When will you start?"

He answered her, "I'll start right now. I'll put myself out there as a consultant, an independent contractor. God knows I've written enough proposals in my day. I'll write my own."

"I love you and I believe in you," was her only reply.

And that was what became known as the first meeting of their new company. Nathan would be the president and chief executive officer and his wife Kathy would be the secretary and treasurer.

The first thing the couple did was to go online and, using Nathan's computer skills, build a website to give their start-up credibility. Next, they sent emails to everyone they could think of, telling them of their new venture together and specifically what services they could offer. Less than a week later they had responses, eight in total, asking for their immediate help with computer-related tasks. Some were from individuals like themselves, looking to start out on their own and others were from seasoned companies. Still many others were from a host of Nathan's former associates that he had come to know during his last ten years working as an analyst. Nathan and his wife Kathy formed an LLC and that became the start of what would eventually grow in to a world-wide consulting firm called, K&N International, employing over three hundred professionals within the next three years.

To celebrate their business success, Nathan gave Kathy a brand-new car as a present for their fifteenth anniversary. It was a Porsche 911 Carrera Coupe, the car of her dreams. He simply told her,

"Thanks for believing in me, Babe, on the day I came home having lost my job. I couldn't have done it without you."

Chapter 70

Chase in the Woods

I can feel my muscles tensing. I can feel my feet aching. I can feel sweat running down my face. My heart is pounding. With every step I take I can feel the leaves crack, twigs snap and my captor's fast steps getting closer. These are no ordinary men. Their footsteps move in unison. When they first began chasing me, I heard two voices. Now I can hear only one, but their footsteps still remain the same. I had taken this chase into the woods crawling on the ground, praying that the tall trees would block the full moon's ever illuminating light. My prayers had paid off. I careen behind one of the many tree trunks. With my back against the trunk, I catch my breath. I can't help but observe how well the shadows are hiding my body.

My focus turns back to the men chasing me as I hear one of them say, "Dammit! We lost him. Let's turn back!"

His associate speaks, "No, he's somewhere in here!"

The first man responds immediately, "Screw that! I'm not wasting my night on some renegade we'll never find!"

"Fine, then go!"

At this point, I hear a cacophony of footsteps on the other side of the trunk that I'm pelted to and resting against. I then hear both men march away in unison the same way they did before. With their footsteps getting more distant, I look up at the trees around me. I offer them thanks for granting me shade from the moon and helping me continue my escape. I peek my head out from behind the tree trunk to see how far away the men are. As I do, I come face to face with one of them.

As we look at each other in the face, eyes wide, I look past him to see another man on horseback. I know this man has no intentions of keeping my secret and as he goes to yell, I lunge at him. I grab him by the neck and force him down rumbling on the ground. While I have him by the neck, choking him, I'm stalling. I need to come up with an idea as to what my next course of action will be. Without my knowledge, the man pulls a blade from his boot. He uses it to slash my right cheek, but I don't let go. He tries to get from under me. At this point I look up at my surroundings. A pointed rock sits next to me. I grab it. With multiple swift smashes to the man's head, he no longer struggles. He doesn't move but neither do I. I am frozen. I am scared and I don't know what to do. I get from on top of him.

I pray he will move but this prayer falls short. As I look at the man, I can't help but think to myself that this was a man who was taught to hate me. This was a man, who like me, didn't know any better and was doing what his life guided him to do. This man did not deserve to die this way, he deserved to be taught to see his fellow man as equal. It's unfortunate that no one was able to teach him until this point. As I am wondering what to do with this man, I look the way he came to see his colleague coming back slowly. He has yet to enter the woods.

This time the horse can be seen taking a leisurely pace. I look back at the man on the forest floor. I know this man is dead. I know I will soon be if I let the other man capture me. With this brief assessment of my circumstances, I run. I run like I never have before. I make a promise to myself. I will make it to freedom. If not for me then for my fellow man who I left in the woods.

Chapter 71

Summer Memories

At a time that seems so long ago and so far, far away, so many things have changed when I think of summer. As a child, a teenager, and even into my college years, the most memorable times where those spent at the cottage at Giant's Neck Beach. Being there probably accounted for a third of my entire life and it was all so normal. But to speak about what happened then, today, seems absurd.

You see, my father and his brother and a few of their cousins had built the cottage by themselves. They used mostly scraps of wood and insulation and other materials that were being tossed away at the construction sites where they all worked. So, the construct of the place was a real mish-mash of building products and was set up on stilts in a wooded lot about a quarter mile from the Long Island shore in the township of East Lyme, Connecticut. There were similar impromptu cottages on the street, as well as some more refined residences. For the most part though, they were just seasonal places, as was ours, without any heating systems. Simple summer retreats.

The location of the cottage was at bottom of a hill, a valley of sorts, and the short walk to the shore just meant climbing up the hill and down again on the opposite side. The same on the way home. We made the walk usually two times a day, once in the morning, coming back to the cottage for lunch, and returning to spend the afternoon at our private beach. While we were there at the shore, we did all the usual summer activities such as soaking up the sun getting a tan, swimming of course, snorkeling, clamming, crabbing, and digging in the sand, building castles. As kids, we waited patiently in the afternoon for the ice cream truck to arrive—my mother always managed to have a buck for each of us to get a treat when we heard those bells on the truck ringing and went running to greet the ice cream man. It was all the stuff that was so ordinary back then but is completely missing today.

I recently returned to Giant's Neck, after being away for almost ten years, to that same members-only beach we frequented on a daily basis, to see that a huge sign had been erected at the entrance. There was a long list of prohibitions enumerated in deep black type. It forbade doing nearly everything we had done on that beach as kids. Included on the list was swimming! That is, unless a life guard was on duty. There were no life guards at all back in the day. I felt a pit in my stomach. It was like we were criminals having lived such a happy-go-lucky existence all those years ago.

But at the cottage, back then, even the summer nights were magical. We would often just walk into the woods that abutted our home-made dwelling, and drag out old tree trunks and branches that had fallen and chop them up for burning in the fire-pit—something else my father had made out of foundational cinder-blocks. There we would build bonfires and break out the guitar and sing songs, and, especially during my college years, we'd enjoy a few beers along the way.

What was particularly enchanting was walking back to the beach at night, trailing right down the middle of those lonesome roads, feeling the warm tar beneath our bare feet. Upon reaching the shoreline, we could see the canopy of majestic stars that filled the sky over the sea. We could hear the mysterious sound of the waves crashing nearby. It all added to the overall mystical experience.

Alas, those days are all but a mere memory now since time has passed and legal ordinances have changed it so much. One more of those deep black typed rules on the sign clearly states that you're not even allowed on the beach after sunset anymore. If caught, a hefty fine would ensue.

Yes, I will always treasure all the great summer memories that old beach house brought us. That is, until the tragic fire that was caused by the lightening strike that burned it too, to the ground.

Chapter 72

Painting the Inn

It was a great summer job while I was on the usual vacation break from my teaching position. During most of the year, I was a high school math and science teacher. But in the summer, I took to the outdoors and had my own house painting business. So prosaic. It was just me. I worked solo. In a typical summer—if the weather held out and there wasn't too much rain—I could manage to get four good-sized houses done. With a profit of roughly five-thousand dollars each, that was a nice chunk of change. I usually settled on painting single-family dwellings that were two-stories max, simply because I only had ladders and could only reach that high. That is, until the summer of 2005.

That particular summer, I had a chance at a once in a lifetime opportunity. It was to completely scrape down and paint a four-story inn on Cape Cod in Massachusetts. The job was so big that I allowed myself the entire month of July to complete it, or the equivalent of painting two houses. Except that the payday for painting the inn was a whopping twenty-five thousand dollars profit! More than double of what I would make in the month doing houses. It was called the Camelot Inn. And since it was on the main drag of Route 28 in Harwichport right in the center of Cape Cod, I would also get a lot of exposure for my business. I put some signs out front stating my name and the number to call. I knew that since it was such a busy road in the summer, that it would be the ideal showcase of my work for future jobs in the area.

Granted, there was a challenge. To paint the inn, I had to go up four stories rather than the two I was accustomed to reaching, but I had an easy fix for that. I got a great price on renting some scaffolding from a nearby U-Haul service center. It would get me up to the second floor with ease and from there, using a platform on top of the scaffolding, I could then place my ladders on it to reach the top two stories. It was the perfect solution to getting up so high. Or so I thought.

One day, being at almost the top of the ladder, which was on top of the two-story scaffold, I was reaching with my brush extending to reach the tip of the peak of the fourth floor. That's when it happened. The ladder started to slip. I immediately dropped the brush and grabbed onto the molding that was around one of the fourth-floor windows to stop sliding, but it was too late. The bottom of my ladder gave way and I was suddenly losing my footing. Next, the ladder slid out from under me and crashed to the ground as I was left hanging from the window sill, dangling from four stories up. Because of the sizable drop, letting go was not an option.

So, I then did the next best thing I could think of in the moment. I started to scream as loud as I could. Thankfully, being summer, and Route 28 being a very busy road with lots of cars passing by with their windows open, someone heard my cries for help. A guy jumped out of his car, leaving it stopped right there in the middle of the road, and ran over to help me. He was able to get my ladder back up on top of the scaffold and position it under me. I then got my feet secured and climbed back down to the top of the scaffold. When I think back on it, I am thankful I was able to hang on for what had to be at least five minutes screaming for help—and that the guy passing by in the car heard me. It was the scariest thing that ever happened to me.

After finishing the inn, I went back to just painting houses. Single-story, ranch-style only.

Chapter 73

At the Altar

The journey to this moment was a lifetime really. As I stood on the altar, a series of memories flashed through my mind. Each one was suddenly more vivid than they had been in the past. Perhaps it was due to the commitment I was about to make publicly before family, friends and of course, God.

There were scenes from my childhood growing up on the farm and tending the animals and sharing the chores with my brother and sister. Then mind-flashes from high school flared through my brain, like my favorite classes and teachers' faces, along with those of my best buddies. Memories of playing baseball in little league and midget football games gave me a warm feeling inside. Then junior high came to mind along with the best recollections of high school following next. Things like getting my license, that great '71 Plymouth Roadrunner I drove around in and of course, my steady girlfriend that I took to both the junior and senior proms during those formative years. What a blast we had during the summers at the beach and the crazy parties with all our friends.

Then on to college went my thoughts. I remembered the intense studying for exams in my double major as a pre-med student as well as the strange ways my buddies and I found to release the pressure by our silly antics. There was the experience of NROTC and all the Navy training that came with it, especially the grueling tests I went through before becoming an officer and finally graduating. I can still see the look of satisfaction and pride in my parents' eyes as I handed them my diploma. I was the first in my family to ever graduate college.

Of course, after that, my mind drifted off to perhaps the happiest chapter of my life. There were fond recollections of meeting Christine Marie and the romance we lived that led to and blossomed through our marriage. Our wedding day has always been one of my favorite memories leading up to this day and it was the last time I stood at the altar like I was standing now. The birth of our children, their growing up and the numerous events, holidays, vacations, and gatherings that our family shared all seemed to rush through my mind at that moment as well.

These were all the fleeting thoughts I had while waiting for the bishop to utter his words of finality to me. As my mind raced, my stomach began to churn in knots as I was realizing simultaneously the gravity of the commitment that I was about to make.

It was then that all the sad memories suddenly rushed upon me. First the loss of my grandmothers, both of whom always treated me like I was special—their oldest grandchild. Then the passing of my parents at relatively young ages and the fact that they never got to fully appreciate the lives of their grandchildren deepened my grieving thoughts. Of course, most finally, was the death of my wife after twenty-eight years of marriage. I was realizing once again, that Christine Marie, who had succumbed to breast cancer nine years ago, was still the love of my life. I thought more deeply in that moment at the altar again, about how I managed to finally deal with that, the greatest loss I had ever experienced. What did it was my faith. Faith in God alone is what had gotten me through the anguish I felt all those years leading up to where I was standing now.

So why should I be beside myself in this moment as I waited on the bishop to utter the words that would herald in my new way of life? I had already decided that after nearly thirty years of marriage that being with another woman wasn't going to be an option for me ever again. Instead, I decided that no, God was calling me now to something entirely different. Perhaps something even greater.

I would accept that thought, rest assured and take the vow I was about to make. I would become a priest.

Chapter 74

Lottery Tickets

The days since the Korean War had long since passed on and so had most of Travis Leary's Marine buddies. Now confined to a wheelchair at eighty-eight years of age, and more or less dependent on his forty-year-old grandson for his livelihood, whom he lived with, it sometimes seemed as if he was just waiting to die. His grandson, Jacob, was still single and had a magnificent sprawling estate complete with a housekeeper who doubled as Travis' aid and somewhat companion. Because Jacob was an airline pilot who flew for United Airlines, he spent considerable time away from home. Having been first an Air Force then commercial pilot for over twenty years, he not only made a handsome, triple-figure salary, he had saved up a considerable amount of money over all those years which allowed him to afford the regal lifestyle he now enjoyed. He had also been to most parts of the globe through his multitudinous travels in the air.

Grandpa Travis lived vicariously through his grandson and his airline visits to exotic places, though he rarely ventured outside of the house by himself anymore. That is, aside from the one place he did go on a regular basis just about every morning. That was, to make his way down the block to the main street and then wheel another two blocks down from there, to the fancy drug store that also sold lottery tickets. By using the top speed of his wheelchair scooter, he could usually make the half-mile trip along the pristine sidewalks of the upscale neighborhood in just under fifteen minutes. Once there, his daily ritual ensued.

He would buy the *New York Times* simply because he loved the crossword puzzle more than anything else in the paper. He would also buy a single lottery ticket. He loved the scratch-off type. It was going on ten years now that he had been purchasing lottery tickets in this way. Travis had won fifteen dollars here and a two-dollar prize there, all totaling about a hundred dollars over all the years he bought tickets.

Not much of a return on investment for the five-dollar tickets. But as his grandson would say, "If he enjoys doing it, at his age, what the heck."

This day, he purchased as usual, the "Lucky for Life" lottery ticket that promised $1,000 a day for life. It doesn't take a genius to figure out that comes to $365,000 a year. It simply was the favorite ticket for Travis. If he won, it meant he would be instantly rich.

So, after motoring his wheelchair back home the way he came, he went into the house and to his ritual spot at the small table in the corner of the kitchen where the housekeeper, Milly, was busy making him lunch. Travis would enjoy his peanut butter and jelly sandwich, cut in triangles the way he liked, as he slowly scratched his ticket.

The time had come to cautiously see if he had won. He wanted to fully enjoy the moment so he took his time. He had a bite of his sandwich and he then reached into the pocket of his vest and took out his lucky quarter which had seen many a scratch-ticket in its day. He began the process of solving the little puzzle by etching away at each gray covered square until, at last, the prize was revealed.

He won! He actually won! At first, he couldn't believe it. He looked at the results on the ticket again and again until he was absolutely certain he, in fact, had won. His heart started to pound in his chest with excitement.

Now suddenly, he was realizing how much his life had instantly changed. With a thousand dollars a day there was no limit to what he could do. Heck, that was thirty-thousand a month. Thirty-thousand dollars! There would be no more needing to depend on his grandson. He would travel himself now. Who cares where? He would decide on a whim. He could buy tickets and fly with his grandson everywhere he went if he wanted to. The world was his oyster.

The next morning, before he could even cash in his winning ticket, Travis died of a heart attack. "Isn't it ironic?" as the Alanis Morissette song goes.

Chapter 75

Left Frozen for Dead

I don't even know what to think right now. My body is shaking with cold, way beyond shivering and it's getting harder to move my jaw to talk.

"I don't know how much longer we're going to make it like this," I mutter to Timothy. As I glance in his direction, I can see his lips becoming a faint purple. His teeth momentarily stop chattering and he replies.

"Let's leave. We have to do something. We can't just stay here freezing to death."

"It's ten miles Timothy, and we're weak. We'll never make it."

He replies, "We owe it to our families to try! I'm not going to just sit here huddled in a cave waiting to die. I'm leaving! With or without you!"

"You'll never make it. Don't be an idiot! Someone could show up any minute now."

"Yeah, let's just put the chances of our survival into someone else's hands. Get real man! Nobody is coming for us. They would have been here by now. I can feel myself shutting down. It's time to go."

So, we left our food and the gold we found in the cave and began marching to an assassinating windchill that had to be nearly fifty below. With each breath, the skin inside my nose burns deeper. My feet feel prosthetic; I'm moving numb limbs.

As we march, the hallucinations are becoming reality. I am delusional and euphoric. Is it my brain shutting down? Or is there something empowering about trudging through a frozen tundra knowing your life is on the line?

"I'm done Branden. This is it for me. I can't go another step," Timothy croaks as he falls forward onto the rock-solid ground.

I turn him over and slap his face. "Think of Ellie! Get up," I plead. But it is too late. His eyes are lifeless.

Suddenly, the necessity to continue takes precedence over the swarm of emotions begging me to mourn the loss of my best friend. I want to breakdown, but a force inside of me authoritatively screams I must keep walking. If I don't, I will end up like him. I do my best to get up and stagger onward.

After about an hour, the sun has fallen and the result is it's gotten even colder. Then I am able to make out the crescent-shaped branch of a tree over the trail that is entirely familiar. It was one we passed just two miles after arriving at the cottage and setting out for the cave. I'm close. I'm captivated by a surge of energy unlike anything I've ever experienced before. It's incredible the resources our bodies reserve for the times when we need them most.

Flooded by adrenaline, my pace becomes brisk. Images of reuniting with my family flash through my mind. I see a warning sign stating that there are wolves and bears nearby. I remember seeing the sign just after we left. I am close. Then, finally, there it is!

I can't believe my eyes. I reach the cabin and it's empty. Everyone has gone home. Again, I'm alone. At least I have shelter. I reach for the doorhandle and twist it with the limited strength I still have. It's locked. I can't survive much longer out here. I begin hyperventilating, shaking my head back and forth, back and forth, moving it up and down in circles. Then suddenly, I see a rock the size of my hand. Without hesitation, I pick it up and launch it into the window. The glass shatters and I hurl my limp body through into the cabin.

"Heat, heat, heat!" I pant repeatedly. My system is so shocked that I've forgotten the sensation of warmth. I look up from the floor I'm lying on, and my heart sinks as I see the window without any glass. What have I done? This cabin is my lifeline and I've put a hole in it.

Cold air is rushing in by the second, this cabin is a sinking ship.

I crawl to the back of the room and open the door to the closet. I cram in and shut the door. I'm going to sleep, comfortable with the fact that whether I wake up or not depends on how early the cabin attendants come to work in the morning.

Chapter 76

Imprisoned

I go to bed each night and wake up a few hours later, usually around three o'clock in the morning with a sinking feeling that nothing changed while I was asleep, that all of this is still true. My kids hate me, my wife of over twenty years had divorced me, my life as I knew it is gone and I am still in this place.

The escape to sleep has had a comforting effect simply because in my dreams I've been able to be away, anyplace other than here. But lately, to my increasing sense of dread, even that has become a place I am fearing to go each night. That's because it has not been the escape to freedom it was before, especially several months ago. Now more and more of my dreaming is of being incarcerated, bound or imprisoned in one form or another. If not in a jail-like setting, then shackled in some way with chains around me or handcuffs binding my wrists. And the more I dream of the people I love, the less loving they are toward me in those dreams.

So, the sense of resentment and disgust I've felt daily now for the past two years in my weakened state, I likewise am feeling more and more in my dreams. It terrifies me to think what this means. I've had times of reflection, while awake thinking about my children especially and even my ex-wife, and the times they repeated how much they loved me, and I could almost re-sense what it was like. But then I realize that they hold no such feelings or resolve toward me any longer. The grief that sweeps over me is so intense sometimes that I can't help but to end up sobbing. Though I try and make sure that I am out of sight of anyone who would see me.

At least in my dreams I was getting the sense of being loved by them, until recently. I woke up one night about a week ago, and realized that my sobbing in my dreams had translated itself into actual physical expression which caused me to stir awake engulfed in tears. My face was soaked. I've thought about this and the source of my depressed feelings. They are not out of guilt or out of a sense that I did anything directly to harm my loved ones, in any way. Because I didn't. I know I reacted foolishly to an overwhelming sense of hopelessness preceded by feeling used and betrayed. But I've not held these feelings against anyone I love, and have not deliberately done anything against them directly.

To numb my own pain, I chose a self-destructive means, turning to alcohol and the outcome of that choice I am deeply regretting now. Perhaps if I had been more sober during the events leading up to my final decision to accept "the deal" I was offered by the court, I would not have taken it. I know now I should not have. What I thought was the best way to protect everyone and every institution I loved and worked for, turned out to be a big mistake. In the end, it didn't matter. I had relied on my family to stand by me and support my "taking the bullet" but that proved to be a foolish assumption on my part— probably one influenced by an unclear mind, in turn influenced by my use of alcohol as a medication against my worry and fear that I would lose everything. Which, ironically, is what happened anyway.

The positive outcome is that I am now completely sober and thinking straight. But even that has been bittersweet because in a clearly thinking mental capacity, I now realize what I chose to do, to accept the plea offer, was the wrong choice. It has turned out far worse than I could have predicted. Instead of having a family that stood behind the man and father who did everything in my life to support and love them, they completely abandoned me for whatever reason or reasons I've never been made aware of to this day. They simply won't talk to me. So, I spend my days in pain with anxiety that is almost unbearable.

And now, even going to sleep in order to escape is no longer working.

Chapter 77

Bucket List

Whoever said that having a "Bucket List" was a good idea? Especially one that has not only items to be achieved but also includes the age by which to complete them. I don't know what I was thinking when I came up with such a list, but now that time has passed and all but one of the items on the list has been accomplished, I feel compelled to finish it completely—in spite of how stupid I was in deriving the list in the first place.

It was back, over twenty-five years ago, when I was forty and coming up with such lists were really in vogue. Admittedly, I was unsure of where the next twenty years would go back then, so I came up with a rather rigorous list of things to do before reaching the ripe old age that I am now. Being sixty-five, my perspective has changed dramatically. There were scores of things on my list that I thought back then would be "lots of fun." Now I find myself more often saying, especially concerning that last remaining item, "Will it?"

Don't get me wrong. There were many things on the list that I have accomplished and I'm very happy that I have them crossed off. For example, back when I was forty, I was sure that I could achieve the item on the list that said I would visit all fifty states. It was not only doable, since by then I had already visited most all of the continental U.S. through my job as a traveling sales rep, but I had a lot of years ahead of me to visit the rest. The thought of getting to all the states offered some kind of excitement to me and now I can say that I did achieve that goal. In fact, I brag about it all the time. I've finally been to Alaska, which was the last state to check off, as this past year my wife and I visited the state via a cruise for our anniversary. So that item is now crossed off the list. No sweat.

Then there were the others that seemingly appear on numerous lists. Things like bungie jumping, which I did immediately after making the list at age forty; sailing the Caribbean, which I didn't achieve until age fifty-five, since I had to buy a sailboat first; owning two great dogs, a Golden Retriever and an Akita-German Shepherd mix, both mutts bringing me much joy over the years; owning a tricked-out Jeep, which I finally bought two years ago; climbing Pike's Peak, again, accomplished in my forties; and a whole host of other items that have all been checked off. All except one.

There is one item on the list that sticks out like a sore thumb that I had indicated would be accomplish by the age of sixty-five. Again, at the time, only at age forty, it seemed like it would be a ton of fun and I would easily accomplish it before turning sixty-six. But alas, I have not. What is it? What is that single most glaring item on my list? What else? Skydiving. Classic, right? I have not yet made the leap, so to speak, and I feel enormous pressure to do so. An added problem is that there is a municipal airport less than two miles from where I live in Oceanside, California. There is a skydiving plane that goes up with jumpers, numerous times every day. I have a constant reminder, seeing their colorful red chutes slowly descending from the sky all the time!

The fact of the matter is, I feel like a complete chicken now. I was so bold back when I was forty and made the list. I should have jumped way back then. But here I am today, six months away from my sixty-sixth birthday and the clock is ticking. I'm trying to figure out how to get up the courage to do this, the last remaining item on my list of sixty-five "to dos" by sixty-five. Maybe I shouldn't have been so cute in making the list have as many items as I had listed include the top age to complete them by. I suppose I could just adjust the list. I could reset the top age to eighty. Then maybe I'll be so out of it mentally to not even know what I'm doing.

Chapter 78

Childhood Sweetheart

I remember vividly back in the first grade when Lynn pointed her finger at me and said to her friends standing by, "I'm going to marry, you!" My cheeks flushed and my heart raced and I tried to be cool, but her words pierced my little heart. Fact was, she was the prettiest girl in the class with her curly blond hair and her fluffy pink dresses, though I had very little use for girls at age six. But the incident remained imprinted in my mind nonetheless.

Flash forward eleven years and here it was, the season of the junior prom, and I still didn't have a date. Now there are three other girls I am interested in, or I should say, are interested in me, but only one, not any of them, makes my heart race and my palms sweat. You guessed it. It's Lynn.

Prior to all this, ironically, we had become childhood friends as she and her family had moved into the house right next store when we were in the third grade together. Yes, she became, quite literally, the girl next door. Since the school we went to was only a quarter mile away, we used to walk to and from school together along with our brothers and sisters. A little neighborhood gang of sorts. Still, as we got older and moved on to junior high, we never dated. As if you could date at that young age. But what I'm trying to say is, we were never boyfriend and girlfriend, except for maybe one night.

It was the annual end of the year eighth grade dance held at the high school. It was the only time each year that eighth graders could go to an actual high school dance. I didn't want go by myself or with my dufus friends at the time so I determined that I would ask Lynn if we could go together. After all, we were neighbors and friends. It took a lot of nerve but I finally mustered up the courage to ask her, with a face beet red and a frog in my throat, I managed to get the words out asking her to go. She was surprisingly casual in her response and just said, "Sure." We ended up going together but we both spent most of the time apart hanging out with our own friends—boys with boys, girls with girls—just watching all the high school kids dancing the night away. Finally, it was the last song of the evening, a slow dance, and I finally asked Lynn to dance. So, we did. I had never been more nervous before in my life. Yet that one dance sealed the deal for me. I was in love but far too shy to do anything about it.

That summer came and we drifted apart doing things with our family and friends. I went to summer camp and talked about her like she was my steady girlfriend but she wasn't anything close to that, since we barely even spoke. Then high school came and I met another girl and we dated for a few months but it wasn't too serious. Once I got involved with sports, the whole notion of dealing with girls, kind of took a back seat. Don't get me wrong. I still had a spot in my heart for Lynn, though I never really acted on it. I got my license early my sophomore year and got more into cars, again with girls being only a side issue.

Then came junior year. The year of the prom. In our little town which had the smallest high school in the state, where everybody knew everybody else, it came with a lot of pressure. You simply had to go or you were a looser. And back in those days, nobody went by themselves or "as a group" like today. There was only one girl I wanted to take, even though there were three others vying for my attention. You got it. It was Lynn. Thanks to the constant irking of my best buddies, they convinced me to go for it. "You've wanted to date her since the fifth grade," they said. They were close. Truth is, I wanted to date her since she declared she would marry me some day—that was in first grade.

I made up my mind. I would ask Lynn to the prom. But my heart was torn with utter excitement on the one hand, and a deep fear of rejection on the other. Then came the moment of truth. It was a Friday afternoon only two weeks before the prom and the bell rang to signal the end of the school day. I would do it then.

As I approached her, standing in front of her locker sorting through some books, I fumbled the words in my mind, still filled with trepidation, when she suddenly looked up at me with her big blue eyes. She smiled, and it melted my heart.

Chapter 79

Riding the Bus

For me, there can be nothing more extraordinary than taking the bus. You see, I don't own a car so public transportation is my main means to get from Point A to Point B. I live in the Northern County of San Diego, and have a thirty-day pass that only sets me back $23 per month which gets me unlimited rides on the bus, any bus, and the trolly system. Not only that, I can connect with the San Diego proper system with the same pass as well. I'm not sure exactly how they can afford such a deal, but it sure does get me a whole boatload of miles of access throughout the northern part of San Diego County, like all of Oceanside, and the rest of greater San Diego all the way down to San Ysidro and the Mexican border. Like I said, it's a sweet deal!

One would consider that taking the bus on an almost daily basis is quite ordinary. Let me tell you, sister, it is not. Oh sure, a ride is a ride is a ride, nothing out of the ordinary there. It's what happens inside the bus environment that is anything but ordinary. Some of what I observe while just sitting there, minding my own business in my seat, is outrageous, strange, and sometimes borders on frightening.

Strange? Well for one, there are the scores of people who are always trying to get a free ride. They get on the bus and start to fidget around in front of the driver as if they're looking for change. Just the other day, I observed one such patron, a woman who had a towel wrapped around her head and a big, wide, brimmed hat atop of that, get into an argument with the driver. She told him that she only had fifty cents and that's all she always paid. "Look Lady," said the driver, "the bus fare hasn't been fifty cents since I was five years old and I'm fifty-five now. Either you have the two-dollar fare or you don't. So, sit down so we can get underway. There are folks onboard who need to get to work." That was the key phrase that resonated with me … "get to work." In other words, lady, "Get a job!"

That's just one example of a fare-dodger that happened recently. I have a ton of other examples. Like the same guy I see nearly every day at the same stop. He's always wearing his green backpack and has a yellow bandana folded around his forehead. He steps on and waits, hoping the driver will go, and then proceeds to open up his empty pockets as if he just lost his change. He hopes that the driver will say, "Just sit down." And often times that's what happens. But there was one driver the other day who would have none of it. He just sat there waiting while the clown emptied all his pockets, pants and jacket, only to have no change. The driver then told him to get off the bus and come back when he had the fare. Bravo to that driver!

There are far worse things I have witnessed happening with bus patrons. Like the time the guy who was on the bus and rode it all the way to the final stop but refused to get off at the transit station. We had to wait a half hour for the police to arrive to try and get him to leave so we could go. When the cops finally did show up, the guy suddenly was able to get up and get off the bus real fast. Still, it held up the bus full of people waiting to go for thirty minutes.

Then there are the people who insist on playing their phone's music loud, without using earbuds. That happens almost daily. It's always some obnoxious song that they're listening to, squealing loud enough for half the bus to hear. Unfortunately, most drivers are reluctant to do anything about it. Though I have witnessed a few who will simply stop the bus and refuse to go until the music stops. Again, bravo for those drivers!

Another staple are the self-talkers. They usually sit at the front of the bus and have loud conversations with themselves. They go on and on talking, sometimes even yelling with arms waving, to nobody. Perhaps it's mental illness, but it shouldn't be permissible. Who wants to listen to that? Often times it is quite vulgar as well. And there are kids on the bus who don't need to hear it.

There are the smelly people, another regular occurrence. Apparently, many bus riders have never learned about self-hygiene and bring a foul odor with them to their seat. I've actually seen other patrons get up and move away from these types. And don't forget the downright scuzzy looking people, many in bizarre outfits. The list goes on and on.

There are hundreds of other unusual things about riding the bus that I could relate if it were not for the constraint of time. You see, I've got to go now. Got to catch my bus!

Chapter 80

Duck Hunting

The first shot feels a little bit off. This early in the year the gunstock doesn't find the pocket of your shooting shoulder quite as easily as it will in the mornings to come during the rest of the season. It is also hard to keep your head down with the first dawn rising and the initial flight of ducks swirling in front of you again. It's been months since you have had that experience. Also, you are not in short sleeves anymore either, like you've been at the skeet range all summer. You're bound up in hunting layers and chest under-straps, your feet mired in the mud beneath them. It all feels a bit unnatural.

But that will change. You'll get your groove back. Soon enough all the "firsts" will be behind you. First hunt of the season, first shot of the season, first miss of the season, first duck in the water. All those weeks of looking forward to this and here we are.

This morning is all we've thought about for days. It stole away our sleep last night. It will haunt our stories tomorrow. It's all coming back to you now—the redolent funk of mud and swamp and wet gear and crushed leaves. The rhythmic hollow thump of a dog's tail on the blind floor. Even the mosquitos buzzing in your ear. It's all part of the morning ritual on a fine day for hunting.

Then the sky glows and the trees emerge from the far side of the pond. Suddenly, there are wings overhead. "Shooting time!" Someone warns us, hushed and hurried. And the first birds appear, and the first duck sails down, and the gun comes up, and in that moment it's all on.

No one minds waiting. Waiting is a big part of what we do. Starting with the last minute of legal light on the last day of the season, we wait for opening day. We wait through the northward spring migrations, through summer trips to the beach, through the heat. We wait on the seasons to change. We wait for the sun to rise. Duck hunters don't mind biding our time. But this is torture. This is waiting on an entirely different level. No one wants to wait on the weather.

For many of us it's been a slow-slow-slow start to the new year. Warm. Wet. What ducks are around are as stale as an old biscuit in the bottom of a blind bag, and there aren't many ducks around across the country any more. We call our buddies and scroll through duck hunting forums on-line looking for a good report. Hoping for a sign. A good spot. We're not ready to throw in the towel. We don't mind waiting because we've been here before, when the skies were empty. We know it can change in an instant.

So, we're not going anywhere. Except back to the blind, where we'll wait a little bit longer. Old Man Winter might be tough, but he's not as tough as a duck hunter bound and determined to be there the very minute all the waiting becomes all worth it.

In addition to the habitat being right, your dog, Penny, has come into her own. She's a four-year-old golden retriever and for her it is the sweet spot of her hunting life. She is fully trained and obedient but still has a young dog's exuberance. Picking up ducks is exciting for her, but it's no longer new. She knows her job and there is no need to worry about her doing it. She's a pro.

The greenheads weren't long in coming. They began as a compact bunch in the north, black silhouettes against the gray morning sky. They came in fast, purposefully, already shedding altitude. They're clearly happy to see this silvery lake with its wind-blocking rim of reeds and rushes shielding it from the elements.

Then suddenly there they are. You hail them with your Buck Gardener 6N1 whistle. They passed, wind rushing, swung around to the south, and glided down to the bobbing decoys on wings barely flickering. Then cupping, back-pedaling, green heads and russet breasts are now visible, olive bills like clothespins of color on the lush brown hens. With one drake already on the water wiggling its tail and three more on the deck, orange feet splayed for landing, you sit up and point the pump gun—a trusted twenty-gage loaded with number three bird-shot. Not too much recoil. The first bird never saw it coming. You pump and take the second by swinging past it as it banked right, just before the rest of the flock caught the wind and blew back, climbing away. Two for two. Not a bad start.

The crazy thing is you can still do this hunt. Maybe not in the ten-dollar wades and a three-dollar box of shells like in the old days. But wetlands and the mallards? They're still there. Despite forty more years of "progress," the heart of the duck factory of your youth is still there. It's all there. Free for the finding. Free for the hunting. No reservations needed. No jacket or tie required. Only patience.

Chapter 81

Old Wedding Picture

It was really quite odd. I saw the picture hanging on my maternal grandparents' wall all the years I visited them in the house on Tremont Street in Hartford, Connecticut. Having lived there for over fifty years, it was their "official" wedding picture. Almost old enough to be a Daguerreotype. In fact, it would be the one and only wedding picture that they had. It was taken in 1920, on Armistice Day, the 11th of November, which was almost exactly two years since the couple had come to America from Poland when World War I ended.

They came from different parts of the old country. She was from the south having lived in the village of Wieliczka, which is near Kraków, for the entirety of her sixteen years. He was eighteen and from a small village in the north called Krępiec, just south of the port city of Gdańsk. They both decided to catch a ship bound for America. They were fleeing the war-torn nation, making their escape out of the country, after the devastation that had rocked their two regions during the war had left them both homeless. They met onboard the ship Rotterdam which sailed out of the city in the Netherlands bearing its name and was on its way to Ender's Island in New York.

He, Stanislaus Galaski and she, Sophia Sudół, hit it off almost immediately upon literally bumping into each other while in the line for dinner one evening onboard the ship. Both, quite fortunately, had been traveling second class. With the voyage lasting nearly a month, they had ample time to get to know each other. They obviously were young, and something magical seemed to well up between them. The long, lonely journey across the Atlantic in April was cold and dreary but it didn't dampen their attraction toward one another as they got familiar in a very deep and personal way.

By the end of the trip, Stanley knew he didn't want to be alone in America. He wanted Sophia to be with him. He reasoned that the two had a better chance starting a life together rather than each of them being on their own. Fortunately, Stanley had a brother who already lived in America. His brother, Constance, lived in Pennsylvania and was a coal miner. He had come to America four years prior, just before the war broke out. He had a good job as an anthracite miner in the northeast mining region of Luzerne which, at that time, was always looking for more help. So, Stanley would have a job waiting for him if he and Sophia could make their way from Ender's Island to Pennsylvania. They had enough money left on their arrival in America to buy two train tickets and met Constance in Wilkes-Barre where the mining was taking place just south of Scranton in Pennsylvania.

While Stanley went right to work in the mines, Sophia got a job in town as a seamstress. The two saved as much money as possible and planned to have a modest wedding. In the meantime, Sophia's sister Helena had also come to America and had a job in a factory in Hartford, Connecticut. She was able to find two additional factory jobs, one each for both Sophia and Stanley at the Underwood Typewriter Company. The jobs paid much more than they were making in Pennsylvania and had considerably less risk for Stanley. So, within a year, the couple relocated to Hartford. Sophia moved in with her sister and Stanley had a room at the local YMCA. Both lived within walking distance to work. The two scrimped and saved and were eventually able to rent a place, which was half of a duplex on Tremont Street. Just two weeks prior to their wedding, Stanley moved in.

Then, on November 11th in 1920, the two were married at Saint Cyril and Methodious Church, a newer and predominantly Polish immigrant parish that was founded in 1902. Even though it was a Thursday, there was no work at the factory that day due to the fact that it was a celebratory day in honor of the Armistice two years prior. The wedding was small and the reception was held in the church basement, which doubled as a gathering hall after Masses. Only a few friends and Sophia's sister were in attendance. But the couple still dressed formally and Sophia had a beautiful wedding dress that she had hand-made. One of their friends from work was also a photographer and had offered to take a picture of the couple as a wedding present.

As they posed for the picture something must have happened to distract the couple on either side of the altar where they were posing. The second that the picture was snapped the two were looking in opposite directions. That was the picture that continued to puzzle me every time I saw it hanging on the same wall of the living room in my grandparents' home. What were they looking at? And, why were they looking in opposite directions? And why no smiles on their faces? Whatever happened in that moment was always a mystery to me and will remain that way since they have both long since passed away and I never had the nerve to ask them.

Chapter 82

Saints Alive

What do all these people have in common with me? They impacted the way I felt about life in general having grown up while certain key modern world events took place from the 1960s through the 1990s. They caused feelings and attitudes that have been nurtured by their example and remain with me well into adulthood. The short list of influential historical persons who were alive during my lifetime that I can relate to the most are the ones who became saints. They were much more than just role models for me, resembling family members that you know and love but don't get to see very often. I can say this because they were, in a sense, actually part of my family since we all shared the same faith as Catholics.

Pope John XXIII, Padre Pio, Pope Paul VI, Óscar Romero, Mother Teresa, and Pope John Paul II were all my contemporaries as they lived and became saints during my lifetime. I knew about them during my formative years as a youth and witnessed them become first venerable because of their heroic virtues, then saw them beatified, and then, finally, canonized as saints.

Usually, it takes centuries before a person is recognized officially as a saint in the Roman Catholic Church, with a few exceptions. These were all exceptions, as their causes were accelerated by most common standards. They all became an important part of my own life's history. To me, perhaps the greatest of these saintly superstars was Pope John Paul II. He was pope for most of my adult life when I was a youth minister and teacher of religion in Catholic schools. His papacy started in 1978 when I was still a junior at Boston College and lasted until his death in 2005. By then I had become a professor at a Catholic seminary. His teachings and life example were instrumental in my continuing formation in the faith as well as in that of many of my students. Furthermore, he was from Poland and all of my grandparents and ancestors were from Poland as well. Having a Polish pope for the first time in history was something we all treasured.

Pope John Paul II was the founder of the World Youth Days which were meetings of high school and college aged youth that he held in different countries throughout the world every three years. The first gathering I attended with him was the World Youth Day, held in Częstochowa, Poland just after the fall of the Soviet Union in 1991. Poland was a free nation at last! This held particular significance for me. At that time, I was a youth minister and had a youth group of about a hundred-fifty high school aged students. Going to the gathering of youth from throughout the world in Poland simply was going to happen in my mind. And it did. I made the trip with ten of my students and two adult chaperones. It was the trip of a lifetime.

We flew out of JFK airport in New York to Brussels and joined together with a college group from Franciscan University of Steubenville in Ohio. We then traveled by bus together through Germany and saw part of the fallen wall in Berlin. Then it was through Czechoslovakia, which was still under communist rule where we had an audience with Jan Strásky in Prague, who would eventually become the country's last prime minister before the split of the nation into two free countries. When we finally made our way to Poland, having a bus, we were able to visit several sites before the World Youth Day gathering at the Marian shrine in Częstochowa. The event attracted more than a million youth from around the world, but most were predominantly from Poland since the nation is ninety-eight per cent Roman Catholic and the people there were on fire to see their beloved Polish pope. As was I.

One of our stops while traveling through Poland was to visit Auschwitz. I cannot adequately put into words the feelings I experienced seeing that death camp in person brought out of me. I'll simply leave it at that. I was moved to tears, sobbing as I stood inside one of the gas chambers that was used to murder so many millions of Jewish people. Everything has been left there intact, as it was back then.

Then, after seeing Auschwitz, we traveled through the beautiful Polish countryside that the nation is known for, until at last we reached Częstochowa. There were students everywhere! Singing joyfully and greeting us with open arms. Some even asked for our autographs because we were Americans. I never felt so much love from such a large group of people. What struck me in that moment was the stark contrast to what we had witnessed at Auschwitz earlier that very same day. All that separated the horrors of that place with the joy and rejoicing of this place was time. Roughly fifty years of history had made all the difference in going from a war-torn occupied country to one experiencing a brand-new way of life—a rebirth.

As we joined our new-found Polish friends amid the throngs of youth gathered in the streets of Częstochowa, a feeling of immense joy swept over me. Now we were waiting for the pope, my hero, John Paul II to arrive and greet us—with singing and dancing and prayers going out all around. Again, for the second time in the same day there would be tears in my eyes but for the completely opposite reason. This time it was due to boundless joy.

Little did I know it then, but for the next three days we would be celebrating life together with a future saint. One that we could confidently come to say was like family.

Chapter 83

Witness Protection

My new life in the witness protection program has been a monumental change from my past. I had been more or less homeless and a volunteer at an inner-city soup kitchen in the heart of San Diego's roughest neighborhood. I had gotten the job as the cook. And although there was no payment for my services, there was the benefit of having a room and bed to sleep in upstairs in the shelter. The place was called God's Extended Hand and was part of an interdenominational ministry to the poor of the city, providing two meals a day to about a hundred patrons who lived in the streets. My task each day was to cook the food in the facility's fully functional kitchen. I was a sous chef in the past, so I knew my way around pretty good. I always managed to get something nutritional prepared while being both unique and tasty at the same time. I would put together a meal with pride and a great amount of respect for the crowd I was serving. One that never failed to show up twice a day, every day.

Then came that one night, not too long ago that changed my life forever. I was lying in my bed upstairs, about to drift off to sleep, when suddenly I heard gunshots, two of them in rapid succession. I went to the window (thinking back on it now, I realize how foolish that was) and saw what was transpiring on the sidewalk below. The lights from the front of our building illuminated the scene so that I could clearly see what was happening. I saw the man holding the gun that had just fired and then I saw him shoot it again at another man who was only a few feet in front of him. Two more shots. A total of four. Because of the bright building lights and the fact that he was right there beneath me just outside my open window, allowed me to get a good look at him. I will never forget that face. It was distinct and different, not one that could easily blend in with the crowd.

I didn't know it at the time, but would find out later that the shooter was connected with a major drug cartel. Nonetheless, I had just witnessed a murder. Moments later the police showed up and sealed off the area. A few of them came inside our building and asked if anyone had seen what happened. I volunteered the information I knew and told them I got a good look at the guy who did the shooting seeing everything from my room's window which was right smack in front of the scene. Before I knew it, I was down at headquarters looking at a notebook of photos of potential suspects fleeing the scene that the police had just taken into custody. That's when I saw him! I ID'd the man and at that time I had no idea how that one act would completely change my life.

After that, I was told they needed my testimony in court to help put him away for good, but doing that came with a huge risk. You see, the rest of his gang in the cartel would kill me to prevent me from testifying. It was then that I had been moved from my meager room at the shelter to an undisclosed apartment building in another town to await trial. There were always two policemen with me. Then, after I testified, they would put me into the witness protection program. That would mean changing my name and my location all in return for my swearing under oath to what I had seen. The fact that I saw the man commit the murder would become public.

In the end, he was convicted of first-degree murder and the entire cartel was going to be exposed. After the trial, I was whisked out of the courthouse, immediately taken to the airport and put on a private jet to my new location where I would not only live the rest of my life, I had to do so with a new identity. At least I got to choose what my new name would be. I changed it to Clayton Bragdon, which was the name of a childhood friend who of mine was killed in a tragic motorcycle accident. I thought it appropriate to give Clayton a new life along with me.

I've always liked motorcycles and bikes so I chose to have a new career as the proprietor of a bike shop. One that also rented mopeds and bicycles. As to where I would locate, I was graciously given four choices and the one I decided to take was easy. At first, I thought that it had to have as good or better weather than San Diego, which would mean someplace a bit more south. So, it was the U.S. Virgin Islands that had the greatest appeal, namely the city of St. Croix.

I knew I could adjust to island living and the fact that I have been here loving my surroundings for over a year now proves it. And, although I still look over my shoulder all the time, it really isn't necessary as it has been safe. Nobody here knows who I really am nor anything about my past and I want to keep it that way. Loose lips sink ships and I'm not about to spoil the safe new life that I enjoy now. From a homeless volunteer in an inner-city soup kitchen to the owner of a tropical island paradise tourist hot spot. What one murder could do.

Chapter 84

Adoption Decisions

It was near the end of August in the year 2005, and my wife and I were evaluating our life's circumstances after just celebrating our twenty-fifth wedding anniversary. We had a beautiful home with four bedrooms in a quaint little farm town in Connecticut where everyone seemed to be friendly towards one another. We had raised four magnificent children who were rapidly all growing up into young adults. It all seemed to go by so fast.

My oldest son was now a corporal in the Marine Corps and deployed in Iraq. My oldest daughter was away at a Catholic college in Ohio entering her third year, and my youngest daughter had just graduated from high school and was at orientation for college herself. Only our youngest son, who was in eighth grade and being homeschooled, would be left at home, now alone.

My wife and I were nowhere near ready to retire yet and figured that we still had a few good years of active parenting left in us. So, we talked about it, prayed about it, and then we finally contemplated it seriously. Why not adopt a younger child?

We then spent the next six months going through "the process" as they call it. After commodious reflection along the way, the more decided we became. Adoption was right for us. It was what we really wanted to do with our lives at that juncture. But adopt from where? What age child? The more involved we got with the process, the more we realized there were lots of considerations, not to mention all the rules and regulations we had to follow just to be deemed qualified and suitable, thorough FBI background checks notwithstanding. Finally, with all the details worked out and our financial situation approved, we were ready to adopt. The next question was who? What child? And, from where?

We decided we didn't want to adopt a baby or toddler. That was a stage we were all too familiar with and didn't desire to experience again. We also didn't want a child older than our youngest son so that he wouldn't lose his place in the family structure. So, it came down to a child anywhere from six to twelve years old, preferably a boy since we had the notion it would be good for our youngest who was still at home to have a brother to play with. As it turned out, the U.S. had very little to offer with these parameters and we were advised to seek an international adoption instead.

Both my wife and I being of Polish descent and active in our parish community which was also Polish, had come to learn that here was a real need in Poland to place children in adoptive families. Since the country was also struggling after its break with the Soviet Union, many children without parents were still being locked away in orphanages instead of foster family homes. We learned through our parish priest, who had many active personal ties to the country, and to some specific orphanages in particular, that we would be an ideal fit. The only stipulation was in order for us as Americans to adopt Polish children, it was required that we had to help keep their heritage active. That wouldn't be a problem at all with our family since we were already doing that on our own. Especially during the holidays, we kept all the Polish traditions alive in our home. So, that's what happened.

After a few more months of going through adoption workbooks, websites featuring pictures and descriptions of the eligible children, and working through a nearby agency in the states that coordinated Polish adoptions, we were finally paired. We decided we would adopt not just one but two children, brothers who didn't want to be split-up. It was a real stretch financially at the time as it was already costing us over $15,000 to adopt just one child. Doubling the adoption also meant double the price to pay. The two boys had the same mother but different fathers and were wards of the state in Poland, living in an overcrowded orphanage. They were both younger than our son so they met all our hopes for keeping the family structure intact. So, despite the added cost, we would adopt both boys. After all the necessary preparations were complete, my wife and I went to Poland to meet our two new would-be family members.

While we were in Poland and working out the necessary paperwork to adopt Andrzej, aged twelve (who was only a month younger than our youngest son), and Marcin his brother, who was six, we learned that they also had a sister who was two years older than Andrzej, named Agnieszka. She was fourteen. The Polish authorities did everything possible in their power to encourage us to keep the three siblings together, even to the point of offering us the option to adopt the sister of the two boys free of charge. What a deal! At that point we figured, what was one more? My wife and I simply looked at each other and smiled as she said, "Well, we have the empty bedrooms, might as well fill them all with love. Family structure be what it will."

So, that's what we did. We adopted all three of them on the spot. That July 25th, Christmas in July we called it, we went from having four delightful children to having seven wonderful children in no time flat!

Chapter 85

Rose's Yellow Rose

Each day Rose waited for the mailman to arrive. It was always at the same time give or take a few minutes, around ten-thirty. This morning when the mailman delivered the letter, it was labeled "URGENT" on top. Rose couldn't wait to open it. She got her letter opener out of the draw and slide it in along the edge of the top, slicing open the envelope. She was neat about it since she would save this letter like she had saved all the others.

Rose, a beautiful young lady, was having a relationship by old-fashioned mail correspondence with Tom, who seemed to be a wonderful young man. This had been going on for little over a year. Tom lived overseas and they never met in person. They didn't know what each other looked like as they decided to keep that a mystery until the day they actually met in person. They did describe themselves to each other. Rose thought by the description Tom gave to her of himself, that he was a fine-looking young man. The other descriptions of themselves that they had shared over the months led both of them to conclude that they were indeed a good match for each other.

As Rose feverishly opened the letter and began to read it, she saw that Tom indicated that he would be flying into LAX the day after tomorrow to take care of some business that the firm he worked for was engaged in. It was pure luck that Rose lived in Los Angeles and this would be an opportunity for the two to finally meet. So, in the letter, Tom asked if she could please be at the airport to greet him when he arrived.

From previous letters, Rose indicated that whenever she went someplace nice, she would always wear a yellow rose. It was kind of a joke and play on her name, but it really did make her look special. She had shared this fact with Tom a number of times. Tom indicated that when he arrived, he would simply look for the woman in the crowd at the airport wearing a yellow rose, her trademark, and that's how he would know it was her. He wrote: "I will look carefully at all the women waiting at the gate, when I see the most beautiful one standing there, I'll know it's you. Your yellow rose will only serve to confirm my judgement." It was sweet. It was typical Tom.

The letter went on to say that perhaps they could share a dinner since his business meetings weren't scheduled until the day after he arrived. That gave them the entire afternoon and evening to be together. As Rose read each line of the letter, she got more and more excited. Immediately, she started questioning herself. What will I wear? What will he be wearing? Should I use make-up. Get my hair done? And on and on.

Anticipation, anxiety, fear, and joy kept disturbing Rose's attempt at sleeping the night before the meet. When she finally did get up the next morning, she suddenly remembered that she needed to pin a yellow rose on her lapel as she got ready. She always had a bouquet of yellow roses in her living room so she took one of them and cut it to fit on her jacket. She decided on wearing a rather attractive skirt suit, with a flowing yellow blouse underneath that only helped to accentuate the rose.

She nervously arrived at the airport a good forty-five minutes before Tom's flight was due to land. After parking her car in the commuter lot, she went to where the signs indicated his flight would arrive. There was already a group of other people congregating and waiting like she was. Before long, she found herself packed in the middle of the crowd. Her anxious thoughts then started to dissolve into ones of doubt. Why was his last letter labeled "urgent" she wondered?

Rose was a beautiful woman on the inside as well as on the outside. She thought to herself that no man had ever appreciated her inner qualities but only her outer beauty. This led to her experiencing much pain in the past. Would Tom fall into that category? Would Tom only like her for her outer beauty? Would he continue to appreciate her as her external beauty faded with age? Had she made a mistake in coming here like this? The questions only led to more questions. Doubt building on doubt.

Then, the passengers from Tom's flight started to emerge through the walkway as they began flooding into the terminal. That's when Rose spotted an unattractive and obviously homeless woman milling about where the trash cans were. An idea popped into her head. She went over, greeted the woman and asked if she could give her the rose that was pinned to Rose's jacket. The woman just smiled, so Rose did just that. She pinned her rose on the homeless woman's lapel and the woman smiled again and said, "That's the nicest thing anyone has done for me lately. Thank you very much ma'am."

Then Rose made her way to the edge of the crowd and stood back waiting to see what Tom would do, if anything. That's when she saw a tall, rather slim, well-built and very handsome gentleman approach the homeless woman. He gave her the flowers that he was holding in his hand, a bunch of yellow roses, a hug, and a kiss on the cheek.

Somehow, just then, Rose knew that everything was going to be just fine.

Chapter 86

The BB BAC

Perhaps the best organization I ever joined was the Baby-Boomers Backpacking Adventure Club. BB BAC for short. As you might have guessed, membership is only open to baby-boomers which made the current average age of all the active members in their sixties, seventies and early eighties. We are a tough lot—seeking backpacking and hiking adventures all over the globe. Last spring, the choice was to go mountain climbing in France up one of the steepest and broadest mountains in the country called Mont Blanc. The name literally means "White Mountain" because the summit maintains snow throughout the year. It is the highest mountain in the Alps and Western Europe rising nearly 16,000 feet above sea level. It is the second-most prominent mountain in Europe after Mount Elbrus, and the eleventh most prominent mountain summit in the world. It derives its name from the Mont Blanc massif which straddles parts of France, Italy, and Switzerland. We would follow a popular trail called the Goûter Route from France into Switzerland, taking three days and two nights to reach the summit.

I had the experience of driving through Mont Blanc two years before as there is a tunnel that goes right through the base of the mountain on the interstate highway, which is actually an international roadway linking France and Italy. The tunnel stretches for over fifteen kilometers (about ten miles) and is one of the longest driving tunnels in the world. That was a harrowing experience—to be driving in a tunnel for that long. But driving through the mountain wasn't enough for me. I had to climb it. I couldn't stop imagining what reaching the summit would be like. So, when the BB BAC chose Mont Blanc as its springtime challenge, I eagerly accepted the invitation to go along. Of course, in the spring, the top of the mountain would still be considerably snow-covered which meant there was always the threat of avalanches. Just one of a series of dangers we could encounter.

I remember it like it was yesterday. We began our trek that sunny afternoon on April 27, 2020. I remember it was a Monday, since the French guides kept saying it was "Lundi". We were making the trip in spite of the onset of the Covid scare that was starting to capture the world's attention. That proved to be a mistake.

Due to our rather conservative schedule for climbing, most of us being rather elderly, it would take us three days and two nights to reach the summit. (Normally groups could make it in two days.) After climbing through the first day, on inclines that were not too steep, we set up camp and spent the night together—a total of fourteen novice climbers and three guides. All of us BB BAC members were already feeling it. Leg muscles were cramping up and I can't explain the level of exhaustion I felt after hiking up a slow but steady incline for eight hours straight. And I was one of the youngest members of the group being only sixty-two.

But the taxing, tired legs and body was nothing compared to what two of our club members experienced. They were a couple, Jean and John, married over forty years and in their early seventies. They were starting to feel really dragged out after that first day. By the end of the second, with only one day to go, they got really sick. You guessed it. They had contracted the Covid virus.

It was the end of the journey for them and the rest of us in the group thought it was the end for us as well until one of the younger members of the group, a guide in his late fifties, suggested that we should take a vote. He was very athletic for his age and was from Somalia, way out of his natural element. His suggestion was that we should use the "method of democracy" as he put it, as to whether or not we should all go back of if some of us, who felt no symptoms, should forge on another day to the summit with one of the guides, namely him. Whoever didn't want to go on could make their way back with the two other guides. John and Jean of course would be included in the returning group.

So that's what we did. We voted. I fell into the "forge on ahead" group, which turned out to be a total of eight of us which was a slim majority out of the fourteen total. The guides didn't have a vote. Six of the others, including Jean and John, headed back down the mountain. It only took them the rest of the third day to go back since it was all downhill.

As for the rest of us in the forge on ahead group, we reached the summit early the next day. It was an experience I will never forget. Seeing the incredible view from the top of one of the highest mountains in the world was beyond any words I could use to describe the sensation I felt. Needless to say, I was overjoyed that we continued on to complete the climb. Fortunately, for all of us who made it to the top, we all dodged a bullet in regards to catching the virus as well. Nobody who voted to forge on was affected. Unfortunately, everyone who returned back down the mountain with Jean and John did catch it from them, including the two guides.

All I could think of after the trip was over and we were safely back down the mountain at basecamp, was thank goodness for democracy in action on the way to the summit of Mont Blanc.

Chapter 87

Big Jim Goes Shopping

Big Jim was never called slim. Though "Slim Jim" would seem like a proper nickname as he wasn't very heavy-set. But he was tall. At six-foot-five with shoes off he was, in most regards, a big guy. A big guy who didn't like being called slim. So, the nickname never stuck. And he had a voice that equaled his physique. Loud! Again, "Loud Jim" was not a good nickname, so just calling him Jim would have to suffice. That's what most people did.

The thing about Jim was, he didn't much appreciate waiting in line. In fact, he hated lines of any kind and made it known that he'd rather go without something than to wait in line for it. Then came the time that the question of waiting in line all reached a climax for him. It happened while he was grocery shopping.

Jim was at the local Vons supermarket on 30th Street and Howard, in his hometown of San Diego, California. Even though he lived in the "laid back" city, he had no patience for most things, especially lines at the grocery store. So, on this particular day while getting ready to check out with his handful of only four items in his shopping basket, he knew he would have to get in a line. As he approached the cash registers, he was searching for the shortest line. No line at all would have been primo, but that was unlikely, given it was a busy Saturday morning. You would think, given that it was a normally busy time, that there would be several registers open—say at least five of the eight at the front of the store. But there wasn't. Only three were available. At least one was designated for fifteen items or less, so that line was shorter than the other two as they both were at least six people deep, all having full carts.

As he joined the shortest line, he also noticed that there were only two people ahead of him. Acceptable in Jim's mind. Not too long, considering. And a quick look confirmed that both patrons ahead of him didn't break the fifteen-item only rule either. No sweat. He figured he would be through the line in no time.

Of the two people in front of him, one was a woman just in front of him who looked rather mysterious. She was dressed in a formal black outfit. Jim surmised that maybe she was on her way to one of those receptions following a funeral. The kind where people gather at the house for some food and to share memories. She only had three items in her hands. There were two loaves of a recognizable popular brand of cinnamon bread and a pound of butter. She won't take long, he thought to himself.

In front of her, about to check out, was an elderly gentleman who looked rather frail. He also had a hand-basket with about five items in it, mostly vegetables. Jim thought to himself that the guy probably heard if you eat a lot of vegetables, you'll live longer. It was a funny contrast in his mind as he considered that the funeral lady was right behind the real-old guy about to "check out." Jim allowed himself an inner chuckle. Sometimes waiting in line could have its upside, he thought.

The old guy started passing his items to the cashier who was beginning to ring him up. "It won't be long now," Jim murmured to himself. Being normally so loud, the two in front of him heard it. He chucked inside again thinking about the old guy followed by the funeral lady and what he had just said. Then suddenly, the cashier stopped ringing up the old guy's items. It seemed as if there apparently was a problem with the little printer that spewed out the receipts. Some sort of malfunction. The cashier sighed loudly and started tapping the machine as if that would help.

A one-minute delay turned in to five rather quickly as the cashier now had the printing device open and was adjusting and readjusting the little spool of paper that went into it. Beginning to get agitated now, Jim sighed even louder, so that the casher could hear him loud and clear. Then he started to glance around bouncing up and down on his toes. As if that somehow would hurry things along. But to no avail. His line had grown to seven deep, now that several others had filed in behind Jim. The other two lines had grown longer as well. He surmised that there simply was no place to go better than where he was now— stuck in line. And they all were going nowhere in this line as long as the cashier kept fiddling with the receipt printer. In spite of pressing all sorts of buttons and adjusting nobs, the printer simply wouldn't go. All Jim could do was look around and get steamed even more. He was about to yell at the cashier when the woman in front of him, with the black dress, spoke up.

"Sir, I can see that you're very anxious. Perhaps you would like to go in front of me. That way you could be next. I only have three items and I can wait."

Jim couldn't believe his ears. Then it happened. The cashier suddenly got the printer to work. The sound of the old guy's items being wrung up was singing from it. In less than a minute later, his items were bagged and ready to go.

Suddenly, Jim felt ashamed and ridiculous for being so impatient. Where did he have to go anyway? Oh yeah. Nowhere! He said to the woman in front of him in return, "No, you go right ahead ma'am. You were here before me. I shouldn't be so impatient."

She simply smiled, completely disarming him.

Jim learned a lesson that day. That although he was a big, loud man, he had little patience and felt small. Funny how a simple thing like waiting in line could help that virtue along.

Chapter 88

Time Not Ours

Think about how most of us view time. It is either too long or too short but rarely do we feel time is adequate. Even more importantly, rarely do we see the value of delay. We have somehow fooled ourselves into thinking that we are beyond allowing anyone else to control our time, we even put God in that category. In spite of what he has revealed to us in the scriptures. Take Psalm ninety, verse four for example: "For a thousand years in your sight are as yesterday, now that it is past, or as a watch of the night." We still think of it as our time and not God's. Not that we should take that passage literally, but God is trying to tell us something about how we measure time and what we do with it. Further on in the same Psalm it says, "Teach us to number our days aright, that we may gain wisdom of heart." The points of this "prayer of Moses the man of God," is that time is not ours, it isn't ours to own, we can't even conceive of it in the same way that God does. What he does say is to take precious care of the time we are given in order to gain wisdom of heart. It's all about how we use the time that we have.

Perhaps an example of how this could be realized more fully in the context of this pilgrimage of life we all find ourselves spending our time on would be helpful.

Years ago, I was working in New York City a good two hours away from my home in central Connecticut. I would actually be away from my family for the week, sharing an apartment with a few fellow workers and then come home for weekends. I felt it would work this way economically for the short term anyway, instead of packing everyone up and moving to New York. Still, I valued my time at home with my family and would try to linger to the last possible second before making the long return trip to work away from them. In what was normally a two-hour drive, I was used to giving myself an extra half-hour just in case.

It was an early Monday morning and I knew that if the traffic was somewhat average, I would make it to work in New York City in plenty of time to do the presentation I was scheduled to give to some important clients from Santa Clara, California visiting our little start-up company. Naturally, and perhaps anyone can relate to this in one way or another, only an hour into the trip, I ran into a massive traffic jam. Immediately, anxiety started setting in because I could see that there was no end to the snaking line of cars in front of me with the glow of continuously pressed breaks lights contrasting the early morning fogginess. One minute turned into ten, ten turned into thirty, until the wave of panic surging inside me was overwhelming. This all took place in the early 1990s, a time before cell phones were prolific, so calling ahead to explain I would be late seemed dubious at best. Besides, there were no rapidly approaching exits to gain access to a pay phone anyway. We simply were not moving!

In my mind I began thinking, no, *blaming* God for making this happen on this particular day when I needed to be on time. He was trying to make me late, I reasoned. Didn't he realize that I was already under a lot of pressure to convince the guys from Intel who came all the way to New York to see the value of investing in our product? Didn't God hear how, in no uncertain terms, the president of our company made it known to me that this was a do-or-die situation for our little fledgling firm? Meaning my job was on the line. I know the Almighty understood that I was pushing my abilities as the marketing director, but this delay and being late was surely going to kill us. And my career.

Most people will get upset over being unnecessarily delayed. We know where we want to get. We know the time that it will usually take to get there. But when something beyond our control causes a ripple in our plan of time, we feel justified in judging someone or something to be held accountable aside from ourselves. Even though we know deep down inside we have no ultimate control, we begin to believe that we do, and feel entirely justified at expressing our contempt at whoever we conjure up in our own minds caused the delay in "our time" in the first place.

But what if it was God?

After the looking at the clock on the dashboard for the thousandth time, and seeing that well over an hour had passed creeping along without the needle reaching any actual double-digit number indicated on the speedometer, it suddenly came to my attention that there were no cars coming from the opposite direction. Not being able to see because of a bend in the road ahead made the moment that much more frightening. Whatever was causing the delay was far worse for those poor blokes going north, heading in the opposite direction as me. Then, as I finally rounded the turn in the highway, the cause of delay suddenly became all too real.

The pile of tangled up metal in the left most lane on our side of the median appeared to be what was at one time a motorcycle, with its longer parts completely twisted and bent into some kind of grotesque looking torture device. The police on the scene were funneling our three approaching lanes of traffic into one, using the gravel shoulder of the road as the only passage. My eyes raced around the scene quickly identifying what happened when they came to rest on the solid, three-car-deep, line of traffic on the other side of the highway being held in place by a single police cruiser turned perpendicular to them. In that few seconds of time, everything seemed so much slower. It was as if time had almost stopped. My head made a natural gesture of bowing as my surveying gaze continued down the road in front of the police car until the horror of what caused the delay was clearly in view.

In the middle lane, some kind of meg-shift, formerly white blanket covered the body of a man whose legs lay lifeless outside of its shroud. The crimson stains which dominated the covering over him registered all too vividly what had happened. To this day, I can still picture that scene with the lifeless lump of human flesh that was once a man fully alive resting completely still, squarely in the middle of the center lane like the oncoming traffic behind him. In that moment his life stopped. So did the lives of every one of us on the highway that day. I was going to be late. Really late. He was going to be late never again. The importance of my efforts that day quickly shrunk to insignificance.

At least I still had time on my side of eternity.

Chapter 89

Dad's Last Day

The phone on his desk at Engineering Automation Systems rang. Two quick buzzes, an internal call. Michael Rybak picked up the phone and heard the voice of his boss, CEO Chuck Hevenor on the other end. "Mike, you need to stop whatever you're doing and leave quickly. The hospital just called, it's your father, he doesn't have very long."

Michael thanked his boss for relaying the message and hung up the phone. He sat there just stunned for a minute. Then he hastily saved the file that he was working on and shut down his computer. He grabbed his coat from the rack, his keys from the top draw of his desk, and dashed out of his office cube. He made his way briskly down the stairs to the main entrance rushing all the way to his car. It was a half-hour drive to the hospital, even in the Audi Sport Quattro, under normal conditions. But today it only took him twenty minutes as he drove the whole way with his high beams on and flashers blinking, using the full extent of the car's three-hundred and two horses under the hood.

On the way, he thought how he had just seen his father, Hank, the night before. The two had talked for hours about almost everything in life as they saw it, and Michael was truly grateful that they had. He never shared on that level with his father before, who offered so many thoughts and stories about his life and experiences. Hank was very grateful he had lived a full life, had a wonderful family, and had done just about everything he wanted to do. When the conversation ended, they watched part two of the NBC *Marco Polo* miniseries on the television in his private room before Hank had asked Michael to pray with him.

The two then prayed the *Our Father*, *Hail Mary*, and *Glory Be* together. Michael recalled the many times in his childhood that his father had gotten him and his brother up in the middle of the night on a Saturday, once a month, to drive to Saint Maurice Catholic Church, a few miles from where the family lived in the small town of Bolton, Connecticut. Hank belonged to the Nocturnal Adoration Society. A group of men pledged to spend one hour in adoration of the Blessed Sacrament from sundown on Saturday to sunrise on Sunday, the first weekend of each month. Hank's watch hour was from two o'clock until three o'clock in the morning. When the boys were around ten years old, he would invite Michael and his younger brother Peter to join him and pray silently in the church for the hour. Michael was thrilled to be awakened in the middle of the night to go out with his dad. There was also the lesson it taught. It was a great exposure to active prayer he was being educated in by having the experience. He couldn't help but think that it had a profound impact on the rest of his life. Now he wondered if all those years of prayer would pay off for Hank who was on his death bed. Michael was certain and rest assured his father knew the Lord.

The drive to the hospital was uneventful as there was nobody in the high-speed lane of Interstate 84 and I-384 at that time of day. Michael simply sped along without so much as a car here or there which he passed right by, doing around eighty miles per hour—well over the mandated speed limit of fifty-five and using only half of his car's top speed.

He finally reached Manchester Memorial Hospital and parked his car in the visitor's lot where he had parked so many times in recent weeks. He jumped from the car and jolted into the building. No need to check where Hank was, since he was just visiting him in his room the previous night. He grabbed the elevator going up to the fourth floor of the right-most wing. The floor of the terminally ill.

The wing was well known as the Cancer Treatment Unit at Manchester Memorial Hospital. Almost a world-class hospital. They had boasted of a high recovery success rate. That is, if you caught the cancer in time, during stage one or two. The problem with Hank's was it was way too late, advanced stage four. The fact that they didn't catch it in time was a non-issue. His lungs were filled with hardening particles as Hank was suffering from mesothelioma, also generally referred to as asbestosis. The cancer was like a timebomb. Symptoms didn't surface until twenty or more years after a period of prolonged exposure to asbestos. By the time he showed the first signs of symptoms, Hank was already terminal. There was no cure. The disease would eventually impair the ability to breathe entirely.

It wasn't only Hank who was afflicted. His brother, three cousins, and some of their wives would eventually succumb to the cancer because they all worked as pipe coverers, using asbestos throughout the 1960s and early 1970s before it was outlawed due to the danger it posed. The women caught the fatal disease because they would wash their husbands' clothes shaking out the particles first, thereby breathing in the deadly fibers. Mesothelioma would eventually wipe out half of the Rybak family tree.

Hank wasn't the only mesothelioma patient in the Cancer Center. There were two others with him on the fourth floor. It was also well known in local folklore that rarely did anybody ever leave that particular floor alive. Nevertheless, Michael ran down the hall to his father's room. Number 402. It was one o'clock in the afternoon, September 13th, 1984.

There Hank Rybak was flat on his back. In the same position as when Michael left him the night before. His eyes were closed and he was breathing ever so lightly. Michael quickly looked around the room. The only other person there, sitting quietly in a chair in the corner, was his uncle. Uncle Eddie was Michael's Godfather and Hank's younger brother. He also had mesothelioma.

"How is he?" Michael asked.

"Not too good," Eddie replied. "He's started taking long, deep breaths and they have the rattle."

The sound of near death.

Suddenly Eddie spoke up again after a long minute of silence. "I'm glad you made it. He loved you being here for him and talking last night. He told me earlier this morning he feels at peace now. He hasn't been awake since then. About nine o'clock."

Michael just dropped to his knees by his father's bedside and took his dad's hand between his own. At that moment he was saddened to think of the times he had taken this man, his father, for granted. But at the same instant, he felt a deep joy that he could be with him as his father passed from this world to the next. Michael believed in God and an afterlife. Thanks, a great deal, to his father.

Then it happened. His father breathed one long gasp inward and breathed out his last.

Michael Rybak then stood over him, reached down, and kissed his forehead, as the tears welled up in his eyes.

Hank was gone.

Chapter 90

Junior Community Service

It was my junior year of high school and all the guidance counselors said that it was time, the big year, to build a resume for college applications. Their repeated encouragement was centered on each applicant participating in as many extra-curricular activities as possible. They would say, "Not only be active in sports, but try to be in as many clubs and do as many community service projects as possible." I remember my guidance counselor, Mr. Barron being particularly on my case about it.

The reason for his attention and my need to be involved in extra-curriculars was because I had my sights set high for the next year's college applications. I wanted to attend one school in particular, Boston College. If I didn't get in there, as it was highly competitive, I had my second choice of Holy Cross, which was equally as competitive. It is well known that both archrival schools are Catholic institutions, so community service is built into everything they do. Rumor had it that they wouldn't even consider an application or transcript unless it had listed community service of some kind, no matter how high your grades were.

As of the meeting with Mr. Barron, early that junior year, I had amassed a rather commendable array of extra-curriculars including having a varsity letter in four sports, an executive position, Vice President of the student council, and held active leadership offices in the Latin and French clubs. But sorely lacking was anything that could be considered community service related. It was true I was a Boy Scout, a Life Scout specifically, but that was considered outside of school so not allowed on my official school transcript. I needed community service and I had only my junior year to achieve it. I swallowed my pride, and during one of our September meetings together, I asked Mr. Barron for help.

He suggested that I join the Big Brother/Big Sister program and that it was an officially recognized extra-curricular community service group in the school. I was rather intrigued by what the club would entail exactly and all my questions were answered during the week of orientation and training that we received. Most of it was safety stuff including a crash course certification in first aid. The rest was more psychological in nature, expressing how to be proactive and communicate better with kids younger than us. I had a younger brother who was a year and a half my junior and a sister four years younger than me, so I had some practical experience in dealing with pre-teen youth. But the kids we would be pared with were much younger, most between the ages of eight to ten years old. I felt a bit intimidated by that, but in the end, I knew I could deal with them okay.

When the week of training concluded, we had small ceremony when each of us got an envelope with the name of our little brother for the boys and little sister for the girls, complete with information about them inside. I was now officially paired with my new little brother. Kurt was his name. His data sheet had a synopsis of his interests, foods he liked, family situation and hopes for the program. As I read through the summary, I became aware that Kurt was ten years old, was a kid who seemed to like sports, baseball specifically, had pizza and ice cream as his favorite foods, was an average student in school, but was living only with his mom. He had no siblings. His father and mother were divorced, and the father had no contact with the child for over five years now. I remember feeling sad for him about the lack of a positive male role model in his life and at the same time feeling a bit intimidated that perhaps I was to be that type of influence now. So here I was, a seventeen-year-old high school student about to be a big brother to a kid whose life experience was almost the direct opposite of mine.

About a week later, it was time for our first scheduled meeting together. I went to Kurt's house which was located on the main thoroughfare through our little town, a very busy street. I could tell right away that there would be no tossing the baseball in his yard, since the house had no yard. Just a short driveway connecting the busy road to the garage. I parked my car and walked up to the front door and rang the doorbell. Kurt's mother answered the door and introduced herself as Jenny Mitchell. She greeted me with a warm smile and thanked me for showing up. I told her my name was Randy but that my friends called me Randy. She chuckled at my poor attempt at humor as she then went on to explain that there had been two other scheduled meetings with her son but the other students failed to show up. I later came to find out that they were from the next town over, which had a much larger high school and somehow never got the communication right. Be that as it may, there I was, ready and eager to meet my new little brother.

Suddenly, the boy appeared. His mother introduced us saying, "Kurt this is your new big brother, Randy. Randy, this is my big boy, Kurt." Kurt smiled sheepishly at that point and I noticed that he was standing there complete with a baseball mitt on his left hand. I used the prop as a means of introduction.

"I see you must like baseball, since you've got your glove on. Who is your favorite team?" I asked.

"I like the Yankees," he proclaimed. "I don't like the Red Sox!"

"Well, that's great," I returned, "You and I will get along just fine. I don't like the Red Sox either. I have my glove in the trunk of my car, and some bats. How about we take a ride to the park and field some balls?"

"Gee! Can we Mom?" he asked his mother. Jenny was just standing there, smiling at the fact that the two of us were apparently hitting it off.

She stooped down to face Kurt eye-to-eye. "It's alright with me, provided you sit in the back seat and wear your seatbelt. I'm sure Randy is a cautious driver."

"Yes, I am, ma'am," I returned. "Been driving for almost two years now and I have a spotless record. That's even my own car that I just recently bought with my own money that I earned working at McDonald's. Maybe we could go there and grab a burger afterward." I said this to try and make an impression that I was responsible and would take good care of her boy.

"Awe right!" Kurt beamed.

"Get your jacket Kurt, and be sure to use the bathroom before you go," Jenny stated. Then, looking at me, "I really appreciate your doing this for him. He doesn't have many friends. Certainly no one who can play baseball with him. He loves baseball. Wait till you see his room."

"It probably looks like mine. I'm a big fan too and have lots of baseball posters and stuff. Not the Yankees though. I'm an Orioles fan. At least Kurt and I have a mutual hatred of the Red Sox!"

"Your secret is safe with me," Jenny said.

A minute later Kurt came running around the corner right up to the door dragging his coat behind him. "I'm ready to go!"

So, off we went. I drove him to the local schoolyard baseball diamond and hit him some ground balls that he surprisingly was quite good at fielding. I thought to myself that he should be in little league and I knew that I would probably be the one to see that through. I was. He did play baseball the following spring, and long story short, Kurt and I became very close. When I look back on it, I learned just as much from him as he did from me. He taught me to be a responsible man. I simply couldn't bear the thought of failing him. Too much depended on it. And, thanks to Kurt, the following year, I was also accepted at Boston College.

Chapter 91

Polish Christmas

For Polish people, whether living in Poland or residing in other countries, Advent is really the beginning of Christmastime. It begins four Sundays before Christmas day, usually just after Thanksgiving in the United States. It is a time when people try to be peaceful and remember the real reason behind the celebration of Christmas. An effort is made not to have excess of anything. Since Poland is a largely Catholic country, there is some fasting that occurs for those who are religious. Individuals give up their favorite foods or drinks. Some people also go to church quite frequently. In predominately Polish churches throughout the world, there is the tradition of the "roraty," which are special Masses (or communion services) held at dawn and dedicated to Mary since she was the one who received the good news (that she would have the baby Jesus) from the angel Gabriel.

Also during Advent, Polish people prepare their houses for Christmas. There's lots of serious cleaning as bigger chores such as washing windows and ensuring that the carpets are spotless are the norm. Everything must be pristine clean for Christmas day!

Advent Calendars are, of course, quite popular. Some people like to make the calendars for their families, so they are more personal and fun. Often the children will construct the calendars as art projects in school. It is exciting to open the door revealing each new day during Advent and see the holiday fast approaching. Sometimes there are small candy treats behind each door.

Saint Nicholas' Day is also important and, according to tradition, is celebrated on the 6th of December. Children hope that they will get a little present from "Mały Mikołaj" (Small Nicholas) often left in a shoe placed near a fireplace or at the front door. Oftentimes some sort of candy is the gift. Candy canes are very popular. Of course, children of all ages expect they might also get presents on Christmas Eve.

Just before Christmas, usually the week of, children in schools and preschools take part in "Jasełka" (Nativity Plays). They are very popular and often more secular than religious. The Christmas story is also sometimes put into modern times.

Tangerines (or Clementines) are popular during this time of year. The smell of tangerines in schools or workplaces is widely thought to mean that Christmas time is about to start. Again, in Advent, it's all about anticipation and that includes sights, sounds, and even scents.

Christmas Eve is a very important and busy day. In Poland, it's now often the most important day over Christmas—even though it's not officially a holiday. It is a day of fasting and abstinence (not eating anything) and meat is not normally allowed to be eaten in any form during the day, that is, up until sunset and the evening meal.

Christmas Eve (night) is known as Wigilia (pronounced vee-GHEE-lee-uh). Traditionally, everyone wears their best festive clothes which are bright and colorful. The main Christmas meal is eaten on this evening and is called "Kolacja wigilijna" (Christmas Eve supper). It's traditional that no food is eaten until the first star is seen in the sky. So, any children present look at the night sky to spot the first star. Looking for the first star is also a reminder of the three Wisemen who followed the star to see the baby Jesus.

On the table there are twelve dishes—they are meant to bring good luck for the next twelve months. The meal is traditionally meat-free, this is to remember the animals who took take of the baby Jesus in the manger. Everyone has to eat or at least try some of each dish. For Catholics, the twelve dishes also symbolize Jesus's twelve apostles. Like in many Catholic countries, Christmas Eve is often a "fasting day" in the church calendar, meaning that some people don't eat anything until after sunset (when the Church-day officially ends).

One of the most important dishes on the table is "barszcz" (beetroot soup) and it's obligatory to have it. The barszcz may be eaten with "uszka" (little dumplings with mushrooms). Carp, cod, or some form of fish or other seafood is also part of the main dish of the meal. In more elaborate gatherings, shrimp or oysters can be served as well.

Pierogi are also extremely popular. These can be filled with any combination of mushrooms, cheese, mashed potatoes, kapusta (a mixture of sour kraut, onions and spices), or blueberries.

Herring is very sought-after and usually is served in several ways: pickled, in oil, in cream, or in jelly. Each household has their own recipe and they say it is "The best in the whole wide world!"

The most popular desserts at Kolacja wigilijna are "makowiec," a poppy seed roll made of sweet yeast bread, "kutia," mixed dried fruits and nuts with wheat seeds, "piernik," a moist cake made with honey (that's like gingerbread) and gingerbreads (which are usually dry, very hard, and decorated).

So much for the foods. There is an even more important aspect of Kolacja wigilijna that is celebrated before anyone sits down to eat.

At the beginning of the meal, a large wafer biscuit called an "opłatek," which usually has a picture of Jesus, Mary, and Joseph on it, is passed around the table and everyone breaks a piece off and eats it after offering a Christmas greeting. Sometimes a small piece may be given to any farm animals or pets that the family may have. It is the most solemn time of the meal.

The tradition of the Oplatki originated in Poland as early as the seventeenth century. Generally, the eldest member of the family will begin the ritual by breaking off a piece of the wafer and passing it to another family member with a blessing. Then, in turn, each family member goes up to everyone else repeating the gesture. The blessing can simply consist of what you desire for your loved one in the upcoming year—such as good health, success, or happiness. The purpose of this act is primarily to express one's love for each member of his or her family.

The significance of the Oplatki Christmas wafer is that it shadows the Eucharistic meal Catholics participate in at each Mass. Just as the Eucharist is shared as one family in Christ and Christ's love is received through the Eucharist, the Oplatki allows for one's immediate family and friends to come together and share the love they have for one another.

An empty place is often left at the meal table as well, for an unexpected guest, "Niespodziewany Gość." Polish people say that no one should be alone or hungry, therefore if someone unexpectedly knocks on the door they are welcomed. In some houses, the empty place is also there to commemorate a dead relative or for a family member who couldn't come to the meal.

Sometimes straw is put on the floor of the room, or under the table cloth, to remind people that Jesus was born in a stable or cow shed.

The worst part about the Christmas Eve supper is that there is no opening of the presents before it has finished. Older members of the family (who traditionally begin and end this meal) always make it last a long time. In most houses, before the presents are opened, the family sings Christmas carols together. Children really want to open their presents and sometimes more carols are sung just to tease the children. Another form of the celebration for Catholics is to include participation in the midnight or evening Mass at the local church. This can take place either before or after the singing of carols.

There are very many carols sung in Poland and each region has own favorite. The most popular ones are "Wśród nocnej ciszy" (Within nights silence), "Bóg się rodzi" (God is born), "Lulajże Jezuniu" (Sleep baby Jesus), and "Dzisiaj w Betlejem" (Today in Bethlehem). The oldest carols are from medieval times, but the most popular ones are from the baroque period.

Then there is the exchanging of gifts. Usually, everyone gets to open just one gift that is specially marked under the tree, since in modern times, Santa will be coming soon and bringing any additional gifts overnight. Turns are taken, starting with the youngest and going up to the oldest, as each person opens their individual gift while the others attentively watch and celebrate with them.

By the end of the night, everyone is tired from celebrating Christmas in such a rich and festive way and is ready for bed to rest up and continue the celebration in the morning and throughout Christmas day. One thing for certain can be said about Polish people. They know how to celebrate!

Chapter 92

Sharing With Marina

I denied it to myself, but the truth was that no matter how close I got to Marina, there was someplace inside her that she never opened up to me. I thought of the long nights that we would spend together, like two children, talking through the early hours of the morning, as if the night was our special universe and nothing else existed, or mattered but us. We had talked and talked, but she would never tell me anything of substance regarding her past—no more than the most minimal details. I never asked her about it because I felt that she didn't want me to. Maybe when she was ready. I had let her reticence constrain me, and also my own fear that I might find something out that I didn't want to know. Maybe it would be just the usual things that lovers are jealous of, but then again, maybe it could also be something I couldn't handle. And because of that, I had never broken through to her. I had let so much go by, so much of her that I had refused to know out of fear of asking.

Yet, I honestly did try to reveal myself to her. Little by little I confided the layers of hurt that had been pent up inside me—the continued pain that I carry with me even now each day. Sometimes she would surprise me in the way she could understand my surface-level pain. Like the fact that I no longer had any contact with three of my four children. She told me that it must be a terrible blow to my heart especially because I was "such a feeling man". I clutched at those words because it is the truth about me and somehow, she knew I felt that pain. There were numerous times when I would tell her stories of my children and she would remark that she too could feel my joy and how much I loved them because my face showed it in the expression of thoughts.

One time I showed her pictures of the religious icons that my youngest daughter had painted and apparently, I went on and on in my explanation of the process she went through and the depth of learning she achieved in their creation. Marina would say to me, "I see you love your daughter so much that you can't hide the expression that your heart is leaving on your face." Simple, strange, yet piercing expressions like that made me feel like finally, somebody understood me at my core, at the deepest level, my soul even. She was somebody who truly cared at least by her perception of me and perhaps she was worth the risk of trusting completely. Something that, I admit, I was never able to do with any other person.

Marina's way brought me such comfort of heart, especially in the face of the continuous pain of being without my children in my life. Then there also was the emptiness I felt from losing my wife to cancer just three years prior. It all only compounded my grief that seemed to never let up. Marina's added assurance that she and her daughter would be my new family now, I drank up like a magic elixir, believing that it would take away the continuous pain that I felt. Yet she never reciprocated with me in revealing her vulnerabilities in the same way I did with her. I did get deep enough responses from her, about half-way to where I wanted to go, but something always held me back from simply asking more. The loss of my wife, after so much time and trust together, over twenty-five years, held a grip on me still. A grip of fear of going any further. I didn't want to lose a woman who had gotten so close to me again.

So, the root, the long-standing, underlying repressed cause of my problems never were revealed to Marina. In that way, my dead wife still had a hold on me deeper than she. But even my wife, now gone from this life of mine, in such a final and conclusive way, also never heard the "whole truth", the entire story with all the painful details, because I still could never bring myself to tell anyone everything that had happened to me. Instead, I realize now, I behaved in ways that, maybe subconsciously, that made me feel normal. Like it was all okay, and after all, it happened so long ago. But I could never bring myself to actually tell anyone. I skirted the issue a few times with my wife, by giving the headline of the story but no details that would reveal the ominous and substantial weight and impact the whole truth had on me. Up until just last October when Marina got closest to hearing it from me (aside from some slight attempts at full disclosure with my therapist that I had been meeting with prior to my soul-bearing with Marina). The lurid details remained buried in my psyche.

It is said, and indeed it is a life-guiding axiom for me, that "God works in mysterious ways." What amounted to staging a much more forthright attempt at exposing the inner demons that I had repressed for so long by opening up as much as I could with Marina, was actually cracking the outer shield of my own self-devised inner defenses. With the "perfect seal" now broken, I was able to tear away at the layers of protection and reveal, first to myself once again, and then to another person, the source of my disordered thinking and illusionary constraints for protection that had been in place for such a great part of my life.

After the initial shock, not unlike going through the grieving process (since one does grieve the loss of a familiar and reassuring way of life with all sorts of safeguards) including the denial, anger, resentment, and depression, I finally gave way to acceptance. With the acceptance also came the realization that nearly everything, quite literally, that I once had in the distant past was now gone. Not just the material, but the psychological dependencies, self-image, and most importantly, practiced defenses had vanished.

The glimmer of hope, the spark at that point, was the chance to see it as an opportunity, a rare and sacred blessing really, to rebuild my self-esteem from scratch and to do it right this time. That meant facing the absolute truth and dealing with it constructively no matter how painful that may be. Sort of like going through physical therapy after a traumatic injury. The limb may have been severely damaged, almost to the point of destruction, but after mending it back together, a proper amount of rest and rehabilitation, and the hard, painful work of exercising and rebuilding the limb to fulness again is the necessary step to full recovery. Oddly enough, the recovery, probably due to the process itself, is what makes the mental capacity as well as the physical strength even more resilient and formidable than it had ever been before.

So psychologically having gone through the process with the help and innate skill of Marina's subtle guidance I reached a point of readiness to face the incident of the past, when I was just a child, so long ago, that I had buried in the back of my mind. I was first able to face it again by myself, and then to relate it to another person. That person was Marina. So, there we were, at three o'clock in the morning as I dared to allow my mind to journey and face the entire detail of the events that had been hidden, buried really, since I was eleven years old. I allowed the horrific experience that I endured then to resurface and play out in my mind through surprising detail again. It was painful, it was devastating. Having had the new experience of sharing it with another human being, one that I trusted really did love me, had an overwhelming cleansing effect take hold of me. I had finally realized that I was ready to disclose to another person (similar to the fifth step of AA) the full nature of my experience.

In her rock-solid manner and deeply compassionate disposition, Marina was the first person to allow me to release the anguish that had been fevering inside me all these years. Yes, I was sexually abused by our family doctor when I was just a child. So now, in answer to the question, "What happened?" I can answer without holding anything back, including the embarrassment I have felt all these years. I now can not only tell the story but also can express it without bawling like a baby as I do so. For that I have my new bride, Marina, to thank, since it was her who had a comparable experience in her young life. So, yes not only had we shared a surprisingly similar tragic past, but also, we had a dynamic positive future ahead of us. Together.

Chapter 93

No More Contingencies

In considering my next mission, my next act in life's drama, the notion of risk and danger are no longer a factor. There are no more contingencies, nothing to hold me back. What does that mean? It means that I am now willing to go anywhere in the world, no matter how challenging or how perilous it may be. Without a family now, the risk to myself is not the factor it was before when I knew I was needed (even wanted) to be there to provide for others. Safety, security, and maintaining a home for my family used to depend solely upon me. But that all has been altered.

The family situation has changed drastically. Both of my children have grown into adulthood and besides, they want nothing to do with me anymore. Why? Because I fell down. I got sick with an uncurable disease, a virus of sorts, that will never leave me. It altered my mind and I behaved in ways that I now abhor and regret. Thankfully, the virus, that disease, is now in remission as long as I keep it that way. That part is under my control if I continue to take the steps necessary. It will stay at bay.

But it is too late for life as it was. The family I once had is gone now. I scared them all away in the height of my alcoholic nightmare. I'm an embarrassment, a bad memory, an annoyance. I can't and don't blame them. I acted like I wished I was dead too. But miraculously God saved me. Again. But my family having no desire to even speak to me does, in fact, speak volumes. It says, "I wish you were dead." Though that is a deep hurt, one that I feel all the time, it is not an excuse for me to fall again. So, I won't. I am setting a new path to take, a new course for the rest of my life. I have recovered.

Where will I go and what I will do now will not be limited by the danger of the region. In fact, it would be preferrable for me to go somewhere that is unstable. My sense of self-worth is coming back but I still feel unworthy of simple things like safety and wellbeing. I don't require much, and neither do I need much to get by. After living in prison, the pleasures in life, even the simple ones like a warm meal or a comfortable bed, nice clothes, even a daily shower are a distant memory now. They are not necessary for my happiness, not that they ever were (although it was nice to have a slice of bacon from time to time). With the familial heart attachments and the physical comforts jettisoned from my life now, I am equipped for anything. Some might say I am even hardened. But that is not the case, at least not in my deepest desire to love, or in the depths of my soul—which governs over all aspects of who I am today.

If a missionary is needed in a dangerous place where life may be threatened by the pitfalls of the elements or by the political environment, then I'm your go-to person. It would be no different for me to serve in such a place as Chad as it would be to serve in a lush locality like the island of Bermuda since the external realities are not factors in the reason to serve in the first place. And now, thanks to the ironic grace that my family has bestowed upon me by ostracizing me from their lives, I no longer have that responsibility in the way of serving either. I do this for them anyway, as a prayer offering. My life needs to be a prayer now in a way like it has never been before. A tragic past doesn't mean that it is a prologue for the future. On the contrary. I have come to believe it was a necessary factor in freeing my mind to even consider what I am about to do now. The future holds an abundance of opportunities for growth and happiness provided I keep my mind straight. That is what propels me now.

What most people can see of the world in a lifetime is astonishingly limited. Yet I have been blessed to see an uncommonly great amount. Good and bad. Happiness and sadness. I have had to forgive myself in order to get to this point. How often we spend months, years, even decades ruminating over something that God has entirely forgiven. I have heard people say that to forgive is not to forget, but my experience has been the opposite. When I forgive from my heart and not just my head, I no longer see the offense but the goodness at the core of the person. Maybe that is what it actually means to see as God sees.

What motivates me now is to do something fulfilling, something that matters, not for me, but for life in general, before I die. I also need to take myself out of the equation because my death doesn't really matter when you consider the bigger picture, the grand scheme of things. That's how it is with death. One day, bang. Everything is gone. Memories, hopes, dreams, homes, loves, property, money. Our family and friends may shed a tear, hold a ceremony, and they go on with their lives. We become a few fading photographs in an album if we're lucky. Or these days, stored on a disk somewhere. And then, those who loved us die, and those who loved them die, and soon even the memory of us is gone, the memory of them is gone, and on it goes.

It is like those old photo albums in antique shops—daguerreotypes of men, women and children. Nobody knows who they are anymore. Like a person who has left a handprint or footprint in the sand before the tide washes it away. Gone and forgotten. To what purpose? It touches to the core of our own sense of mortality and how we live in that short time we are mortal. It's the most sobering thought that has awakened me to change. To do away with the routine I had grown so accustomed to and to spark a new flame in my desire to do something for the betterment of the world's condition and not just my own self. That is why I choose to be a missionary now and to go to a place like Chad and spend the rest of my life trying to make a difference, no matter how small it may be.

In Chad, for example (which is a small country on the interior of the African continent), the poverty rate is sixty-five per cent of the total population of just over twelve million people. The average life expectancy is only to age forty-eight. Only forty-nine percent of the people are literate, there is only one doctor to care for every thirty-one-thousand people, less than two passenger vehicles are accessible per thousand, and there are less than two telephones per thousand as well. Imagine that. The Gross Domestic Product number is even more shocking. The GDP of Chad per person is $696 in U.S. dollars. Compare that to the United States, which is first in the world, where the GDP per person is $69,287 and you begin to get the idea of just how poor the country is. Even access to clean water is a major commodity and is in short supply. In other words, it is one of the poorest nations on the planet, an LLDC.

What is an LLDC? The CIA publishes a manual of the world's destitute countries. So instead of "third world" there now are new categories. LDCs are "less-developed countries", meaning that they are in the bottom group of the hierarchy of developed countries. There are officially 172 LDCs, or the vast majority of the countries in the world's total of 195 nations. Then there are the LLDCs. They are the "least-developed countries". They are at the bottom of the barrel, dead in the water. There are, sadly, 42 of them. What does this mean? Over half the people on the planet live in abject poverty.

We pay more to farmers in the United States not to grow crops than we do for humanitarian relief efforts overseas. Of the total federal budget, foreign aid represents about one per cent, with the vast majority going to two countries, Egypt and Israel. For some perspective, consider this: Americans spend a hundred times as much money on make-up, fast food, or video games in a year's time than we do on feeding starving children in third world countries in a decade! We could wipe out a dozen serious childhood diseases in undeveloped countries with less money than we spent on Beanie Babies when it was a fad in 1993.

All of these thoughts had been assaulting me until I finally gave in to God. I really tried, through serious prayer, to listen to what God had been trying to tell me about the purpose of my life. It was then and only then, by putting all distractions out of the way, that I actually "heard" what he had to say. God said to me, "I hope you've begun to think differently about your life and recognize that you are meant for more. You don't simply exist to take up space on the planet or pursue your own selfish desires. Instead, you are called to be an active participant in my work here on earth. What you do each day can fulfill the purpose for which you were uniquely created. It is up to you to accept your role and be empowered by my Holy Spirit to serve with supernatural strength."

It was then that I determined that I would accept the calling and live every moment for God's purposes and glory over my own. Chad would be my new home and missionary would be my new way of life. It is a place in the world that desperately needs help and perhaps I could do something about it.

There would be no more contingencies.

Chapter 94

Others May, You Cannot

Anytime I need to fly, I try to get either a window or aisle seat. That didn't happen on my most recent flight from San Francisco to New York City as I was late getting a reservation and got stuck with seat 29E, a middle seat in the very last row of the Airbus A319-100, that has fairly narrow seats to begin with. Although I tried to get it changed when I got to the airport, the attendant at the gate merely smiled and informed me that the flight was booked solid and I was lucky to even have a seat at all. That there were a considerable number of folks waiting on stand-by. Upon boarding the plane and making my way down the aisle and securing my one carry-on bag in the luggage compartment above, I took my middle seat and sat there anxiously waiting for who I would be surrounded by. That is, to see what form of human beings would grace me on either side. Would the six-hour flight be pleasant with nice neighbors or would I be miserably sandwiched between two unpleasant passengers? Time would tell.

Finally, I saw an elderly woman approaching my seat as she eyed the numbers on the bulkhead. "I believe that's me in seat 29F," she said with an unexpected sweet voice. I stood up and moved out of the way for her to slide in and take the window seat. She was small and thin and a bit frail, so there would be no need to worry about her crowding me. After she sat down to my right side, I resumed my place in the middle and buckled in since I wouldn't have to move for whoever got the aisle seat.

Then I saw him approaching, unmistakable by the Roman collar. I surmised the older gentleman was a priest because he was clad in solid black aside from the white square on the collar under his neck. Sure enough, he graciously nodded to me and took the seat next to me on my left. Thankfully, he too was thin and so there the three of us sat in a row without any intruding on personal space. Once the priest was settled in, he also buckled up and took out a small-sized, yet thick, prayerbook that I recognized as the Daily Office. He proceeded to turn to one of the sections that was marked by color ribbons and started to pray. Or so I assumed.

Then I casually glanced at the woman to my right by the window and she noticed me and said, "Hello there. My name is Judy. Nice to be flying with you."

I smiled and returned, "Hello Judy, I'm Morgan, the pleasure is all mine." In that moment, I thought maybe I should introduce myself to the priest since he obviously heard Judy and I exchange welcomes. But he looked like he was intently absorbing what he was reading in his prayerbook and I didn't want to disturb him.

A few minutes later the stewardess went to the microphone and read us the "in case of air disaster" routine and a few minutes after that, we were taking off into the wild blue yonder. All the while, the priest on my left was completely absorbed in the pages of his Daily Office and Judy was starting to fumble through her pocketbook. She took out a wad of pamphlets that looked like those prayer tracts that evangelical types hand out to people because I could see the word "God" in big letters on the one at the top of the pile. Then Judy turned to me suddenly and asked, "Can I give you something to read and consider on the flight?"

I shrugged my shoulders and said rather sheepishly, "Sure. What can it hurt? We've got a long trip ahead."

So, she lifted the elastic band that held the pile together and slide one of the pamphlets out and handed it to me saying, "There's not a lot to read but there's a ton of stuff to consider. Hope you enjoy it."

She handed me a little tract, a three-fold paper pamphlet of sorts entitled with big, bold letters, "OTHERS MAY, YOU CANNOT." The title alone had me intrigued. So, I started to read it. At the top was a Bible verse which read, "If anyone wishes to come after Me, he must deny himself, and take up his cross and follow Me. For whoever wishes to save his life will lose it; but whoever loses his life for My sake will find it (Matthew 16:24-25)." That seemed like a pretty intense verse, one that invoked a feeling of apprehension over how I had been living and doing many things that I thought were so important.

What I mean is, I consider myself to be mostly good toward others, I'm a practicing Catholic so I'm Christian, and generally speaking, a morally sound person. But according to the verse, I knew I was falling way short. Here sitting on my left was a man who obviously took that verse quite literally by the lifestyle he had chosen. Apparently, I was definitely heading in the opposite direction as the verse called for me to do with my life. Then I took comfort in the fact that maybe the woman had handed me the tract for a reason. So, I accepted that was the case. That God himself wanted me to know something and that he had used the woman, Judy, sitting right there next to me to do just that by handing me the words he wanted to say on that little piece of paper she had given me.

Then I took the next few minutes to carefully read the rest of what it had to say, which was:

"If God has called you to be truly like Jesus in all your spirit, He will draw you into a life of crucifixion and humility. He will put on you such demands of obedience that you will not be allowed to follow other Christians. In many ways, He seems to let other good people do things which He will not let you do.

"Others who seem to be very religious and useful may push themselves, pull wires, and scheme to carry out their plans, but you cannot. If you attempt it, you will meet with such failure and rebuke from the Lord as to make you sorely penitent.

"Others can brag about themselves, their work, their successes, their writings, but the Holy Spirit will not allow you to do any such thing. If you begin to do so, He will lead you into some deep mortification that will make you despise yourself and all your good works.

"Others will be allowed to succeed in making great sums of money, or having a legacy left to them, or in having luxuries, but God may supply you only on a day-to-day basis, because He wants you to have something far better than gold, a helpless dependence on Him and His unseen treasury.

"The Lord may let others be honored and put forward while keeping you hidden in obscurity because He wants to produce some choice, fragrant fruit for His coming glory, which can only be produced in the shade.

"God may let others be great, but keep you small. He will let others do a work for Him and get the credit, but He will make you work and toil without knowing how much you are doing. Then, to make your work still more precious, He will let others get the credit for the work which you have done; this to teach you the message of the Cross, humility, and something of the value of being cloaked with His nature.

"The Holy Spirit will put a strict watch on you, and with a jealous love rebuke you for careless words and feelings, or for wasting your time, which other Christians never seem distressed over.

"So make up your mind that God is an infinite Sovereign and has a right to do as He pleases with His own, and that He may not explain to you a thousand things which may puzzle your reason in His dealings with you.

"God will take you at your word. If you absolutely sell yourself to be His slave, He will wrap you up in a jealous love and let other people say and do many things that you cannot. Settle it forever; you are to deal directly with the Holy Spirit, He is to have the privilege of tying your tongue or chaining your hand or closing your eyes in ways which others are not dealt with. However, know this great secret of the Kingdom: When you are so completely possessed with the Living God that you are, in your secret heart, pleased and delighted over this peculiar, personal, private, jealous guardianship and management of the Holy Spirit over your life, you will have found the vestibule of heaven, the high calling of God.

—By G.D. Watson (1845-1924)"

Wow! I just sat there stunned. So many thoughts went pulsing through my head. As I read each line of that little tract, a rush of emotions came over me. I truly felt as if it was speaking to me directly. No, that God was speaking to me directly. After all, that's what I said going in. That he had put me in the middle seat for a reason. Everything that I considered to be so wonderful about me in life, especially my ambitions, seeking honors and recognition from others, was laid bare before me. Now I was awakened to a new way of thinking. But here, on this simple plane ride across the country I was sitting between God's messenger to me and one of his committed disciples. How much more tangent can you get?

I read the tract again. And again. Each time lingering on a specific section that spoke as if it was centering on an aspect of my life. I stopped to consider what I could do about it now. Perhaps the biggest realization was that I was seeking recognition from people all the time. What I needed was to change my way of thinking and seek recognition from God. The words before me offered a means to do just that. I began to feel as if I had been wasting a lot of time. Time pursuing things that were not lasting. Taking relationships for granted. I knew one thing for certain. I had to get my soul straight. I had to turn back to putting God first in my life again. I had to stop kidding myself that I was a good person because I did things that I thought were good enough and not really even knowing what God wanted of me. I had honestly never taken the time to find out what was my true calling anyway. This all came to me as I realized I was sitting between two people who had found their true calling and were actually doing it.

When I finally looked up and around both the priest and Judy were smiling. The kind of smile one has when everything is going well and the feeling of contentment is overwhelming. They were happy. Happy for me. As if they knew what I had just been pondering for the last two hours. Yes, that's how much time had passed without me even realizing it. In that moment the priest spoke up, "Excuse me," he said, "I couldn't help but notice you have been reading a prayer tract there. And I can tell by the title at the top what it must be. Is that the famous tract written by George Watson?"

"Yes, it is," I returned, "This wonderful lady on my right gave it to me to read. I have to say it contains some powerful words. Words that can change a life."

"Oh, I know," said the priest, "It changed mine. I keep a copy of it in my wallet to occasionally remind me of what's really important."

In that instant, a powerful feeling came over me and I felt the presence of God like I had never felt before. I just looked the priest in the eye and said, "Father, I'm a Catholic. Will you hear my confession?"

He responded, "Of course." Then he leaned over me and spoke directly to Judy. "Sister Judy, could you put your earphones on for a few minutes. I'm about to hear a confession."

It was then I realized they were traveling together and had reserved seats on oposite sides of the row so as not to be right next to each other. Perhaps to allow an unsuspecting wayward traveler like me to be between their soul-saving efforts.

Chapter 95

California Coast Highway Crash

They were finally there. The three good buddies from Boston College had made it all the way to California from Boston, driving the whole way. Rick, Johnny O, and Mitch decided they needed to do something special the summer of their junior year to make it a summer to remember. They took the entire month of July off from life as they knew it, and decided to travel cross-country in Johnny O's Volvo station wagon. The goal was to see as much of the country as possible. The trip of a lifetime. After meeting up at B.C., they packed for camping along the way and set out taking the northern route westward. The trip was to be as cost-effective as possible. There would be very few motel stops, a few relatives to necessarily stop and visit along the way, and lots of sleeping out under the stars at KOA campgrounds. Beer, of course, would be a given.

The journey took them through Indianapolis and Chicago, the Badlands of South Dakota including stops at Wall Drug and Mount Rushmore where Johnny O had cousins. After short visits and numerous parties, it was on to Yellowstone, Grand Teton, over the Rocky Mountains to the Great Salt Lake, and across the desert via Interstate 80 to Sacramento. California at last! After making their way south and seeing San Francisco, the trio stopped in Salinas to spend two days partying with Mitch's cousin John Furrick who was his grandmother's sister's kid's kid. He was Mitch's age. From there, they decided to take the coastal highway down to San Diego where Mitch had to check-in at the Navy base for a weekend, as he was required to do, being fully immersed in the NROTC program at school.

After leaving John's house in Salinas, they traveled south through the Big Sur region following the Route 1 loop along the coast. It was there, that the traffic started to pick up while everyone slowed down as the long, winding, cliffside road with breathtaking views made its way up and down along the spectacular coastline. It amazed Mitch that they would even allow a road to go through the area which had such huge drop-offs. He was driving, taking his turn behind the wheel when he got stuck behind a slow-moving green Ford Maverick with a couple sitting next to each other in the front seat. Ahead of the Ford, was the line of traffic slowly winding its way along the coastal pass.

As he looked in the rearview mirror, Mitch noticed a car weaving in and out of the traffic line behind him, a few cars back. Fortunately, the car that was immediately behind him, a Chevy Monza, was a good twenty yards distanced and not riding his tail. But the approaching car, making its way, zig-zagging in and out of the traffic from behind, kept advancing until it was right behind Mitch. He saw it was a Porsche. It started riding his tail, practically touching the rear bumper of the Volvo. Even though there was a double line in the middle of the road, meaning no passing allowed, that didn't stop the Porsche. It sped up to pass Mitch as soon as a car coming in the opposite direction went by heading north. Mitch reflexively slowed down. He didn't care if the maniac in the Porsche passed him.

Sure enough, the Porsche accelerated and zipped past the three of them in the Volvo. He was probably doing at least eighty, as Mitch had slowed it down to about forty miles per hour. As the Porsche pulled in front of Mitch and his buddies, it caught the rear bumper of the Maverick just ahead. What happened next was surreal.

The Maverick sedan suddenly spun sideways, jumped the guardrail, and flew over the cliff on the right. The Porsche tumbled over and over, landing on its roof in the opposite lane. An oncoming car suddenly screeched to a stop while bumping into the Porsche and causing it to spin around while on its roof. At the same instant, Mitch slammed on the breaks to avoid hitting anyone. The break-enforced slide caused their car to spin sideways and come to within inches of hitting the upturned Porsche. Miraculously, there wasn't a single scratch to the Volvo. And because everyone was securely belted in, no injuries.

Once the dust settled, the three friends quickly got out of the car. Almost upon instinct, Johnny O went to the drop-off where the Maverick had gone over, while Mitch and Rick went to check on the now upturned Porsche. The single driver of the sports coupe was still belted in and appeared to be okay, as he sat hanging upside down in his car. Seeing that he was in no danger, Mitch ran to the Volvo and retrieved his medical kit from the back by opening the hatch. Being a volunteer fireman and an EMT, he had brought along his emergency kit, fully equipped, just in case. Just in case just happened. Then he and Rick ran over to Johnny O who simply said, "Looks like they're pinned in down below."

Upon looking over the drop, Mitch could see that the Maverick was standing on its nose with the trunk and tail lights in the air. It had landed head-first after tumbling down the ravine.

"I've got to get to them," Mitch shouted. "One of you come with me, the other get help."

With that, Johnny O insisted he would go with Mitch. Rick turned and went back toward the line of cars that had now stopped in both directions. Passengers were starting to line the side of the road where the drop-off was, looking at what had happened to the Ford below. Rick started calling aloud for anyone who could help. In one of the cars, three up the line, there were two Canadian women medical students from McGill, both doing their residency at Saint Francis Memorial Hospital in San Francisco. They responded.

Rick introduced himself as being one of the guys in the car right behind the one that went over the cliff. He informed the docs that his buddy Mitch was an EMT and that he was already making his way to the car below along with his other friend John.

"We'll have to stabilize them and make sure that their backs aren't broken," the blonde doctor said. Her friend, a brunette with real short hair, agreed and added her opinion.

"Right now, they are most likely going into shock. If your buddy is an EMT, he knows that, and he knows what to do. We're most likely going to need to get them to a hospital as soon as possible. That means getting a chopper in and out of here. See if you can find somebody in that line of cars with a mobile phone and call 9-1-1. Barring that, maybe someone has a two-way radio. Call for a medivac chopper!"

As Rick proceeded to do as instructed, the two doctors made their way with their medical kits to the side of the cliff.

Meanwhile, after reaching the landing below, Mitch and Johnny O had come upon the car which, fortunately, had both the front side windows open. The windshield was totally smashed, but the shatterproof glass had held together. Only a few shards had made their way in. The first thing Mitch checked for, was to see if the couple was still alive. They were both obviously breathing, but both were unconscious.

Next, he tried to pry the driver's side door open. By reaching up and pulling down, the two of them were able to open the door. The car appeared to be stable on its front end because it had dug well into the loose dirt. There was no apparent smell of gasoline, so hopefully, a fire wouldn't be following any time soon. Now Mitch could assess the driver's condition.

He was bleeding near his left shoulder but not profusely. He looked over at the woman in the passenger seat who was slumped over as well but wasn't bleeding. At least not noticeably. He went back to his kit and took out a gauze sheet and tried to apply it to the driver's shoulder. He was still seated and leaning forward due to his seatbelt holding him up. Mitch managed to get the gauze in under his shirt, right against the wound.

Then both Johnny O and Mitch started to shout to the driver to wake up. "Are you alright? Can you hear us?" the two echoed. Mitch returned to his bag and pulled out some ammonia inhalant pads. He pressed one under the driver's nose. He responded by jerking his head and finally came to. He looked lost. Mitch then told him that he'd been in an accident.

"Help is on the way. We need to stabilize you and get you warm. Can you hear me?"

The man nodded a slight nod and tried to speak. "My wife, is she okay?"

"She is just like you. She's pinned in the car. You both need medical attention. Right now, you need to try to keep awake, in case there was a shock to your head. What is your name?"

"I'm, I'm Paul. Paul Banks." He looked to his right and said, "That's my wife Debbie. Is she alright?"

"We're going to check her right now. Same as we did to you."

Mitch grabbed another inhalant and made his way, with Johnny O following, over to the passenger door. The two did as before, opening the door by pulling it down. Debbie was not conscious, so Mitch passed the inhalant under her nose. When he did, she suddenly jerked awake.

"Wha, where, what happened?" she asked.

"Just relax Debbie," Mitch stated. "You were in a bad accident but you're okay. We're going to get you out of here. Just remain still."

Just then, the two doctors had finally made their way to the car. They were accompanied by three other men who came with additional ropes and blankets. Mitch looked back and could see they had tied a rope over the top of the cliff to scale down the side. They created a rope lift of sorts. One of the doctors, the blonde, spoke up.

"I'm a doctor. I understand that you are an EMT, so you're probably better equipped for this kind of situation than I am. Let me take a look at her. My friend here is also a doctor. She'll look at the driver. What have you been able to ascertain?"

"I'm Mitch. Glad to see you! They are both going into shock, which is to be expected. I couldn't see any serious injury at first glance, aside from the gash in the driver's shoulder. His name is Paul, she, here, is Debbie. They are apparently married. I just revived them using smelling salts and was about to ask them the usual concussion questions when you two got here."

"We've got to get them out of the car and lying flat on their backs.

We're both going to check and see if anything is broken first."

The two doctors did their cursory check of the couple and found nothing broken, but both Paul and Debbie had hit their heads on the seat headrests quite hard during the recoil of the crash. They both had concussions as a result. Paul's shoulder had a piece of the car's plastic door molding cut into it. Fortunately, not near a vital artery. The doctors dressed the wound up tight using Mitch's kit supplies.

In the meantime, Rick had located a driver with a cell phone, eight cars down in the traffic heading south above, and had called for an emergency medivac chopper. It was on the way. The police had not yet arrived, as the word was just getting out that there was a bad accident on Route 1 in Big Sur. The police were hampered in their approach, due to the line of traffic stopped in both directions of the single-laned, bi-directional road.

After another ten minutes, Johnny O and Mitch returned to the top, using the provisional rope line that was constructed, and started directing some cars to move, to form a suitable landing area for the chopper that was fast approaching. Slowly, the nearby cars moved to the shoulder of the road, until a makeshift landing pad in the middle of Route 1 was cleared.

Finally, a state police cruiser made its way to the accident site, lights and siren blaring while coming up the shoulder. The car stopped, and two troopers got out, as Mitch informed them of what had happened. He called their attention to the driver of the Porsche, who was sitting aimlessly, cross-legged atop his upended car. The officers then went over to have a few words with him as the sound of the approaching chopper was becoming more apparent.

In less than five minutes, the chopper touched down in the middle of the road adjacent to where the Maverick had gone over the side. Immediately, three EMTs jumped out, carrying two stretchers and their kits slung over their backs. They made their way to the rope line and proceeded to rappel down the side of the cliff.

By now, another two police cruisers had also arrived. The troopers were split between helping to secure more ropes down the cliff to bring up the stretchers, and tending to the growing line of spectators who had left their cars to see what was going on. They resolved that there was no way to move the traffic with a helicopter perched in the middle of both lanes.

After another ten minutes, the EMTs had managed to get both the victims of the crash to the medivac helicopter and secured them on either side of the chopper, with back braces and head restraints attached. Then the three EMTs jumped back aboard, and the chopper took off a few seconds later, heading for the nearest hospital, which was the Community Hospital of Monterey Peninsula.

The driver of the Porsche was promptly handcuffed and put in the back of one of the cruisers while the remaining troopers tried to get the traffic moving again around his car.

The three friends took one last look at the crashed car below as Mitch gathered up his emergency kit and put it back in the Volvo.

"I'll drive," said Rick. "You two look like you could both use a beer."

Chapter 96

On the Road to Damascus

What was once a school was now a battlefield. Lieutenant Mickey O'Brian's face was pressed as close to the hot concrete and sand-laden floor as humanly possible. He didn't even notice how the small piece of random charred glass, laying on the same surface, was cutting a four-inch-long, ruby-red trace diagonally right below his right ear as it scratched the surface of his face's flesh. The emblematic scar to follow would remain for the rest of his life. What his eyes did notice, in the immediate background, was his desert camo helmet lying more than three feet away, which fell from his head as he hit the deck a few seconds earlier when the sudden multiple cracks of bullets being fired at him came from somewhere behind the dusty cloud ahead.

His first thought was that his helmet hadn't fallen but instead was blown off. Then his eyes became focused on the more immediate threat that was less than a foot away. The transient helmet worry disappeared into the back of his brain. Despite the last round of bullets whirling just inches above his now exposed head, his left eye was glued to the advancing grim reaper intruding on his personal space. His right eye remained closed, as the dust from the previous round of fired shots had caused an unwelcome sand storm against his right iris. The greater problem at hand was the advancing scorpion making its way toward him inch by inch, its tail arched like a fishing hook, lured for an attack.

Ignoring the ghastly insect's impending and deadly threat, he managed to tilt his head leftward and back toward his chest and glance comprehensively behind him. The recently fallen concrete column supporting the ceiling was protecting him from the continuous blast of bullets streaming from his bow. Just then, another shower of multiple gunshots whizzed past him. But the fallen concrete column with its sixteen-inch sides provided a temporary barrier at best, protecting him from lethal harm from the enemy lying in wait ahead of him. As his left eye focused downrange and behind, Mickey saw his old friend

Master Sergeant Dan "Digger" Phelps signal to him. His hand was raised with the first finger extended right. Then he waved his flat hand laterally, followed by three extended fingers: the two, three, and four digits specifically.

By the signal, Mickey knew that Phelps had one of his Marines advancing on the right flank against the enemy that was so generously providing the continuous buzzing stream of bullets that sounded like bees building a hive to their glorious queen just above his helmet-less exposed head. Mickey's left eye drifted back to the more immediate danger before him and noticed that the scorpion stopped its advance, but it remained just inches ahead, poised for attack. As his mind processed the last signal from Sergeant Phelps, the three fingers extended, he realized something big would happen in three seconds.

It did.

Simultaneously, both Lance Corporal Tony Clark and Private Patrick Cummings rose from behind Mickey next to Phelps, secured behind yet another fallen column, and fired two rounds of rocket-launched grenades from their well-equipped rifles.

A few seconds later, a firestorm erupted at the exact spot that Mickey's reason to keep his head down originated. Still looking back, Mickey noticed the wall behind his support group of Marines had a line cut through it due to the continuous stream of bullets from the bad guys.

In that same instant, the structure suddenly gave way. It started to crumble as another overhead support beam swung forward toward the enemy's machine-gun nest. Then everything went black.

…

A half-hour later, as Mickey regained consciousness, he realized he was on his back, lying outside, under the desert sun in the open air. He looked about, puzzled by the situation.

"Glad to see you finally decided to wake up, sir." The medic, Kim Anders was being sincere, yet Mickey's disorientation was still settling in.

"What the hell happened?"

"Well, sir, the grenades fired by my men took the enemy out, and the crumbling ceiling collapsed, providing a ready-made tomb for them. May God grant them eternal rest."

Yeah, and may perpetual light shine upon them.

Anders' smile was both revengeful and comforting at the same time.

Mickey just sighed and passed out into a much-needed, and healing, version of deep sleep. His last thought lingered. *Why does my head and body hurt so much?*

What Anders didn't tell him, as the medication was expressing its intended effect, was that several large chunks of debris from the ceiling collapse also engulfed Mickey's body. It was a miracle he survived the three hundred-plus pounds of concrete that had showered down like a meteor storm on top of him. Sadly, two of Digger's troops did not have the same fortunate outcome. Thankfully, neither did the scorpion.

Mickey dozed off to sleep again.

. . .

Two hours later, he woke up due to the bustling and shouting outside the medical tent.

"What the? Another attack?" Mickey's first coherent words were direct and amazingly accurate to the point.

"Yes, sir! We need to evacuate now! Sir!"

The answer came from the Marine quickly advancing toward him who was ordered to get him out of the cot and ready for evacuation. By his chest tag, Mickey noticed that the corporal's name was "SLOAN."

"Sloan, do me a favor, show me where to go since I have no clue where I am!"

"Aye, sir! Follow me, then jump in, and lay low!"

Mickey did as he was instructed while piecing himself together and fighting off the grogginess of just having come to. Again, he found himself lying face-down, this time in the back of the beat-up M1060 HMMWV (High Mobility Multipurpose Wheeled Vehicle) or popularly called, "Humvee" (or HV in military circles) for short. He just dove into the back according to Sloan's direction, without so much as giving any thought about why not to assume a normal riding position. As he slid into the floor, he noticed there were no windows on the vehicle and Sergeant Phelps was up ahead driving. Sloan hastily joined him on the passenger side.

The jump squad's three tattered armored vehicles then quickly sped away; several explosions signaled that it was wise that they did so. Leave, that is, in a timely fashion. Meaning now! The enemy's grenade launchers were on target alright. Their firing count was just a few seconds too late. As Phelps continued to steer the Humvee through an increasingly narrower mortar fire maze exploding about them, and accelerating amid the enemy fire, Corporal Sloan was on the squawk box. He was giving the active coordinates of their position relative to the enemy's late, but insistent, and quite resilient mortar fire aimed at them, to the air support that was shadowing their advance.

"Roger, Reaper Two, the position is thirty-six degrees Whiskey—six, four, zero, niner. Forty-five degrees November—three, seven, zero, zero!"

Sloan's transmission of the enemy's firing position went to a U.S. Navy Grumman F-14A Tomcat aircraft from fighter squadron VF-142, also known as the "Ghostriders," part of Carrier Air Wing 7 (CVW-7). They had taken off from the nuclear-powered aircraft carrier USS Dwight D. Eisenhower (CVN-69) deployed in the Mediterranean Sea and were moving just under the speed of sound en route to the scene.

He received the usual confirmation, "Roger that Hedge Hog. VF-142-Reaper Two has the bogey's twenty."

Two seconds later, Marine flight Lieutenant Larry Byron, the F-14A's pilot, known as "BC Eagle," alerted his back-man, Navy Chief Warrant Officer Aldo Beretta, "Crapshooter," to key in the coordinates for their wing-mounted Rock-eye and CBU cluster bombs. They would smoke real havoc on the bad guys.

"Whenever you're ready Lar, the dirty ladies are active!"

Beretta had keyed in the coordinated line of attack for the jet's firepower from the ground coordinates he received from Sloan while signaling his pilot partner to fire when ready. With the ground target in his sights, Byron heard the active tones and immediately pressed the tiny red extended button on the right side of his hand con.

As Sergeant Phelps directly advanced upon the area where the enemy fire was coming from, a sudden burst of flames came out of nowhere and confirmed that the F-14A had a direct hit on its target. A complete wall of fire. CBU's were truly a bitch! Thanks, Navy! *Good-bye Haji!*

The sudden quiet, at least as far as mortar fire went, was welcomed by both Phelps, who could now attend to driving to their next destination, and by O'Brian, who could now fully sit up and do what he was there to do in the first place: analyze the situation. He didn't notice that he was still bleeding, rather profusely, just below his right ear.

Private Cummings assumed the role of triage medic noticing Mickey's ear was bleeding. "Sir, let me help you with that."

He leaned toward O'Brian, who looked puzzled as they both somewhat bounced about in the back of the HV. Cummings had a gauze pad in his hand that he had removed from his upper right pocket. Mickey suddenly realized his right ear hurt like hell. The glass from the floor back at the school had left its deep mark, and so far, no stitches were in place.

The ruby-red, body-life liquid, spewing forth, confirmed his wound was Purple Heart material. But that was furthest from Mickey's mind at the moment. He assisted Cummings with the compress and looked forward out of the front of the window-less HV as Phelps increased speed to arrive at their intended destination ahead of schedule.

They were traveling due west, on the road to Damascus in Syria.

Just like Saul. Mickey thought at the moment.

After what seemed to be an hour of bouncing and skipping over the dusty dirt road, Sergeant Phelps turned up the narrow incline ahead that was an apparent extended driveway into an old deserted Catholic school campus of sorts, complete with what was left of the extirpated statues of fallen saints at the gate. As they turned in and approached the front entrance of the convent/school safe house, Mickey had another blast from his past.

He suddenly remembered the many retreats he had been on. It was always at a place like this. The Catholic Church truly had the market cornered on remote retreat places to escape, learn, rest, and move on. A quiet spot to take time, get away from the world, and just pray. Pray to God that he would help. This place though, was well beyond remote.

Stopping in front of the school and putting the HV into park, Phelps opened the conversation, "So, geek Lieutenant, Navy? It's a good thing you outrank me, otherwise, I would have you do pushups for that travesty back at the last s-house."

Mickey appreciated Phelps' candor. It was a refreshing change amid all the other recent and very unwelcome changes in standard protocol he experienced on this fine autumn day in the sun-drenched Middle East. No leaves changing color here.

"Yeah, Sarge, I was wondering when you would give me a chance to do what I was sent here to do!"

"Hey, you Navy pukes have your comfortable, what do they call them? Oh yeah, staterooms!"

"At least we sleep on beds. Not like you jarheads, who just pass out drunk wherever you happen to be."

As Mickey spoke to Phelps, he had no idea that his words would become the final ones that the sergeant would hear in the life of mortals.

A sudden click. A burst. The all too familiar snap-sound of a rifle firing echoed in the distance. Instantaneously, Phelps had a crimson hole in his forehead. The sniper had made his mark. A perfect shot.

As Phelps left consciousness and life on Earth, Mickey suddenly realized what had just happened. He hit the deck instinctively yet again. The trained instinct saved his life a second time in one day, as the next bullet raced just above his head while he was on his dive to the floor of the HV. Indeed, it was a day of near misses.

Like a precision running machine, Sloan sprang into action and began shouting orders to the other Marines as they quickly disembarked from their vehicle and the other two accompanying HVs followed suit. Out of one, Private Darren West positioned himself on the ground under the carriage and had already begun to view and adjust his own M40 A1 sniper rifle's long-range scope as he surveyed the trees ahead where the shots had originated. He couldn't contain himself and shouted, "Damn! I've got a bingo!"

West had located the sniping bastard spread across an inner crop of branches, halfway up a tree, amidst the cluster of similar trees about a hundred yards downrange. The enemy sniper was looking through his scope setting up for a third shot.

West had instinctively squatted down and then lay flat on the ground beneath the engine compartment of his own HV, and without taking his eye off his sight, zeroed in on the acquired target.

He yelled to Sloan, "Permission to fire, Corporal!"

Sloan was a bit stunned as he realized he was being addressed for permission since he was not accustomed to being in charge of the unit, that is until Phelps was killed a few seconds earlier. It took a quick leap of his brain to register that he was now in command.

"Fire at will, Private!"

With that, West had already determined the range of the target and was adjusting the sight of his rifle accordingly. Then he placed the scope up to his eye again and determined that the best shot was right through the sniper's brain via the bridge of his nose since his head was bent forward of the rest of his body looking through his own rifle's sight. West exhaled, depressed the trigger slightly, ensuring his target was locked, and then followed through with the shot.

Bang!

As the shot rang out, Mickey began to realize what was taking place around him. He had been focused on the now mortal remains of his savior friend, Sergeant Digger Phelps who was the enemy sniper's first target. West continued to look through his scope after the shot and saw that the sniper ahead suddenly jolted forward and then fell out of the tree to the ground where he remained motionless.

"Splash one for the good guys!" West shouted with vigor to his unit, as much as to his new boss, Corporal Sloan, "Target eliminated!"

Sloan recognized the takedown and assumed his new command position all within one breath as his Marine battle training kicked in. "Digs is down. KOA. Copy all. Thank you, Lance Corporal West." (Sloan used his newfound authority and instantly insinuated the promotion of the private due to his act of justified revenge.) To the rest of his command, he barked out, "Justice is served at least. We need to take cover in the school in case there are more of them. Now!"

Mickey O'Brian looked toward the inanimate body of Master Sergeant Dan Phelps as his men were lifting him into the back of the HV, and realized that the bravest man he had ever known, was now before the thrown of the Almighty. Instinctively, he whispered the prayers he memorized in childhood and finished with, "… And may perpetual light shine upon him."

Whisky Tango Foxtrot.

Chapter 97

Silence and White Noise

The late-August orange morning sun peeked from behind the empty hills and found two sets of furrowed brows. On the driver seat, David, the dad, lowered the sun visor, and his frown dissolved. On the passenger seat, his son did the same, and his frown didn't move. Andy's eyes were lost beyond the hills, his arms crossed, his hands fiddling with the white cord of his earbuds.

"I love this time of day," David said.

There was no response from the passenger seat.

The bright sun was flooding the dashboard of his Chevy Malibu. The hills came and went lazily on the horizon as they traveled the straight road ahead.

David sipped from a large coffee-to-go and pushed the oversized cup back into the small cup holder in the middle of the bucket seats, struggling to make it fit.

"The sunrise, I mean," he tried again.

Andy kept his eyes on the hills. The car was silent except for the droning of the wheels. David prayed for the radio to come back to life. The rolling hills took away the reception of the tuned in station.

He pushed the buttons on the radio, hoping it would magically start playing a song, or preferably, the news. God, he hated radio music, but even that would be better than this silence, better than the hum of the radial tires on the road. Nothing but white noise and static from the fading radio.

"Why?" Andy asked.

"What's that?"

Andy sighed. "Why do you love the sunrise?"

"Oh," David gathered his thoughts and answered. "Great memories. Start of a new day." .

The humming kept going strong, the blaring of nothingness. He could hear the granularity of the asphalt in the sound, feel the silence vibrating.

"From when I was just a bit older than you are," he said. "I used to go out. To parties, that is. In my early twenties. And get drunk."

A new patch of asphalt came in the distance and found the wheels with a different texture of sound, as bland as the one before.

"The time to end a fun night is before sunrise," David said. "If you started drinking the night before and you're still drinking the next morning, you're doing it wrong. When the hot sun touches your face in the morning, it's warm and disgusting at the same time. You feel sticky. You feel like trash. You're thirsty, and you're hungry, and you just want to go to bed and sleep in your clothes, which are all messed up from people bumping into you all night and spilling beer. The sunlight is the one good thing you feel. You just want to start life over. Fresh."

He sipped the coffee while the hills came and went following the continuous road ahead. And the dull humming proceeded.

"God, getting drunk sucks. I'll never do that again."

"David, that's lame." Andy's frown was directed at his father now.

"What?"

"This little rant of yours is a lame attempt at keeping me away from drinking," Andy said.

"Wha— No! Not at all."

"Right." A smirk and back to the frown.

The drab droning kept on unaltered except for the changes of the asphalt texture's tone on the tires. A different shade of white noise here and there, a new radio station fading in and out, playing a new song, as monotonous and hypnotic as the one before.

"I mean, you shouldn't drink," David said. "Well, you can. You're going to college. God knows you will. I'm just saying, don't drink too much. It's bad. At least in my experience."

Andy's eyes were on the horizon again, riding the traveling hills. Up, then flat, then down and flat again. Rolling hills. Straight ahead eastward.

David took another sip from the coffee, another struggle to make the cup fit.

"Well, do you even drink?"

"I'm seventeen," Andy said.

"Seventeen. Right."

Andy raised the sun visor. The sun was now on its journey through the vivid blue sky. David raised his sun visor as well.

"And what about that old friend of yours? Do you go out with him?"

"I don't go out. I spend most of my free time on the computer."

"Yeah, but do you talk to him?"

"Who?"

"That friend of yours," David said. "The one from your school."

"There were at least five hundred kids at my high school."

"Seriously? I mean the small kid. The one with the glasses. I think his name was Jimmy."

"You mean Jerry," Andy said. "That was in sixth grade."

The static sang its dull song in David's ears. "Sixth grade. Right."

He tried another sip but there was no more coffee in the wrinkled cup.

"Hey," David said, "do you remember Grandpa's and Grandma's

beach house on Cape Cod? We used to go there when you were younger."

"Yeah. I guess so."

"It's only a half-an-hour drive from Mass Maritime Academy. We should go there sometime when you get a break from school and hang out. I still go there every month or so, to take a look and see if everything is in order. The place is kind of abandoned since Grandma died. Grandpa never goes there anymore. So, I go up there, clean up, and just hang out for a while, drink a beer with my feet in the ocean. It's peaceful. Silent. It's nice. In the off-season."

David waited but there was no answer from Andy. There was just the never-ending droning of the wheels and the annoying static.

"Do you remember the tire swing in the yard?" David persisted. "It's still there. God, you used to love that swing! So did your brother Martin and sister Agnes. You three would take turns and keep asking me to push you higher and higher, and I would do it and you'd all never get afraid. You would, all three of you, stand up and everything. It's like you all had courage. I loved that. But your mom was so pissed! She would say I wasn't being careful with you, that I was a bad—father."

"So, you go to the beach house every month and just hang out?"

"Yeah!"

"So how come you never come to see us more often? It's been almost two months since the last time you were home. And that was just for one day."

David's heart sank, it felt pressed against the tight walls of his chest. There was a surge of pain and nausea, but he kept his eyes fixed on the road and his face as blank as the song on the silent radio. He couldn't tell Andy that he used the place as a temporary escape from Communications Operational Headquarters in Boston since it was only an hour away. When he had an afternoon free, he would drive there, hang out for an hour and drive back just to get a break from the intensity of maintaining his double life as a CIA analyst. Everybody thought he was just a computer engineer working for some research lab run by MIT. Nobody he knew, not even his wife, was the wiser to his real profession.

Andy's eyes were lost on the rolling hills and valleys of northwestern Rhode Island again, as they traveled along Route 44 past Glocester, and David's mind was drowning in the sound of the dull noise.

"You didn't have to do this, you know?" Andy said.

"What?"

"Give me a ride. You didn't have to do it."

"Yeah, well, your mom had a shift suddenly come up at the convalescent home."

"I know," Andy said, his eyes had now left the hills and were on the screen of his phone, his right hand flipping through a list of songs while the left hand twirled the wire of his earbuds. "Someone else, like Grandpa, could've taken me."

Another moment of deafening silence. David took another sip from the empty cup. Another shade of white noise filled the car's interior.

"Yeah, no," David said. "I wanted to. When was the last time we've spent time together? You know, just the two of us, alone?"

"I don't know," Andy said, putting in his earbuds. "I don't remember."

David looked at the horizon, at the up and down of the hills on the straight road ahead. "Right. I don't remember either."

The hills came and went, and then there were only plain fields of gathered crops. And then buildings, and a small town, and another. But there was no silence.

. . .

Eventually they came to the entrance gate of Massachusetts Maritime Academy in Buzzards Bay just over the Bourne Bridge at the beginning of Cape Cod. They pulled up to the dormitory complex, parked the car, got out and stretched after being cramped up for the two-hour drive. Immediately, David popped open the trunk and unloaded the large suitcase to the smooth asphalt and took a handbag over his shoulder. Andy started to unload, his iPhone in his shirt pocket and earbuds dangling next to him.

"Do you need a hand with that?"

"No, I got it."

Andy took the microwave from the trunk while at the same time he was carrying his pack on his back. David closed the trunk of the car and pulled up the handle of the wheeled suitcase. They walked to the brick residence hall trimmed in immaculate white as he beep-locked the car.

"Let me get that for you," David said, rushing for the glass door.

"No need to." Andy pulled the door open holding the microwave with one arm. He let the door go and David caught it with his foot. They walked to the stairs, their steps echoing through the empty hall.

"Are you sure you don't need any help?"

"I'm sure."

They crawled upstairs, one step at a time. Andy leading the way, David following, on and on up the endless staircase.

"Do you know where it is?" David asked when they got to the second floor.

"Yeah, it should be at the end of this hallway."

"And you've got the key?"

"Yup."

David followed Andy through the pristine hallway with shiny tile floors, the light wooden doors all closed, the walls empty, the fluorescent lights buzzing above their heads, a lonely window in the end wall.

Andy stopped in front of the last door and shifted the microwave in his arms.

"Could you knock, please?"

"This one?"

"Yeah."

David settled the suitcase on the floor and raised his hand, but before he touched the door, it flung open. A kid with a headset on was standing inside.

"May I help you?" the boy asked.

David stared blankly.

"Hey, Tien," Andy said. "It's me. Help me put this microwave somewhere."

He shouldered his way past David into the room and rushed for a table to put the microwave on.

"Oh, hey, A. R.," Tien said, "you're finally here!"

David stood outside for a second and then stepped into the room, rolling the suitcase.

"Where do you want me to…" He trailed off, his voice drowned by Tien's and Andy's greetings.

"It's nice to finally see you in person, bro," Andy told Tien while they hugged.

"Look at us, two Youngies. Enjoy the day, because morning formation starts tomorrow at sunrise. Then the real fun begins," Tien replied.

David looked around. Two neat beds, one empty, the other one with an open laptop. A small clothes cabinet, a solid, clapboard desk with the microwave, a window overlooking the courtyard. Nothing on the walls. Nothing allowed for "Youngies." The term for new freshmen in the academy's regiment of cadets. The place looked clean, sterile, and modern.

The phone rang in his pocket.

"Hey, it's your mom," David said. "She probably wants to know if we got here in one piece. I'm gonna take this outside."

He left the suitcase where it was and stepped into the hallway, taking the phone to his ear.

"Hey, Linda."

"Are you there yet?" the voice on the phone asked.

"Well, hi to you too."

Inside the room, Tien and Andy were talking, and David's ear turned the volume down on Linda.

"We gotta find a place to plug in that microwave," Tien said. "And who's that guy? Your uncle?"

"Nah, that's David. He's my absent father, trying to compensate for his absence I guess."

David's eyes died in a stare as blank as the walls in the hallway. The only sound in his ears was his heart pumping, and the buzz of the fluorescent lights.

From far away came a voice.

"Hello? David, are you there? David, answer me! Hello?"

He blinked several times and shook his head.

"Yeah, yeah. Yes! I'm still here."

He walked to the stairs and started down. He needed air.

"What happened?" Linda asked.

"Sorry, I zoned out for a second. What was the question?"

He could hear her rolling her eyes in the brief silence of the phone.

"Are you there yet? Did you get there fine? How is the academy? Are there sailors everywhere?"

"Yes. We're here. And no, nobody is around except the kids moving in. They don't get all formal until tomorrow. Something about a morning formation. And they are not sailors." He tried pulling the glass door a couple of times before pushing it open. "He's settling in, his roommate was already here."

"Oh, he mentioned Tien would be there," Linda said. "Good."

"You already knew his roommate?"

"Well, they've been talking online for a couple of weeks now."

"Right," David said while he paced the sidewalk. "Linda, listen. Don't take this the wrong way, but did you tell him bad things about me through all these months I've been away?"

"What? David, why would I? Of course not! What are you talking about?"

"It's just that … the kid hates me."

Her sigh on the phone carried an emotion he didn't want to take, but it was the only one she had to offer.

"I'm sorry to hear that, David. I truly am. But you didn't exactly help during this time."

"I know," he said, "but I'm trying to help now and he won't let me."

"I was talking about helping yourself."

"Right," he turned and paced back.

"He is a grown man now. He doesn't need your help. He doesn't need a father now. He's going to a maritime college, for God's sake. He'll be a cadet with other cadets above him bossing him around."

"Yeah. No, I know."

For a second there was nothing but silence and a cool breeze caressed

David's face.

"But maybe he could still have a friend?" he said.

. . .

"Are you sure you didn't forget anything?" David asked Andy from inside the car, Tien was standing at the glass door of the residence hall.

"Yeah, I'm sure," Andy answered. "Thanks for the ride."

"Don't mention it. I …" He fumbled for words but nothing came.

The setting sun hit Andy's face the same way it had in the morning and he furrowed his brows to look at David. Everything was silent, and David's crumpled up heart was hurting inside his broad chest.

"Listen, son. I … I know I haven't been around much and the only thing I can tell you now is I'm sorry. I can't go back in time. I can't go back to when you were that kid that I was pushing on the swing at the beach house. I can't go back to the birthday I missed, to when you found out you had been accepted to the academy. I can't pretend I've been a part of your life lately, and I have no excuses. I used to have them, I used to have a bunch of them. I know my work has taken its toll on family life.

"Life, it's weird. It's like a highway in some ways. You get an exit and if you miss it, you sometimes have to drive for miles to get another one. And until you get to the next one, you're asking yourself 'Why the hell didn't I take the last one?' And you hate yourself for not having taken it. And you have to keep driving and driving and asking and hating.

"But I finally took the exit, and I'm here now. Because I kept driving and driving and at some point, I noticed I was driving by myself. My mistakes were my only passengers. I don't want it to be this way anymore. And you're really unlucky because I do have a son, and it's you. But it's a son who doesn't really know me anymore. A son who doesn't feel comfortable enough to call me Dad. A son who hates me."

The soft breeze swept by while a small tear washed David's eyes.

"That hurts," his voice cracked. "That hurts so much, you have no idea. I want to change that. So, if you ever feel like having a beer with your old man, give me a call. I mean, you can't drink but … you know. We can go to the beach house. You can bring Tien with you. We can— go fishing. Surf casting. I'd have to talk to Tien's parents and I don't even know if there are fish you can catch right off shore but, I mean, just call me. Okay?"

Andy's frown had a twinge of sadness now.

"Geez," he said, "What am I supposed to say?"

"I know, it was too much to drop on you. I'm sorry. I just had to get it off of my chest. So, just, you know."

He extended his arm and touched his son's. Andy awkwardly grabbed his father's hand and David pressed it. A hug for hands. He enjoyed it for a second before bringing his hand back inside the car and turning on the engine.

"Take care, son."

"Yeah, don't worry."

"Bye, Tien," David shouted.

"Bye, Mr. R," Tien waved back.

…

David sat with a beer on the small dock of the beach house, his feet in the water, the big white moon reflecting off the glistening sea. The rhythm of the waves crashing against the dock, making a flopping sound. He took a sip from the beer and looked at his feet.

His phone rang.

"Hello?"

"Hey," Andy said.

"Hey! Did you forget something in the car?"

"No, no. It's just … I was thinking about what you've said, about having a beer with you. Tien is very interested."

David laughed.

"So, you know," Andy continued, "if you wanna pick us up next weekend, we have liberty on Sunday, I think it could be fun."

"Yeah, sure buddy! I'm not sure about that beer though. And I'd have to talk to Tien's parents."

"Yeah, no problem. I think it could be fun anyway," Andy said.

"Sure thing. I'll pick you boys up next Sunday morning."

"Cool! Thanks—Dad. Bye."

David held the phone in his hand and kept looking at it for a few seconds with the stupidest smile. He slipped the phone back into his shirt pocket and drank from the beer.

There was not a single annoying sound in the entire world, only the deepest of silences hovering over the moon-kissed ocean. David floated on that sweet song.

Chapter 98

Secret Deployment

The recently promoted Lieutenant (LT 03) Stephen Geer's first deployment for sea duty was aboard the USS Ogden (LPD-5). The USS Ogden was considered a newer ship in 1979, having emerged from the New York Naval shipyard's buildings in 1964. Rather a strange-looking ship, she was five-hundred seventy feet long with a hundred-five-foot beam, and her forward half had a fairly normal super-structure including eight guns to annoy attacking aircraft. The odd part was the other half, which was flat on top and hollow underneath.

The flat part was for landing helicopters, and directly under that was a well deck designed to be filled with water from which landing craft could operate. She and her eleven sister ships had been designed to support landing operations, to put Marines on the beach for the amphibious-assault missions that the Corps had invented in World War I and perfected in World War II, Korea, and Viet Nam. But the Pacific Fleet amphibious ships were without a mission now—the Marines were the beach, generally brought in by military and chartered civilian jetliners to conventional airports. So, some of the 'phibs were being outfitted for other missions. As Ogden already was.

There were a series of trailer vans secured onto the flight deck. When in place, deck parties erected various radio antennas for radar and other listening devices. Other such objects used for clandestine surveillance were bolted into place in the superstructure as well. The activity was done in the open—there was no convenient way of hiding a seventeen-thousand-ton warship—and it was clear that Ogden, like her two other sister ships, was transforming herself into a platform for the gathering of electronic intelligence-ELINT. The ships were particularly at the disposal of Naval Intelligence which made good use of them in clandestine operations around the globe.

In the late summer of 1979, she sailed out of the San Diego Naval base just as the sun was beginning to set, without an escort and without the Marine battalion she was built to carry. Her Navy crew of twenty-four officers and three-hundred ninety enlisted men settled into their routine watch bill once they were underway. Stephen Geer was one of the officers on this first deployment to the China Sea, specifically, the Gulf of Thailand. His mission was classified as he was an analyst and lieutenant in Naval Intelligence.

Established in 1882, the Office of Naval Intelligence is considered America's longest, continuously operating intelligence service. This mission was not to be on the official slate of Ogden's operations. It would be billed as a mere practice beach landing in southwest Viet Nam at the village of Ha Tien. The U.S. and Viet Nam still had tensions between them, to say the least, but the "practice landing" was part of a larger peace-keeping exercise in case of an emergency.

Where Geer and his jump squad of two Marines, two Navy SEALs, and his own Chief Petty Officer, were really going, was to the Cambodian territory of Kampot, the area near the village of Kep. A region just across the border where the United States was not welcome at all. Behind enemy lines. The operation was high-tech in nature but much more significant on several levels, morally speaking. The mission was to make it from the Ogden to the beach, to an inlet waterway that was believed to contain the remains of four Marines from the Viet Nam conflict buried within a shallow. The squad was to retrieve as much of the fallen Marines' remains as possible and return to the Ogden, all without being detected.

Lieutenant Geer had hand-picked his jump squad from intelligence reports and from recommendations he had received from his superiors and his Chief Petty Officer, Chief Craig Jensen. Aside from CPO Jensen, there were two Marines; Staff Sergeant Dan "Digger" Phelps and a sniper, Corporal Nolan Ryder who was at the top of his class of shooters.

The two Navy SEALs on the team were Petty Officer First Class Jim Hudner and Petty Officer Second Class Dan Buckson. Each man had a specialty, and each was considered at the peak of his career and expertise. Diving was their forte.

Geer had met Chief Jensen during a recent intelligence briefing at port in San Diego and was impressed. Jensen was a Viet Nam veteran and knew the territory having spent so much time, two tours of duty, in the nearby northern Mekong Delta region of Viet Nam. He was familiar with two of the Marines whose remains they were going to retrieve.

Marine Staff Sergeant Phelps was also a Viet Nam veteran having the same amount of battle experience as Jensen. The two knew each other as well. Having two NCOs was a luxury for Geer since he would have been lucky to get even one on a virgin deployment. The SEALs were both from the same SEAL Team platoon, which was known for their special reconnaissance abilities, particularly underwater operations.

Although the mission had a seemingly benign objective, it was to be covert. That was because the Marines whose remains they were seeing to retrieve were technically in Cambodia. Even though they were just barely behind enemy lines, the United States and Cambodia were still at military and political odds in 1979, as they had been throughout the Viet Nam conflict. It was agreed between both nations that the Cambodians would not enter Viet Nam and the Americans would not enter Cambodia. That was not the case. The four dead Marines were indeed where they were not supposed to be and nobody knew how they got there. Lieutenant Stephen Geer's jump squad was about to go in to get them back.

How would they find them and where would they begin to look? The second part of the question was easy to answer, thanks to the fact that the United States had a CIA operative in place in the Cambodian coastal village of Kep. To the east and south of the village was a series of rice paddies. The CIA operative, a Cambodian local, named Arun Sok, using a common, unassuming Cambodian name, had been in place since 1965 and had gathered intel mostly at the local bar. It was near where the Marines were killed while crossing the paddies and approaching the village while still technically in Viet Nam. But were they killed and then dragged across the border? That was the question.

To make a point, the locals had left them piled up together on the side of the rice paddy irrigation system to serve as fertilizer as they decayed.

Rice paddies in Cambodia often used the local village's sewage as a source of fertilization, funneling the waste through a series of canals that surrounded the paddies located on a lower point geographically than the town. So, the intelligence pinpointed approximately where in the rice paddy irrigation system the bodies could be found. But the mission of the lost Marines took place in 1966, almost fourteen years before this new mission by Geer's jump squad to go and retrieve them. What would be left would be nothing more than skeletons in uniform. At least they knew generally where to find them, thanks to Sok, who had been there then and was still there under cover now.

But how? How could they detect exactly where they were? They knew where to begin to look but finding decomposed bodies fourteen years later would take some special kind of technology. It just happened to be the technology that Lieutenant Stephen Geer was an expert at, thanks to his last job working as a Navy contractor for PerkinElmer in Norwalk, Connecticut for the prior six months. Geer's expertise? GPC technology. He wrote the language to operate GPC to do what needed to be done. It was no accident that Naval Intelligence, the branch of the Navy that he worked for, gave him this deployment. GPC would find the fallen and Geer was the expert with GPC.

GPC? Gel Permeation Chromatography. Generally speaking, it is a type of size-exclusion chromatography, that separates analysis of substances based on their mass, typically using organic solvents. The technique is often used to separate polymers and analyze them as well as the desired end product. The process considers things like molecular weight and dispersity as well as other factors. In other words, it can distinguish between different substances combined together and then submitted to the GPC process. By taking a sample of the soil in the rice paddy, GPC could determine if an organic specific substance, (ie. human remains) was in the sample.

What is entailed is taking a sample and allowing the GPC system to determine the composition of what is in the sample. With a predetermined baseline, thanks to the software that Geer designed and programmed at PerkinElmer, you could then decipher a match. Simply stated, they could sample the soil in the paddy and compare it to known human composition and find the exact location of the buried, decayed remains of the Marines.

While at PerkinElmer, aside from completely impressing his boss, Andre R. Muir, who himself was the recipient of not one but multiple patents, Geer had led a project to develop a software language to control hand-held devices to do this. Given six months to complete the project, he was able to finish in just two. The programming language was called, innocuously enough, GPC BASIC 2.

With the language running on the specially designed GPC device, his skills as a Naval Intelligence analyst notwithstanding, he could program it by including a sample of what type of match they were looking for by using the special probe that was built in. A very rudimentary display on the top would signal a match or no match. The device looked like a Craftsman Weedwacker, except the bottom portion scooped up the substance to be checked and passed the sample up the arm to the top of the rig, which included a hand-held electronic GPC analyzer that would issue either a positive (green) or negative (red) signal in comparison to the known substrate that was preloaded within.

It was no wonder that Naval Intelligence had assigned him this particular mission as his first deployment. It was not just a chance to be at sea and in hostile waters for gaining experience, but also to complete what had to be a covert mission, using the technology he developed. It would take all of his skills to master success: those as a computer analyst, Naval officer, and chief among subordinates. He had five deeply talented men answering his command and couldn't help but think that this was a Navy set-up to see how he would handle it. But he didn't care. He would do what he did best and that was to analyze the situation and react in order to have the best possible outcome. It was at the core of his personality.

It was time to meet and go over the mission in the ready room. The reason that the Ogden had a ready room was because it once housed helicopters and still could. *Hell, why not just helo us onto the beach?* Stephen's mind asked him the obvious. No. That would be too simple. Better to risk being seen motoring in on a Navy RHIB (Rigid Hull Inflatable Boat) instead! But that was the state-of-the-art method in order to sneak in quietly, under darkness. *They can't know we are coming, can't hear us.* His mind finally recognized.

As he went over the plan, it was obvious that Lieutenant Stephen Geer was in charge. Beyond that, every man knew his specific role. The team, all dressed in battle fatigues with faces charcoaled, answered to him. Everything was in place. Not a single detail was overlooked. They would leave the ship at zero three hundred hours. Their ride into shore was leaving in a half-hour, which would give the Ogden enough time to get back out of sight before dawn after letting them go. They would recon back at the ship on or before zero four hundred the next day. Who cared if anyone saw them leaving after the excursion? Geer and his team had exactly one day to complete the mission. No sleep required or allowed. They had all been trained for this.

At zero two hundred thirty hours, the team loaded the boat on the submersible deck of Ogden. All six of them got into the RHIB as the surface of the deck was flooded to carry them out, away from the ship. The ride into shore wasn't eventful, and there was no light except the stars above. A new moon night. Obviously planned for this foray into enemy territory. Equipment aboard included the Navy SEALs' diving suits, a radio comm unit, two large water-proof bags for holding the remains, Ryder's M40 A1 sniper rifle, along with four M16 A1s for the two Petty Officer SEALS, Sergeant Phelps, and Chief Jensen. They contained thirty rounds each, along with four additional magazines per man, while all Geer carried was a sidearm, a Beretta M9, and three additional clips. The group had already decided to rely on Ryder as the sniper for any unfriendlies, as otherwise, they were ill-equipped for an elongated battle. That is aside from the two M26 fragmentation grenades each of them also held which could blow a lot of stuff up.

A half-hour after leaving Ogden, the team reached the beach. Almost immediately, the two SEALs, Hudner and Buckson, started digging a large hole to bury the boat at the crest of the beachhead. They were well trained. Phelps, Ryder, and even Jensen joined in, using the paddles from the boat and their hands to help dig the camouflage pit while Geer stood watch with Jensen's rifle. A half-hour later, the RHIB was completely buried and covered up and nobody would have known they were there. The team regrouped and set out due northwest where they knew the rice paddies were.

The jump squad started climbing and keeping low over the wind-swept dunes until they hit high grass on the edge of the paddies. Instinctively, each man crouched low while moving ahead. Sergeant Phelps held the detailed map (thanks to the work of Arun Sok, the CIA operative) along with a small flashlight to check where they were and needed to go. He was familiar with working rice paddies from his experience in Viet Nam. He just didn't know these rice paddies and how they were structured. As it turned out, they were similar to the ones that Phelps was familiar with, elongated squares separated by streams, used for irrigation between them. Keeping his voice low he alerted the others, "We need to zig-zag our way about another half a click."

"Roger that," Geer responded. "Let me know when we're within fifty meters."

They moved on, staying right on the edge of the natural gullies that the irrigation streams provided. Turning right, walking about fifty meters then turning left and going another fifty meters until the exercise became like walking a labyrinth. All of the men took note of the putrid smell. The irrigation streams were tied into the village's sewage system upstream for purposes of fertilization.

Finally reaching the fifty-meter mark on the map, Phelps signaled the others, "We're entering the red zone."

"Corporal, Ryder, take your position," Geer ordered in a whisper. Immediately Ryder broke from the formation with his sniper rifle and ammo bag and made his way quickly up the hill to find a secure position in the tall grass with a view of the entire area.

"I've got our six," It was Chief Jensen. He began moving back to a position twenty meters behind, his rifle at the ready.

Knowing they were closing in on where the remains would be, Geer broke out the GPC monitor from its water-proof shield, while the two SEALs quickly got their wetsuits on. He got the device ready to engulf the end in a nearby rice paddy irrigation stream. After walking another few steps, he submerged the device's probe head into the side of the muck just below the water's surface and took a sample. Looking at the result on the screen only denoted a red tone. Nothing here. He commanded the group using hand signals to move on another ten meters. They did. He reloaded the device and took another sample. Nothing. Moving on again, they were right on top of the place that Arun Suc had indicated on the map. Another sampling. A true signal. It went green! They are here! The remains were right below. The problem now was how to retrieve them.

Suddenly Ryder, from his sniper position, noticed movement. "We have several bogies at six o'clock on the ridge." He spoke into his radio comm from his hiding place deep in the grass about fifty yards up from where the rest of the team was. Being the sniper, he was in position to take out any threat. On the highest ground. But that was not in the cards. Not as far as Geer was thinking.

"Hold your position!" Came Geer's returned and precise order into the mic.

"Roger, at your command." It was Ryder.

"We're not here to take anyone down. Unless fired upon." Geer responded. "Only to recover. Continue to stand down unless they fire. Then, smoke the bastards."

What Corporal Nolan Ryder spotted was a small Cambodian patrol moving directly toward them just at the crest of the irrigation rivulet downstream from where Geer was surveying. He noticed a total of four men walking in a path coming at them about a hundred yards away. He figured he could take them all out without so much as a fight.

"We have a total of four Bogies at your six, about a hundred meters downrange," he relayed to Geer over the comm.

Lieutenant Stephen Geer took immediate action based on Ryder's assessment and ordered everyone into the water at the base of the irrigation channel to try and blend in with the terrain as best they could. Phelps, Jensen, Hudner, and Buckson immediately responded with the two Navy SEALs having the advantage of wearing wetsuits and going beneath the surface into the water of the channel. Phelps alongside Geer, and fifty meters back, Jensen, packed into the bottom of the bank at water's edge as best they could. All men had their weapons at the ready. The sides of the channel were covered with human feces from the sewage which was used as a source of fertilizer from the drains located in the village above. Nothing went to waste here. The three men embedded on the bank were, in fact, covered in crap.

While they made themselves as invisible as possible, Corporal Ryder kept the lead adversary in his sights, ready to fire at Geer's command. The crosshairs of his scope had the head of the Cambodian lieutenant square between the nose and eyes as he walked ever so slowly towards the jump squad's location. The time being close to six-hundred hours, there was enough light to see them clearly and enough darkness to keep the jump squad fairly hidden, their fatigues blending in with the murky grey muck of the channel.

The Cambodian patrol made its way along the top edge of the waterway and eventually came within ten meters of Geer and Sergeant Phelps half-buried in the bank below. Fortunately, they kept some distance between themselves and the bank because of the stench. Suddenly, the patrol paused for a minute, right there, to light some smokes before continuing to walk on, almost half staggering. Geer thought that they were probably drunk.

They then moved on. Once the patrol was past his team, Corporal Ryder ducked down deep into the grass from his hidden spot fifty meters away and breathed a sigh of relief while ever so slowly turning in the opposite direction to keep them within his sights. This time focusing on the back of their heads. After two minutes, the patrol was well on its way and almost out of sight downrange.

"All clear," came Ryder's assessment to Geer over the comm.

The team got up from their positions as Geer began probing with the GPC device again and had another green signal showing a clear indication that there were human remains directly below them.

Almost as if on cue, Hudner and Buckson went diving with hand rakes into the water. Two minutes later, Navy SEAL Petty Officer First Class James Hudner resurfaced holding a human skull in his hands. Spitting out his snorkel, he almost yelled in a hushed voice, "We've got one!" And, "There's more below."

They had them.

Chapter 99

Pilgrimage Accomodations

Bringing the prayerful day's long walking experience to a close, Mark Ryan genuflected once more toward where the Blessed Sacrament was, where it was reserved in the tabernacle of the old church. He shouldered his backpack, and made his way along the center aisle, down the columned sanctuary, and back into the pressing, warm, sun-laden outdoors. The sudden uptick in light and temperature stirred his present circumstances and concerns, which included a place to wash up, gain some nourishment, and to bed down for the night. His only regret was he was unable to attend Mass this day due to his ambitious travel schedule. The sign on the Ave Maria Auberge beckoned less than thirty meters away right in front of him across the street. He was about to go and enter to see if there was room in the inn, when a small group of people approaching, moving with purpose, came within his pass.

There was one fellow, leading at the apex of the others. He was obviously a Catholic priest being outfitted entirely in black, complete with the Roman collar. Instead of continuing to cross over to the auberge, Mark's feet took over bodily control and stayed firmly anchored in place as the advancing troop reached within an arms-length of where he was standing.

"Bom Camino!" First the priest, then the others in the small group cheerfully offered a responding chorus of the traditional greeting.

"Bom Camino! Inglése?" Was Mark's knee-jerk reply.

"Yes, indeed. I am Father Rick. We are from Windsor in Ontario, Canada," said the priest with a warm smile.

"Wow! Fellow Americans!" Mark quickly thought to explain his meaning. "I mean, I'm from the U.S., Connecticut actually. So, we're fellow North Americans. I'm Mark, Mark Ryan. Are you here on pilgrimage?" Mark smiled sheepishly, which was due either to his inclusionary tactic or because he had become a blundering idiot when it came to meeting other pilgrims for the first time.

The good priest charitably addressed Mark's enthusiasm by saying that his group of seven young people, five men, and two women, were college students from Assumption University, a Jesuit institution in Windsor, Ontario, just across the bridge leading into Detroit. They were making their way (as was Mark) on pilgrimage to Santiago de Compostela and had arrived there in Santo Domingo de la Calzada about two hours earlier after leaving Logroño early in the morning and walking the forty-seven kilometers—about twelve hours with a stop midway in Nájera. The exact same journey as Mark had made that very day. They had just rested a bit and were about to take a short walk into the town to see "What was what, eh?" as he put it.

Mark and the group exchanged a few more pleasantries where he learned that the priest and his group were staying at the Ave Maria Auberge across the road from where they stood. The place Mark had just spotted. The priest also mentioned that he planned to offer his daily Mass in that very church at twenty-one hundred hours, less than three hours away. The best news for Mark was, he was going to say the Mass in English! It had been a steady diet of daily Mass for him over the past week, but being in Spain, none of them were in his native tongue. He was thrilled at having the opportunity to attend an English Mass in the somewhat famous Catedral Santo Domingo de la Calzada, where he had just spent an hour meditating, especially on a day he thought he would miss it.

After promising to meet at Mass later, the group went its separate way; Father Rick's youth group to continue their exploration of Santo Domingo, and Mark to finally make it to the entrance of the Ave Maria Auberge.

Immediately upon stepping through the doorway, Mark was ambushed by a force of savory aromas advancing from something amazing cooking nearby to the left. He could single out bursts of garlic roasting, onions frying, sweet-tangy tomatoes simmering with oregano and basil, and fresh celery, cucumbers, and chives mingled together in wonderful wafting waves of enticing nasal attacks. It was intoxicating to him. Or maybe Mark was suddenly realizing just how hungry he was, having fasted all day. He decided to follow his nose, proceeding left through the open foyer, advancing past what looked like a large sitting room with several couches, chaise lounges, and chairs somewhat circularly arranged, through an open door at the other end. It had light gleaming through it like a welcoming beacon to come and enter.

Upon peering through the doorway's threshold to deliciousness, Mark caught a young woman in mid-stroke, stirring a large pot on the stove with a long wooden spoon in one hand while sampling its contents by putting a smaller spoon to her lips with the other.

She was strikingly graceful in both her outward appearance and how she carried herself moving about the kitchen. Her silky, flowing, knee-length dress, having a light violet flowered print, aptly accentuated her shapely, firm, and fit athletic build, in spite of her apron. She looked to be in her early thirties, as she radiated her younger womanly physique with a captivating, yet modest older appeal in her stature. She wore shiny polished, black, low-heeled shoes with white bobbysocks which seemed to be chosen for their walking-on-cobblestone practicality. They made her look entirely feminine, or perhaps they were chosen for their going-to-church appropriateness. Her long, thick, jet-black hair, tightly bound in a ponytail, was pulled back from her face and fixed firmly in place by a soft, puff cotton, dress-matching bow beneath a nearly invisible hairnet. Her pure and smooth olive color complexion was freely expressed, being highlighted due to the setting of the late day sun shining through the kitchen windows. Her focused gaze on the spoon suddenly zoomed in to the background of her vision point of view to see Mark standing in the doorway of the kitchen.

"Ah! You've caught me in the act. It is my crude method of quality control," she stated in perfect English. She must have noticed the small American flag patch on Mark's camo shirt.

Mark detected a sudden increase in the glow of her cheeks. "Well, if it tastes anywhere close to how good it smells we're all in for quite a treat at dinner," he replied.

"I'm Carla. I'm the manager, as you would call it, of this, the Ave Maria Auberge. Welcome!" She put the spoon down and extended her right hand while giving an earnest smile and slight tilt of the head. "As you can see, I am also the cook."

Mark shook her hand gently and asked, "Do you have any beds available? I would like to stay here for the night if possible and of course share in the dinner."

"Yes, we have several beds available for three euros a night, and the dinner is also an option for two more euros. We serve the food at twenty hours if you would like."

"I'll take it!" Mark exclaimed. Then he asked her, "Where did you learn to speak such beautiful English?"

"I took graduate courses at Cambridge. English was a must. That's where I learned hospitality as well. I've worked at several inns and hotels in England before finding this place. It was love at first sight, four years ago. I've been here ever since."

"Well, I would be delighted to experience some of your hospitality in this fine place," Mark alluded.

"Give me a few minutes to get things under control here and I'll sign you in. You're welcome to go upstairs and choose a bed that you would like. Any of the beds without sheets or personal items on them are available. I'll meet you up there."

As hard as it was to leave, Mark gave her a big smile, a nod of the head, and managed to turn away from the delectable appeal of the kitchen and walk back through the sitting room to the stairway. At the base of the stairs were several rows of well sodden shoes and hiking boots neatly arranged in two replete columns on a rubber mat.

As an unwritten law of curtesy throughout the network of pilgrim-frequented auberges, patrons were expected to leave their walking shoes on the bottom level; thereby preserving the cleanliness, silence, and civility of the sleeping quarters upstairs. Mark had eruditely learned from his trusty *Pilgrim's Guide* that to go barefoot, sock-foot, or in flip-flops was acceptable. However, shoes of any kind, even athletic shoes or sneakers, were taboo on the sleeping area floor. He kept a thick pair of grey, woolen ankle socks tucked into one of the handy outer pockets of his backpack for just this reason. Using the purposely provided deacon's bench alongside the adjacent wall, Mark sat and removed his hiking boots and socks. His feet rejoiced in being freed from the harsh, hot, hellish constraints of the heavy-duty, sturdy envelope of leather that had kept them tethered for the past twelve-plus hours. Upon natural impulse, he gave his doggies a quick rub before sliding them into his thick "bunkroom approved" stockings. He then added his pair of shoes to the regiment of footwear and proceeded up the narrow winding staircase that had made a ninety-degree turn by the time he reached the top.

It opened into a large, high ceiling room with two rows of double bunks positioned on either side of the wide center aisle. The surface was well worn, composed of hardwood floorboards except for the center which had a long, thin-piled carpet running the length of the room. It was bright due to the three sets of double windows on either side of the light baby-blue painted walls. Their surfaces were completely bare except for a large crucifix on the wall opposite the entranceway and a painting of the Madonna with child above the door. The immaculately white painted ceiling also helped brighten the place.

Mark noticed that nearly all the beds on the left were occupied with random clumps of clothes, blankets, an occasional backpack, or a body. He determined that a few of the folks were readozing. (Mark's made-up word to describe the state of being where one is about to fall asleep while reading. The eyes were tracing words on the page, but the mind is busy elsewhere drifting off to La La Land.) Others were obviously sleeping as indicated by the faint sound of restrained snores.

The right side looked more sparsely occupied having signs of laid claims only as far as the first two bunks. The remaining six looked empty, both top and bottom. Quick basic math and the apparent symmetry of the bunk layout helped Mark surmise that the capacity of the place was thirty-two beds, eight rows of two-person bunks on each side. Upon closer inspection, he also ascertained that two of the people sleeping in the bunks were female. The rest on the floor were male. Also, at the end of the aisle in each corner of the room were doors with a large "WC" between them on the wall. The door on the right had an internationally recognized stick figure with two legs while the door on the left had a stick figure with a triangle in place of the legs. Men to the right, women go left. The bathroom and showers were just behind the doors. Hence the term, "Water Closet" that the initials "WC" stood for.

Mark walked down to the last bunk on the right and put his pack on top of the bottom mattress, thereby staking his rightful claim to a comfortable night of sleep with convenient access to the facilities. Just as he turned to check out the WC, Carla somewhat startled him by seemingly materializing out of nowhere standing in the aisle with a folded set of sheets under her left arm and an aging register book that she clutched in her right hand with a pen dangling between her fingers.

After slinging the sheets on the bunk next to the pillow, Carla plopped down on the bottom mattress and opened the register, flipping to the page with today's listing of guests. She proceeded to note the date and time of a new entry. Mark Ryan's.

"You need my passport," Mark offered.

"Please."

While Mark dug out his passport and a five euro note from his backpack pocket, Carla began writing the time and date into the register with perfect CPA penmanship. Once he handed his passport and the bill over to her, she began by reading his name aloud.

"What kind of name is Ryan?" she inquired.

"It's Irish. All my grandparents were from Ireland, but I was born in the United States."

"Have you ever gone back to your homeland? It is close by to Spain, just across the Bay of Biscay and Celtic Sea on the north coast, you know."

"Oh yes. I've been back a lot to visit relatives, my cousins, who still live there."

"I have been to Ireland twice. The people are very friendly and accommodating. The pubs are rather interesting as well," she added.

Carla continued writing Mark's name and passport number and country into the register's designated columns. Then she closed the book and flipped it over revealing a pocket-sized flat case that was firmly attached to the underside of the register. She flipped it open revealing an inkpad and a small coin-like disk with a narrow ridge on top. She removed the stamping device and asked Mark, "And your other passport?"

She was referring to the threefold Pilgrim's Passport (or Credencial) that everyone is issued at their starting point on the Camino de Santiago route. As each pilgrim walks along the Way of Saint James, they receive an official stamp showing their progress. Auberges were among the authorized stations, together with churches and selected heritage and religious sites, where one could receive a stamp on his or her passport. Then, when finally reaching Santiago de Compostela, the Credencial serves as evidence of advancing along the route entirely, entitling the holder to a formal document stating that the achievement of completing the pilgrimage route was attained.

Upon seeing Mark's last stamp was at Logroño, Carla stated, "You've come a long way in one day. Usually, people do that distance in two days, with a stop in Nájera."

"I did stop there," Mark retorted. "For refilling my water and a quick nap. I left Logroño at five o'clock this morning before the sun was up." It was Mark's favorite time of day.

"Do you plan to leave at such a time tomorrow?" Carla asked.

"Yes. After dinner and before bed, I'm going back to the church for an English Mass at nine, er, ah, twenty-one, with a priest I just met in town a short while ago."

"Sounds lovely. Can I join you?"

"What about the dinner?"

"We serve an hour before that, and each dinner comes with a bottle of wine. I'm sure the pilgrims will carry on alright without me after I serve the meal. I've been to Mass earlier today, but like you, would like to hear it in English."

"Sounds like a plan," Mark added while taking back his Pilgrim's Passport that she had just stamped. He looked at the logo which said simply, "Ave Maria Auberge. Bom Camino!"

"So, I'm guessing despite your wonderful English, that you are Spanish?" Mark offered.

"No quiero ni puedo abstraerme de mi condición de vasca!" she proclaimed in Spanish.

"What does that mean?" he asked.

"It means I cannot and will not ignore the fact that I am Basque. You see, I come from the city called Vitoria-Gasteiz, it is the capital of the Basque Autonomous Community in northern Spain, as we like to call it. You may have heard it referred to as Basque Country. Even though technically we are Spanish, we regard ourselves as being uniquely Basque. Since you like religious sites and churches, you would love the ones in my city. In the medieval quarter, as we call it, there is the Gothic-style Santa María Cathedral which has a sculpted facade and towering columns. The inside is breathtaking to behold with its vaulted ceilings. It truly is magnificent! Then there is also the Church of San Miguel, dedicated to the archangel saint because he is the champion of justice, a healer of the sick, and guardian of the Church. It has a large, baroque altarpiece and houses a famous statue of the White Virgin, which is the city's patron saint. I go back there a lot to visit my family since it is not too far from here. You go straight up the A-1 about a half-hour drive. So, in answer to your question, I am Basque."

"Wow! I had no idea there were such beautiful sites so close by. I'll have to come back someday with a car and venture into Basque Country. Do you manage this place by yourself?"

She smiled and said, "For the most part, yes. I have a woman who comes in the morning to help clean, her name is Elena. She is a great worker. We can have the place cleaned and ready to go by eleven o'clock most days. But I don't own the auberge, Senior Morales owns it. He rarely comes here though. He is an avid pilgrim and has walked the Camino several times. He wants this place to be a welcome spot for pilgrims and give them a sense of home. It's my job to see to that. That's why we have a community supper every day."

"The place looks great. It's so clean and inviting. I just followed my nose when I walked in so I'm sure supper will be delicious. I've stayed in many different hostels throughout Europe and this place ranks right up there at the top. And look at you. You're obviously devoted, going to Mass twice on a Thursday!"

With that, she blushed and said, "I think I would be a nun in another life. In many ways, I feel like one now. Tell me, Mark, why are you on pilgrimage?"

The question hit him like a sword to the chest. His heart pounded and his mind doubted he would tell anyone at first. But he decided it was time to be truthful with someone about why all this walking he was doing. Even if it was a total stranger. She seemed familiar to him though. Not like a stranger but rather a sister of sorts. He decided she would make an excellent nun.

"I'm walking because I needed to get my life straight. So many things have happened over the last few years that I feel like I am spinning along out of control. Does that make any sense?"

"Totally."

"Yeah, and then there's the fact that my wife of twenty-eight years died suddenly this past year of cancer. Since all our kids are grown adults now and out of the house, I decided I didn't have anything holding me back from the next chapter in my life. Problem is, I have no idea what that should or could be. Another reason for a long walk. To clear my head and discover what the next step would be. I want to do what would be best for me. And, believe it or not, I want to do what God wants."

"It sounds like you are on pilgrimage for all the right reasons. I'm impressed you are keeping God first and center. After all, if you wanted to just walk, there are plenty of places and trails in America to go and see the sights. But you chose this ancient way of Saint James. Countless saints have walked where you are walking. That says a lot about your faith."

"I guess you are right about that. My faith has always been there. Trust me, I've seen and done things in my years so far that would boggle your mind. Some good, some not so good. In many ways, I feel like I have lived five lifetimes because I've done so many different things. I have an insatiable desire to live more than just the average existence."

"Sounds like you've never been a nine to five guy. Is that what they call it when you just work, sleep, eat, and repeat?"

"That's what they call it. And no, I'm not like that at all. You don't seem to be either," Mark offered.

"No, I'm not. In fact, I hate sleeping. I wouldn't do it at all if I could get away without it. Seems like a waste of time to me. Don't get me wrong, I love the routine I have. Even the cleaning and cooking every day brings me satisfaction. But the best part of doing this is being able to meet so many different people from all over the world and get to know their stories. Kinda like I am doing with you right now." She offered a big smile.

"Well, I appreciate your listening skills. I can't remember the last time I felt so comfortable sharing about myself this way. I feel like I could tell you anything."

"Thank you. I truly value you saying that. Just save the juicy stuff for the priest in confession. And speaking of priest and confession, I should go finish getting the dinner ready so I can go to Mass with you. We can cut out right after we eat at twenty hours."

Did she just ask me out on a date? Mark wondered to himself. He stammered a moment then replied, "Wouldn't miss it for the world."

Carla got up, gathered in her registry, after securing the stamp back in its place, tucked it under her arm, and got ready to go back downstairs. Mark just stood by next to her. He wanted to hug her so he awkwardly reached around her and gave her a half hug. Surprisingly, Carla put the registry down on the bed and wrapped her arms around him to hug him back. The two stood there embracing for a long moment. Mark didn't know what to say, so he just kept silent as Carla looked him deep in the eyes and smiled. She then grabbed up the registry, turned, and walked back down the aisle between the bunks. Her ponytail swayed back and forth like a metronome keeping time with her steps.

Chapter 100

In Tockseqated

Highly unusual human behavior has been observed, specifically among the inhabitants of two separate northwestern U.S. cities. Although there is no apparent connection between the two municipalities, with over a thousand miles separating them, not to mention the numerous cultural differences, the people who live in and visit each city exhibit the same strange social behaviors. Scientists and sociologists are admittedly stunned, not only by the behaviors themselves, but also in trying to find a plausible connection, explanation, or probable cause for what is occurring. Adding to the complexity, the local government officials in both cities seem to be completely at a loss as to how to deal with the increasingly troubling situation they face. In short, they have an impending public crisis looming and no clear-cut way in which to deal with it.

First up, welcome to Tockseqated, Oregon. The city named according to a Muckleshoot Native American word, which is pronounced: TOĆ SEE KATE TED, meaning "a deep thirst" or according to a more contemporary dialect, "one who needs to drink soon." Population is just over forty thousand, and the town itself is located roughly sixty miles due south of Seattle. It's a place that many would describe as a typical, laid-back, northwestern coastal community, with a commerce center that could easily be characterized as the cliched, "Main Street USA." The region's only first-world claim to prominence being the Muckleshoot tribe's casino, called "Lucky Shot" that everyone gives a pass to, considering the historical turmoil that the native tribe has been through. There is that primary economic concern, not to mention the fact that over eighty per cent of the locals have their employment or livelihood attached to the success of the casino in one way or another. The population is predominantly middle class, and sports a remarkably evenly-balanced mix of the "regnat populus" at least on the basis of race, religion, gender, and age. There are blacks, whites, Asians, Mexicans, more recently assimilated eastern Europeans, and of course the Muckleshoot tribe (in that order). Many would consider it to be the ideal example of what a backbone "melting-pot" community found throughout America should resemble. Especially one that has admirably overcome the racial challenge of accepting and integrating the indigent Native American population into the social milieu.

The town's main social gathering spot is, in fact, Main Street. Characterized by its expected conventional and impressive collection of fanciful restaurants, artisan shops, specialty stores, and well-groomed, meticulously landscaped, public parks and gardens. It is, indeed, the heart of the town. However, there are several strange and noticeable behaviors being expressed among the locals, and also, to an astonishingly increasing extent, by the visiting population as well. Out-of-town folks that seem to be drawn to and frequent the downtown area, and not just to the casino necessarily, are showing up in rapidly increasing numbers recently. The primary attraction for them is to come into town and then to seemingly act as the locals do in their drinking behavior.

The people of this quaint little city, which has been regarded for decades as a great place to live, and is characterized by its inescapable village-like charm, all walk around in public while holding a drink. Yes, a drink is in everybody's hand. When I say all, I mean literally all. Everybody has a drink! That is the astoundingly, unadulterated truth. There is absolutely nobody about the town proper without a drink in hand. First time I witnessed it, it completely astounded me as I noticed the unique phenomena. So, I decided to stop, look around in a 360-degree view only to see that, yes, everyone moving about in this town was holding a drink, if not sipping it. And it doesn't seem to matter what type of container is used either; albeit a can, bottle, thermos, paper or Styrofoam cup, water bottle for jogging, the always familiar blue or red, white-tipped, plastic party cup, or a mug of one sort or another. Everyone, all the time they are downtown anyway, have a drink in hand. It has gotten to the point where this overbearing public behavior has created quite a stir and is being regarded by some as reaching the level of actually being either a freakish social expression of some sort, or a coordinated covert action, perhaps purposely geared to be a planned rebelling nuisance against the "dry town" laws already in place. Yet, even with this questionable behavior being so prevalent, there are no observable problems that violate the law, or general public decency for that matter, in any way whatsoever. There are just normal people drinking. So, what gives?

The first shocking drinking-related incident I personally observed, came while I was crossing as a pedestrian into the notably central gathering point for the locals downtown. It is called "Nipsip Plaza." The descriptive word, "Nipsip" is apparently yet another word of Muckleshoot origin that has eponymously also found its way into the modern lexicon of geographical reference points in the town. Its meaning being something akin to "watering hole." The central plaza is the typical, large, park-like, courtyard that you could find in any similar place throughout America. This one though, seemed to have a deeper and more meaningful connection to the locals, due mostly to the fact that it was strategically located at the corner of Main and Bourbon Streets, a very busy crossing intersection in the heart of the city. Looking around in all directions, I noticed that there was a rather large advancing crowd, consisting of both average pedestrians walking about, and those who were passing by on the main thoroughfare inside their cars. Normal enough, at least for any small city in these parts, or anywhere else in America for that matter. Except for one very tangible difference. Every single one of the people I spotted, walking about or riding in cars, had a drink of some sort or another in their hand. Really? For me, as an "I spy" reporter, whose job is only to observe and relay the facts, and I am sure for other people who have had the experience of driving into this town or visiting for the first time, it was incredibly strange to see so many people drinking, regardless of what they were up to. Literally, every person I saw was drinking while being in Tockseqated!

The next jolt to shock me was the realization that there did not appear to be any age limit to the ones doing the drinking Everyone had a drink. I kid you not, every person, walking about downtown in this charming city, literally everyone, no matter what age, six to sixty and beyond, all the people who were in Tockseqated, were drinking.

There were old folks, for example, just shuffling their way out of Rusty's Hardware Store with drinks in their hands like it was completely normal, and then proceeding to stagger their way down the main sidewalk in Tockseqated. No big deal. It was almost as if they planned their day for the excursion in order to be in Tockseqated, and did their drinking in public every week at this time, as a matter of some subliminal scheduled activity that was nothing to "get up" about. There were many middle-aged folks as well. All of them going about, doing all sorts of things, like typical weekly errands I suppose, but still unashamedly drinking and traversing the streets while they too were in Tockseqated.

Very disturbingly, I witnessed one young mother, who couldn't have been a day over twenty-five and yes, she was also in Tockseqated, trying to entice her squirming young child to drink more, while struggling and trying to hold her own drink without spilling it in her right hand. Even the toddler, clutching a smaller-sized, straw-imbued cup with both hands, was drinking. Both of them, mother and young child, were constantly drinking while they were in Tockseqated! Shocked? I cannot even begin to relate how astounding it was to witness these public displays of drinking by everyone, all completely unmoved by public opinion, just enjoying their drinks unashamedly, almost triumphantly, all while they were in Tockseqated.

As bad as the mother-child public drinking display was, perhaps the most astounding problem drinking behavior, in terms of being "in-your-face" and quite commonly being openly expressed, were the acts of the local teenaged boys with their skateboards. There they were, sliding along the sidewalks and pulling their stunts, while holding drinks in their hands. Seeing a kid on a skateboard and holding a Mountain Dew would seem to be expectedly avant-garde, the new normal, just about anywhere in urban life. It would probably even be considered as somewhat "cool." Even by adults. Of course, that is what the folks at PepsiCo, owners of the brand hope for. But while being in Tockseqated? It reaches a whole new level of speculation. Why? Because it wasn't just one kid expressing a rebelling attitude here or there and drinking while skating along. No. Literally every kid was drinking something, and the vast majority of them were not just downing Mountain Dews either.

Beyond my own personal belief of what I was witnessing was, in fact real, and to a larger extent, well beyond my wildest imagination, I carefully viewed my surroundings in yet another 360-degree turn. (A common tactic as an observer that I employ quite readily and often, just in case you didn't notice. Hey, it works!) That was when I realized that every pedestrian who was in Tockseqated, no matter what they were doing, or where they were going, no matter what age, all of them, continued to carry a drink while they were making their way around downtown. Literally everyone who was in Tockseqated was continuing to drink non-stop. But it doesn't end there.

Perhaps the greatest wake-up call I had, the one that shook me to my core and illustrated just how severe the problem was, came when I saw and suddenly realized, how many people were driving and openly drinking while in Tockseqated. In fact, I didn't spot a single motorist who wasn't driving and drinking at the same time as they were cruising their way on down the streets of the eclectic town. They were drinking and driving in Tockseqated! It was almost as if, by just entering the city limits, one was prone to adopt this strange social drinking behavior. To satisfy my need for a firsthand explanation, I noticed, and quickly approached, one middle-aged couple tooling along in a vintage Plymouth Roadrunner. (My guess was it was a 1971 model, like the one I had in high school, before the over-famed Hemi completely intruded on the antiquated, purist roadsters of that era.) They were quite obviously, by facial expressions, enjoying the fact that they were driving their coveted classic muscle car on the main drag downtown— while they were obviously in Tockseqated and perhaps thinking that they too were "all that."

I quickly made my way to them, actually leaping over a few sidewalk slumbering folks (a fixture in every city and a constant reminder of the homeless problem everywhere in America) like an Olympic hurdler, finally reaching my goal. I approached the passenger side of their cherry-cool, museum-worthy car, since they had no choice but to stop for the red traffic light. I knocked on the passenger window while the two occupants were seemingly in a trance staring at the light that suddenly had obliged them to stop. (I later learned that, to my fortune, that the light at Main Street and Hennessy Way was an obnoxiously long wait for a stop-light. One that the locals all hated.) The passenger, a bearded dude, who looked like a typical 80's type (sorry for the obnoxious, yet entirely accurate stereotype) sporting a classic mullet hair-style, and the requisite throw-back beard for the sake of some imagined "chick appeal," eagerly opened the window. Then asked me, "Hey man! You cool?" For a second, taken aback by his legal probe regarding my credibility, I jumped into cover mode, explained that I was a reporter and just wanted to ask a few questions. Suddenly, taking the lead like a network correspondent answering my inquiry, the woman at the wheel who called herself Sherry, took control of the conversation and responded. She indicated that drinking while driving in Tockseqated had been elevated to a weekly ritual for the two of them.

"Sure, I like having a drink while I'm driving around in Tockseqated, and my boyfriend Bud here, his last name is Wiser, oh yeah, and me, my name is Sherry, that's Sherry Pinot if you happen to be recording this, it's my fifteen minutes of fame, right? Well, we both, just like, you know, we like to come here to drink and drive around this cute little town. You know, to just be crusin' around, of course while we are in Tockseqated, it just makes us feel ... invigorated! Especially on weekends. Yeah! There's something really cool about being in Tockseqated and driving down Main Street in our equally cool car, all the while letting everybody know that we are like everyone else. Drinking of course. I mean, they can see our cups, right? We get sort of a buzz, or high, or more properly, an elation. I guess that's a smart person's word. Right? Use it. It's also kinda romantic for us at our age. We don't go out much anymore, but we sure do remember cruising around and drinking back in the day as teenagers. Catching a buzz. Right?

"So, coming here, and just driving around in Tockseqated gives us a bit of that old thrill again. You could call it 'a new wave buzz' I guess.

People see us sippin' our drinks while we are lookin' cool in our muscle car driving around in Tockseqated. They nod their heads, lift their drinks as if to toast us, as if to say 'you two are really cool!' Of course, we'll always stop and grab a bite to eat while we're in Tockseqated. Because, hey, we're trying to enjoy the whole experience. You can't just drink and drive in Tockseqated, you gotta stop and enjoy something to eat before attempting the long drive home, like we have, going all the way back home to the Black Out hills thirty miles north of here. Which is, nearby to our house, we actually live in Passeo. You know what they say 'round these parts, 'Don't pass out before making it to the Passeo outskirts!'

"I certainly don't want to be forced to stop on the way back home due to a sudden hunger attack or an unquenchable thirst, if you know what I mean?" (She smiles and winks at me.) "Better to fill up and make sure you are in totally in the tank, ready to go, and drinking as much as possible while you're in Tockseqated. Especially before downing that one last drink before driving back home."

The basic question I realized, and one that I am sure others have also had, kept gnawing at me while observing this incredulously bazaar behavior. What is it exactly that causes these people to start drinking and then continue to keep on drinking without any concerns while being in Tockseqated?

I went looking for an answer, stoutly determined and unabashed. There had to be some deeper underlying reason for this strange behavior. What I got, disappointingly, was what could only be characterized as "the typical" response. It came from one of the many clone-like teens hanging out at Nipsip Plaza that I mentioned earlier. (Just seeing them congregating together called to mind the definition of "teenager" that I had picked up somewhere along the way years ago. Being labeled *a teenager* is actually the time of life where one strives to be completely unique while at the same time trying to be just like everyone else.) The individual boy that approached me was (uncannily individual by definition, and at the same time he was just like the others hanging out) a teen who looked to be fourteen or fifteen. With his betraying, neatly-cut, blonde, unkempt hair and lanky build, he was doing everything possible just trying to look inconspicuous and to be noticed at the same time. He seemed to be mulling around there, doing "his thing" by kicking and spinning his skateboard around in various, apparently avant-garde gyrations, poignantly notable to him alone (or maybe the folks at Mountain Dew), right there in the center of town.

By the growing number of (same but different) teens gathering about Nipsip Plaza, it was seemingly the apparent go-to place for a teen to hang out while being in Tockseqated after school let out. I guess that my observation of the flagrantly obvious dress, and copious mannerisms, that this one high school-aged youth openly displayed (and compelled me to lock my gaze on him a bit too long) also caused him to notice me. He acknowledged my presence vociferously, and much to my astonishment, came up to me on his own, although he was obviously struggling between being brash or sheepish. Yet another of the constant paradox-laden struggles that a teen must endure in the modern social pretext.

He bravely and boldly introduced himself (even extending his hand for a shake, much to my amazement) and told me his name was Jack. Jack Daniels. I looked him straight in the eyes, as he looked to be your average teen. He was just hanging out with some of his buddies after getting out of school, on this welcome sunny, mid-Friday, late afternoon in May. I introduced myself as well, maybe overly stating that I was reporter on assignment here to cover a prospective news article that focused on the various questionable actions of the townsfolk.

He told me without any reservation whatsoever, his own point-blank, uncensored opinion. "Heck man, here we are, you an' me, and here I am, you know? And more to the relevant point of your question, there's me and my buds, an' we're all fully enjoying, after a week of intense study, being in Tockseqated! Naturally, all of us grab our drinks right after school and then come here. Hell, it's Friday! We all know it's most 'specially Friday, and here we are at this place which is the most choicest spot for our viewing of the hotties! Yo Bro, we figured that out a long time ago. So, we're hangin' here chillin' an sippin' a few, all the while waiting to impress any babes that may come along. Let me tell ya', right here is the perfect spot to be waitin' for the hotties to come along! There is no better place to be hanging out, trying to look cool and to be sippin' a few drinks to let them know that, 'Hey Babe, we are totally cool, waitin' for you, while being in Tockseqated.'"

At this point, Jack and his buddies raised their cans, without any cue and in concert, all in one smooth move, took a long swig from their drinks. Then, almost as if they had done this many times before, of course only while they were in hanging out here being in Tockseqated, they all raised their cans in unison, and gave me the "Catch you later, Dude" salute. (The CYLD salute comprises a raise of the can or drink in one's hand as if to toast, followed by completely chugging the contents in one long swig and then tilting the empty container's opening over one's head. Thereby proving it was all downed in one big gulp.)

In unison I heard a comforting, "Catch you later! Dude! We are out!"

Being mesmerized, or more accurately entranced, by their knee-jerk response to my inquiry, all I could manage to do was give them a "thumbs-up." I know. Pathetic, typical 80's response.

After that spectacle, I was about to move on, when Jack suddenly turned back and piped in, "Stay cool man. Nothin' like chillin' with my buds and downing a few cold ones, while being in Tockseqated! You got me?" Yeah. I got him.

Wow. So that was where the youth of this supposedly conservative bedroom town was headed. Everyone, even the preteen youth, were outright unashamedly willing to drink whenever and whatever they wanted, in public, completely uninhibited while frequenting the streets of the town. The town official rank and file simply did not care.

I moved on.

I came across a threesome of what looked to be a nine to ten-year-old group of girls enjoying an after-school, afternoon in the playground, friendly, jump-rope competition. The amazing thing I immediately noticed was that even these young girls had drinks in their hands. Oh my gosh! No way! The two on the ends who held the long rope, twirled with one hand while holding a drink in the other. Somehow, the one in the middle, actually doing the jumping, pig-tails flying upward while jaunting with each launch of her legs, still managed to hold her drink and jump rope in response to the hip-hop cadence shouted out by the two girls on the ends managing the rope. All the while, she was still taking random sips at will without spilling a drop. I was dumbfounded. In my own wildest drinking days, I could not have pulled off such a remarkable stunt. To any passerby, it looked like what would be coined as a typical, seemingly expected event. Just pre-teen girls enjoying a youthful after-schoolyard activity. That is, anywhere else. But not here. All of the girls just had to have a drink in their hands while being in Tockseqated.

So, is jumping rope while in Tockseqated and holding a drink in hand considered to be just another "normal" childhood activity, one to be blindly accepted by the population at large? Was there no limit to how far this massive drinking problem, at least while being in Tockseqated, had spread? Most especially, I was concerned about how many young people were drinking, while they were in Tockseqated. Surely there had to be a way out for them, or more specifically, a way of true recovery.

After finding that the behavior in this town was so strange, I couldn't shake the recurring question (more of a realization really) in my mind, "What is their core problem? Why does every person in Tockseqated need to have a drink in hand all of the time?" Maybe AA could help. But AA is all about alcohol abuse and alcoholism as a disease, and certainly not about drinking while just being in Tockseqated, and at the same time there was the assumed social pressure of constantly needing to hold a drink in one's hand in order to get along with everyone else who did the same thing. After finding the behavior of all the people who were in Tockseqated being nothing less than puzzlingly strange, I stepped up my research in order to find out if there was any other town, anywhere else in the United States, which was showing this similar behavior among their townsfolk.

You can imagine the shock, when, after posing just a few questions out on several trustworthy blogs on the net, which unambiguously asked: "Is this strange drinking problem happening in your town?" I was inundated with a series of substantial affirmative responses. Yes, I found out that this seemingly strange behavior was, in fact, having a wider appeal. It was expressing itself elsewhere, that is, other than just affecting the people who were already in Tockseqated. There was one other town I found in particular, one that was an almost mirror image of the people who were in Tockseqated. And yes, they too, were expressing the same untoward drinking behavior in public.

Remarkably, I also discovered that there was a behavioral adaptation study already being conducted by the company that produces the so-called energy drink marketed under the name, "Red Bull." Their sole marketing interest was to find locations throughout the country that had a high rate of public drinking. The reasoning for the study went as follows: If people drinking in public were obviously consuming Red Bull products, it would be the best possible avenue for advertising to exploit. There is, after all, nothing better than having live, walking, talking, (optimally) people consuming the drink in public, accompanied by apparently spontaneous (and numerous) ad hoc testimonial endorsements. All of which characterize public drinking of the product as "normal" behavior. It would be a marketing godsend. To have actual consumers having the drink in hand and to notice them in the process of consuming it was the best possible way to promote any product. Red Bull was so dedicated to this marketing approach, they reached out to the somewhat obscure government agency known as the Center of Research Among Populations (or CRAP for short) which boasts of having some of the brightest and most prestigious scientists and sociologists among their ranks.

The unwitting taxpayers, through congressional national government approval, had gone so far as to fund the CRAP study—most notably in response to a request to provide an in-depth report stating as to where there had been the highest concentration of public drinkers in the country. Like anything else in congress, the original focus was lost. But the resulting investigation did ironically provide some invaluable information. The marketing geniuses decided, taking into consideration the mutual conclusion of the behavioral study group's data, sponsored by the Red Bull/CRAP collaboration, that the best way to enhance sales (and thereby tax revenue) was to promote outright public drinking.

Surprisingly, the Red Bull/CRAP data that came out of their final study did identify many people who already were in Tockseqated. In addition, they were leading the entire nation, specifically in the category of having the highest rate per capita of persons with drinks in hand while unashamedly continuing their personal drinking in public. They were followed by another small city, also one named according to native American origin, located nearly a thousand miles due west from the good people who were in Tockseqated.

My next stop, on this wild goose "drinking in public" chase, was to go to Kneebreated, located in central Wisconsin. It was the city infamously marked as number two on the Red Bull/CRAP research study identifying where the highest known level of public drinking was presently taking place. There I was, in Kneebreated, ready to find out why this drinking problem was also taking hold. I totally immersed myself into the drinking problem, while being fully determined to be in Kneebreated so I could find answers. I fully engaged just like when I was in Tockseqated.

The city's name, is one coined by the Ojibwe, also known as the Chippewa, made famous by the song, "The Wreck of the Edmund Fitzgerald" by Gordon Lightfoot, recorded in 1976. The famed singer/songwriter includes the lyrics: "the legend lives on, from the Chippewa on down … of the Big Lake they called 'Gitche Gumee' … Superior, they said, never gives up her dead …" The verses refer to the Ojibwe name for Lake Superior and its Wisconsin shores.

There I was, again downtown, fully absorbing my surroundings, this time while being in Kneebreated. The city pronounced: NEE BREE AYE TED, the Objebwe origin of which, means quite literally, "insatiable thirst." You are kidding right? Again.

I was lucky. I arrived in the city's center at a great time of day to catch the swell of the downtown crowd as they decided to break for lunch. Of course, they were enjoying the sights and sounds while being completely brazen about what to do while being in Kneebreated. Sure enough, not only was the downtown setting strangely similar. Again, to what I witnessed while being in Tockseqated, it was, compared to my last jaunt, dripping of the same drinking problem. Being in Kneebreated, I could tell it was, again, also a typical, bustling, "Main Street USA" type of place. Just like the people who were in Tockseqated. They all too, had drinks in their hands! Okay, saw that before. But these folks did more than just drink all the time. And it didn't matter what they were up to. Whether walking, driving, or just hanging out while simply enjoying the sights, all were unashamedly drinking while being in Kneebreated. Strange, strange, behavior. The people who were in Kneebreated were no different than the ones who were in Tockseqated. It's as if they're all drunk or something! But the people who were in Kneebreated also exhibited another strange behavior aside from walking around with a drink in their hand.

There was no person with a free hand at all, as most everyone also held some sort of cell phone as well. I stood there watching, completely mesmerized, at how almost all the people had a cell phone in one hand and a drink in the other. Yet, somehow, they were still were able to function, as if it was a completely normal way to be walking about chatting on the phone, also drinking while being in Kneebreated. Obviously, there seems to be some real serious dangers to this behavior.

I observed one young woman, for example, trying to cross an intersection in the middle of downtown, she too (for the record) was also in Kneebreated. She had a drink in one hand and was looking at her phone in the other, not really paying attention to the traffic, while crossing at the corner of Main and Jameson Streets. All the time apparently feeling completely safe while being in Kneebreated. Cars screeched to a halt, coming from four directions. She was so into her own mind-induced normal feeling, apparently because she was in Kneebreated, that she didn't even notice that the cars had the right-of-way when the light suddenly changed.

It was then that I saw an on-coming car slam on the brakes in order to avoid hitting her, but that driver was really no different either. Even he had a drink in one hand, his cell phone in the other, and yet somehow managing to steer his vehicle clear in order to avoid a disastrous accident. There he was, drinking, looking at his cell phone and driving, all the while he too was in Kneebreated. Very puzzled and disturbed, I decided to ask the leading police authority in the town about this.

I most fortunately located the top law enforcement official, who just happened to be sitting in his cruiser, right there on the corner of Brandy Street and Resolute Way. I casually began my inquiry by engaging in a harmless, safe-level, conversation with the cop, who was in fact the police chief, Jim Beam. I sheepishly made an inquiry about the strange behavior I was observing.

"Yeah, I have to admit, it seems strange to some folks who are not used to being around here and all. I mean, everywhere you go in this town, you see people with a drink in one hand and the cell phone in the other. It seems to be the only characteristic or MO, from our police perspective, if you want to enjoy the downtown life. But I guess we all just kind of got used to it being our own unique way. We've even relaxed the laws a bit so people can drive the short distance home while they are already in Kneebreated. And yes, we allow them to continue to use their cell phone at the same time. Granted, it's not like that in other places. I get that. But maybe here, huh? I mean, all of us who are always in Kneebreated, maybe we are just lucky. Fact is, with all of the preoccupation folks have with their cell phones, and then they decide to take it to the next level, that is, while drinking in Kneebreated, it's a miracle we have the very few accidents we have.

"In fact, the last car crash we had was when Ol' Jose Cuervo, that Spanish old-timer bastard, rammed his all-too-typical '57 Chevy pick-up, into the side of the Crown Royal restaurant last Sunday. Claimed he couldn't remember if it was the break or the gas pedal that was the sideways one. No matter. He's eighty-two. We all give him a pass but he still had an accident. Right? Now here's the real counterpoint. He was the only one in town who wasn't drinking!

"And, more significantly, he doesn't even own a cell phone! But that didn't seem to matter, because he was still in Kneebreated and the law is the law, drinking or not. Maybe if he did have a drink, he would have been better off. Less confused and all. All I'm sayin' is, that if you are a person who drinks while you are in Kneebreated, you probably will have a far lesser chance of something bad happening to ya."

After my visit to both of these patently obvious strange places, where unbridled drinking occurs, in public, without any concern for the consequences of doing so, I decided to find out if there was anyone else who had information about the strange behavior I experienced while being either in Tockseqated or in Kneebreated for that matter.

After further research, I also, thankfully, found out that both the government and scientific communities were aware of this unique problem—more specifically that they made recommendations to profoundly manifest the issue in these two communities. Surprised? Yes. So, there is hope.

As further relief, I learned that recent government legislation is currently being proposed to help the people, especially those who are already in Tockseqated or are in Kneebreated once and for all. The plan is dramatic and unprecedented. It calls for both cities to stop completely allowing anyone to drink in public. That's right. No drinking when you are in Kneebreated and no drinking while being in Tockseqated. It simply will not be allowed in public, at least for now. The initial measure is to at least try this approach, for the next thirty days and then reevaluate the data. The government admits that these measures will be a challenge. To get people who are already in Tockseqated or in Kneebreated for that matter, to stop drinking completely is an uphill battle. That much is known. But, they believe, in the long run, there is hope for these people. If they could only stop drinking all the time.

There are also plans to implement a locally endorsed program to "stop drinking while at home and while already being in Tockseqated" in order to curb the problem. But lawmakers completely agree, that such an ordinance would be hard to legislate, and even harder to regulate. One thing for certain, whether you are in Tockseqated or completely living the life of Reilly, fully immersed in the lifestyle while being in Kneebreated, there is one thing for certain. Drinking while driving will be completely out of the question. Both cities have adopted a similar ordinance that has (thankfully) already gone into effect.

"Thank God! At least the drinking while driving law will apply only to adults over the age of eighteen," said Chrystal Stolichnaya, yet another motorist I happened upon, and a recently naturalized citizen, originally from Russia. "In my native country, we never had any problem with anybody drinking, at least a person willing to talk about such. I am just glad my children will be able to drink in car while being in Kneebreated. Maybe I want this too, for me also, that is, to have drink in car while I am in Kneebreated. But this wish is no longer so. At least drinking is still allowed for the children, since it helps them to stay calm during the long time to sit in the car downtown".

Since they are exempt from the ordinance, the youngsters will still be able to drink as much as they like. The same ruling is true for the kids who are in Tockseqated, where an overwhelming majority of parents petitioned to adopt the same rules regarding public drinking as the folks did who were in Kneebreated. Whether you are in Tockseqated or in Kneebreated, whatever, you better not be drinking while in public if you are over the age of eighteen. It is here-to-fore a crime, and you will be prosecuted to the full extent of the law. But, if you are under the legal age to vote, you'll be just fine. No need to worry. Drink as much and as often as you want within the city limits, whether you are already in Kneebreated or residing in Tockseqated for that matter.

"It seems odd, but it's for the best," said Sheriff Johnny Walker, while being interviewed when we were in Tockseqated.

"I don't mind coming down hard on the parents for their obsessive drinking, but damned be, if I am going to stop a poor little kid from needing a drink while they are in Tockseqated! Our town just ain't that way. We regard social values highly, and thereby take pride, specifically and especially, as we are keeping an all-vigilant eye out for each other, especially the youth of our community. If a young person needs to have a drink while being in Tockseqated, for any reason whatsoever, by golly, then the law as written already says that we all should respect and stand for that kid's right to do so. As for the adults, it's another matter altogether. They should be able to control themselves and wait until they are not in Tockseqated before having a drink. I'm glad that the rules are the way they are now. Less adults behaving badly while being in Tockseqated, and more kids drinking all they desire while being in Tockseqated, it is, by far, a vast improvement in my book. I don't know why we didn't realize this formula for success and implement it a long time ago."

Let's just hope for the sake of the rest of the nation that the experience of these diversely different, yet surprisingly similar, small cities can set an example for the rest of the country—before drinking everywhere becomes a real problem.

Chapter 101

Camino Spirit

ONE DAY ON THE CAMINO SANTIAGO DE COMPOSTELA

I should have collapsed. Been beyond exhausted. Totally tapped out. Physically depleted, mentally adrift, even spiritually spent. Instead, I was completely the opposite—one hundred per cent, fully and sharply aware of every intricate detail of my surroundings. My disposition was increasingly invigorated, fervently enjoying the reverie of replaying the highlights of the passing day's lengthy leg of my ambitious journey. Dispersed in an array of spontaneous prayers prompted by one sudden inspired revelation after another, my supra-liminal mental state carried on a sort of conscious examen. My self-contented internal dialogue expressed profound gratitude to the Creator for the astonishing experience I was completely imbued in, while my senses were bombarded with the welcome toil of progressing through the pure unadulterated beauty of the idyllic Spanish countryside surrounding me. Then, suddenly, the revelation: *This* is pilgrimage!

I realized that my eighth straight day of continuous walking was nearing an end by the sun's rapidly descending trajectory in the cloudless western azure sky, though still positioned way above three o'clock if referenced in northeast New England. It simply got dark way later here. Usually toward ten, or as the locals refer to it, twenty-two hundred hours. There was that lighting hue change and the rising cadence of the incessant fatigue spasms drumming up from each foot, snaring along my legs with every beat of my steps. My entire body was feeling that pleasingly painful glow, uniquely evident after completing a formidable athletic workout; perhaps in some exotic locale where the physical, emotional, and spiritual aspects of one's very being have been exerted and pressed to full capacity. Feeling sore and exhilarated at the same time. It was like a runner's high. Best way to describe it.

As I walked, the recollection of my morning devotion and daily reflection coming from *The Spiritual Exercises of Saint Ignatius Loyola* was repeatedly impressed in my mind. It focused on the difference between living in the moment and the futility of creating a life-long, labored focused legacy. Ignatius made the indisputable point that after a hundred years or so, nobody cares what you did during your life on earth, let alone even remembers you. Think about it. Do you know the intricate details of your great-grandfather or great-grandmother's life? Most of us can only truthfully respond to that query with a less than enthusiastic, diametrically opposed, and ubiquitous, "No, not really." Focusing on living in the here and now, open to God's promptings which will ultimately lead directly to our eternal future with him in heaven, forever, is therefore, the best logical option that we face in carrying out our existence each day. The ultimate future for each of us on earth is that it ends. Physically, it is as if we were never really here.

Think about that. Take a moment to stop and reflect. We are truly just dust, after all, as God tells Adam in Genesis, "you are dust and to dust you shall return." Nothing more, nothing less. But that is only in the realm of speaking of ourselves physically.

The realization in my own life's endeavors that I was feeling at that moment echoed precisely affirmative to what Ignatius had imprinted in my soul with his suggested daily reflection. It also seemed to incipiently become completely relevant and astute. It was almost as if the saint's writing was intimately directed and personally designed for me. Overall, it only served to heighten the exuberance I felt (alluringly aroused by the spectacular scenery of the Spanish countryside, I readily admit) and contrasted masterfully with the painful toll of the taxing calisthenic imposed by my "physical side" being resiliently imparted, mostly due to having walked such a far distance this very day. Those two replete realms of my existence—the spiritual and physical, both inadvertently collided, almost as if guided miraculously and harmoniously. They then joined forces together to sublimely infuse the joyful, prodigious, suffering power of grace that suddenly came from somewhere out there. If I were not physically taxed, while realizing this, then how could I know? A profound mystery had again suddenly (welcomely mind you) invaded my soul.

Where? How? God? Pilgrimage simply does this. It helps us to focus on the big questions we often ignore living our busy daily lives.

I completely believe, beyond my own awareness of being, that it was the Creator's power gently inserting himself in order for me to overcome the taxing physical stress that I was feeling with each of these late-day strides along the Camino Santiago de Compostela. I was truly blessed, thoroughly appreciating in that instant, that I was also fully immersed in the very essence of pilgrimage. I was well on my way. I already had two-hundred thirteen kilometers under my belt with five-hundred and sixty-five more to go. On *The* Camino. *The Way of Saint James!*

The day's jaunt once again started well before dawn in the facile little city/town of Navarrete, about twelve kilometers just west of Logroño, after enjoying a flawless night's welcome rest. Now I was nearly finished making my way across the predominantly mountainous province of La Rioja, a sliver of a region sandwiched between Navarra on the northeastern tip of Spain and the divergent, flat-landed, and considerably larger Castilla Y León province boundary leading west. The next major milestone: the isolated ancient city of Burgos, still three days journey away by foot. A spectacular landing point, based on its history alone. As I entered the outskirts of a mini-municipality called Santo Domingo de la Calzada (which, in English awkwardly translates to "Saint Dominic of the Causeway"), the history of the place was at once intrusively noticeable, and quite obviously initially inspired by the founder's own life of humble service. In 1040, Dominic built the bridge leading into the town as well as a hospital and hostel for pilgrims. Since then, the Way of Saint James has traversed through the hamlet.

As I started walking into the town, the sensation of reconnecting with any form of humanity started to well-up inside me as a joyous refrain, resoundingly taking over the fading verses of my deep mental contemplation. So too did the desire to call it quits on walking for the day, one spent almost entirely alone and traversing one of the most peaceful pastoral planes of the Iberian peninsula's recondite interior topographical panoramas. After following the genius-inspired and obviously holy galvanized contrived route of the Camino—which carved along the edge of the few barren craggy mountains to the south by following a relatively low, impressively flat, valley region of plains that featured some occasional plumes of vineyards, and that was mostly buttressed by the seemingly endless rolling cereal wheat fields to the north—I simply needed to stop.

Time to rest.

Now, recalling the relentless hours walking through the fields, it looked as if, and I believe, that the entire world could harvest their breakfast cereal from the endless plains of wheat in this country. Especially from those that were within my continuous scope of vision that stretched outward in every direction. Perhaps they did. Point is, there was a lot of wheat. Everywhere you looked. Wheat!

Fields of wheat. To make bread? The bread of life. Eucharist.

Aside from the call to reflect on what I had already experienced, I also considered the newly realized perspective of the enrapturing view immediately displayed before me. I was well above keeping up my pace according to my predetermined average daily distance requirement. All totaled, in this one day, I had walked thirty-eight kilometers (the rough equivalent of nearly twenty-four miles thus far) comprised mostly of following burro impressed footpaths over a period of time that now exceeded well over eleven hours. Being late in the afternoon (that is, according to the Spanish definition of late afternoon, meaning close to five o'clock), it was indeed time to stop, have some dinner, relax, and recharge my resistance to torpidity with some rejuvenating down-time before facing yet another beguiling day. The pallid, ruggedly maintained, and somewhat awkwardly intimate, short road leading to Santo Domingo humbly presented itself as a welcome passageway to the perfect place for my next respite.

Decision made. Go there.

The packed clay and thoroughly amalgamated, dry dirt surface of the thoroughfare leading into the modest village, typical of many roads so far afield, opened up before me as I descended a small rise just high enough to allow a striking panoramic view of the entire placid rural community that was just ahead. Its tightly grouped, bone-white, limestone structures with their requisite processed clay, red-orange, tubular tile-shingled roofs, all clustered together in support of each other, and almost seemed intended to stand out with their flower-like isogonic color. They simply contrasted so resplendently against the verdant hue of the vineyard-laden purview in the background. It combined, infused, into an inadvertent artistic masterpiece of a sight to behold. One that innocently worked to distill the prominent, grassy olive retral spectrum, which had boldly decided to express itself dominantly on the lazy, rolling brownish hills resting far in the distance behind. It was the perfect optic. Picturesque.

Especially for one who, like me, is artistically enjoined, and thereby would greatly appreciate the view; it was a visually pleasant and anti-virulent tableau filled with a cascade of natural life elements that were still just ahead in my journey, all waiting to be discovered up close. Crisp, vibrant green clumps of bountiful vegetable gardens filled the foreground. They were sparkled with random tan, cork-brown, and copper streaks denoting the rows of fertile soil carefully and smartly woven between them. To my right, almost dead-center in the village, was a much statelier edifice, similar in color to the rest, but having an impetuous towering belfry. Obviously, it was the church, whose namesake was undoubtedly dedicated to the saint chosen as the town's guardian. And, like so many rural Spanish settlements, it was also the public focal point and moral beacon of the intrinsic identity of its inhabitants.

The hamlet had the pleasing appeal of an oasis compared to the surrounding landscape I had just passed through on this day which was mostly decrepit due to ages of weathered wear, leaving only sporadic windswept rock outcroppings amid scarred patches of shrub-like diminutive trees. It was a vista resembling so many others, commonly strewn intermittently alongside the more resplendent geographical marvels of the Spanish frontier. Each town, I thought, was like a prayer bead strung together in a rosary-ropeway along the entire Camino. (I'm also sure one of the numerous saints that had made this same journey, over the centuries, on this same route to Compostela before me, made the same incipient observation and saw the connection to the Blessed Virgin's arsenal of weaponry to battle sin. I simply couldn't be the first to make the analogy.)

Upon entering the town proper, I immediately noticed the indispensable public water fountain, characteristic of nearly every station along the pilgrimage route. Its marble catch-basin and matching retainer wall featured various sculpted carvings of what likened to be angelic Biblical figures surrounding the protruding spigot from which gushed a glistening stream of cool, clear running water—an aqua rope that naturally tied itself onto the gathering pool-drain swirling below. In what was becoming a natural reflex upon encountering any such water fount along the Camino, I immediately removed my red bandana (presently dubbing as a protective head scarf safeguarding my scalp from the unrelenting barrage of the sun's oppressive rays throughout the day) and thoroughly soaked it in the cool, clean, refreshing, liquid lanyard of life.

Agua!

After gulping from the stream directly and thereby realizing the water's heart-felt curing effect, I began to act like a transient interloper, generously swabbing my face, neck, and arms, thereby freeing them from the sticky film of what was once wet, swilling about, sticky mud particles that had anchored annoyingly upon my skin and then had become a dried, baked-on, version of a road-dust arms and facial make-up. After cleaning my face and arms, I greedily replenished my liter-sized, plastic water bottle and drained it down my throat twice—finally slaking the niggling need my insipid, tumid thirst had cruelly provoked over the prior three hours. (Like an idiot, I had forgotten to fill it at my last stop in Cirueña.) Road dust was finally abated on every level. It felt really good, as they say. Externally and internally I was finally hydrated, fully alive, once again.

Time for a break.

I reclined, form-fittingly and sitting snuggly contented against the embracing trunk and anchor-root arms of a nearby shade tree that seemed to welcome and naturally fit my body form perfectly as I gazed listlessly upon the soothing tranquil stream of water gracefully cascading away from the fountain spout. My mind began to slowly wander into what could only be referred to as my own private zone of completely surrendering to a moment of contemplative bliss. The wear and tear of the day's lengthy trek, one that had rent my muscles into radiating pinching pain pangs throughout my body, was keenly abated by the elixir effect of the recently swallowed and presently sighted draining water. Which in turn, also triggered a resurgent field of energy to well up like a panacea for my soul. A clash of physical and spiritual extremes. The former tattering on defeat and the later rejoicing in renewed rejuvenation. Both coalesced to produce an all-encompassing wave of jointly realized elation. Calling what I felt right there and then a "natural high" doesn't even begin to describe it. No artificial substance could have produced that blessed feeling.

Everything in that moment felt perfect. Just wholly right. Being in "the now" I emphatically realized in a deep, deep way. This was where I was supposed to be, what was supposed to have happened, and what God wanted me to know on every level of my being, before going one more step forward on this pilgrimage. It was a mystical moment of ascetic solitude and stillness that lingered for quite some time, perhaps an hour. I have not forgotten it to this day. I never will. I recall it often.

Then the sudden, the impetuous ringing of church bells awakened me back to the worldly present. Their clanging sounds instilling a consummate key feature of my holy reflection—a summons to approach the altar, the table of life, that I already knew would be found in the heart of this blessed remote village.

After re-affixing my now bone-dry bandana limply around my neck, I gingerly rose and hastily gathered my scattered belongings, very haphazardly stuffing them into my backpack while slinging it over my right shoulder. With stubborn, angry protests and visceral objections from various regions of my body, ardently expressed in the obdurate, dull pain, stifling stiffness, and unremitting throbs pulsating predominantly through my limbs, I nevertheless set off with bounding determination in the direction of the belfry sounds summoning me. The new goal was to follow the main road toward the origin of the bells' insistent resonance. Their augured bellowing intoned a familiar revered hymn after precisely heralding the six o'clock hour: *To Jesus Christ our sovereign king in whom this world rejoices* ... I sang aloud to the exuberant ringing tones as I made my laboring way toward them.

Quickly regaining my full stride, I seemed to enter into a precarious state of being that was paradoxically both trance-like and poignant—schismatically unaware of my waning gait, yet sharply perceptive of every detailed impression being perspicaciously thrust upon each of my bodily senses. I cannot recall a time, ever, when all my human perceptions were more precisely balanced and so finely tuned in.

As my breathing cadence perked up, I noticed the natural perfume essence of the roadside's floral foliage seeing that it mostly consisted of violet-colored Spanish bellflowers, emanating a jasmine-like bouquet. They were intermittently highlighted by the suddenly invading and alternating specious traces of the wild blackberry bushes and the contrasting redolent dill weeds that were ever-present, adding their own bewitching fragrance to the mix. Dill weeds were always evident in Spain, almost everywhere along the side of the roads that I had traveled so far. To think that I actually had to pay for dill, a spice/weed I love, in the States actually annoyed me to say the least!

Then these naturally occurring, and bemusedly all-too-familiar scents collided with yet another invading, yet deliciously enticing, and uniquely Spanish aroma. That of the fresh bread baking somewhere nearby. I already knew that every village had a bakery, an inescapable notable observation due to my own pronounced dietary cravings. So, this village also had the most desired shop-wish in my heart as well. And, best news was, that the dinner bread was always fresh. They baked twice a day in Spain. Again, the lusted loaves were never more than a few hours old, and always ready for purchase, even gooey. The best!

Next, the vortex of the bakery's pleasant "ca sent bon" conflated vexatiously with the pungent, quite fusty, scant earthen scent of the packed clay road upon which I was walking, creating a puzzling mental frame of reference—at once both appealing and at the same time being thoroughly repugnant. The paradox of the battling essences conjured up in my mind the effect that incense in church always had on me. This new experience of realizing my nasal senses operating at their peak would remain imprinted in my memory as an uncanny juxtaposition, uniquely inimitable to this specific location on earth. *This place* of pilgrimage. Santo Domingo de la Calzada.

I realized that the sight, the sounds, and most recently the smells, all forged a life-long lasting, visceral imprint upon my psyche. Of course, the amped-up, living in the moment experience, sparked especially by my morning reflection, was then continuously accentuated continuously throughout the entire day. Each new encounter presented itself as unique, and ultimately became seared into my heart at its very foundation. All because of both my reflection that started the day, and then in the end, by being here and now in this most inviolable place. I was being spiritually driven and felt completely safe in God's hands.

Visually, the impact was equally astounding. Although sunglasses-fortified, my eyes were nonetheless impaired and still stunned, being effectively breached by the onslaught of the powerful July sun. The solar source of life on earth stabbed at my eyes with its javelin-like rays, even covertly, but also unashamedly, working to overtly cast a visually impairing flash of impairing light, reflecting white-hot and fire-opal off of the flat, glossy, bleached walls of the quaint homes and other assorted fictile edifices along the way.

The numerous looming flash points were thankfully all neatly contained at their base by their unique dampening rings of succulent greens, accented with dark, spotted gray, and reddish copper tones that actually comprised the almost expected mix of commonly encountered and purposely chosen assorted shrubs, perhaps out of their owner's hubris: worn, weathered, wooden fences, and the mishmash of prided fieldstone and brick low walls marked the territorial boundary of each miniature estate. The humble dwellings stood surrounded by as much bounty in nature as their diminutive interior plots could painstakingly extrude. Some yards boasted of wished-for prestige with prized orange or lemon trees, while others conveyed themselves more modestly with practical fruits including: apples, peaches, plums, pears, and the all-to-common, in my opinion at least, obnoxious date tree.

The phantasmagoric impact of my surroundings was simply overwhelming.

Whether it was due to a community-wide collaboration to an extend siesta, the relentless searing heat being impressed by the sun, or maybe perhaps even the entire village coincidentally choosing this particular week to go away on holiday, what I did not see was any other person moving about. Not a single person was visible, anywhere. Even though there wasn't a single soul in sight, the pacific hamlet was fully permeated with a vivacious spirit, strikingly evident in the curious mix of diverse sounds that progressively called for my ears' full undivided attention.

It all started with some dispersed jovial screams and the crackling sweet laughter of children playing unseen somewhere in the far-off distance. Then, the sporadic sluggish clanging of cowbells, followed by a sudden engulfing air-whisper in my ear, as the breeze of the warm wind abruptly cascaded about and intruded my personal space. I suddenly became acutely aware of each new distinct specific tone, as if it were a solo aria set apart from the intended crescendo surround-sound ensemble resonating behind in a complex concert—thereby creating its own unique melange of mixed melodic harmonies. The extraordinary, very strange, evolving cacophony included the enticing symphonic tinging of distant wind chimes, mysterious foreboding clinks and clunks, some dissonant burbles, the incipient high-pitched roborant bee buzzing, stepped-on boards creaking, and a rhythmic work-horse hammering.

Then there were rattles and rustles, a splash, a passing clip-clop. An anguished thud. Disparate chortles, chuckles, protruding outwardly expressed groans, followed by speculatively diminutive sighs. All seemed to come from somewhere behind closed doors someplace, making their impetuous way out of an unseen force of open windows.

All a seemingly open expression of the mysteries contained within this unique place. They were then finally accentuated with creaking shutters slamming closed.

There were all the obvious animal noises. The notable and almost expectedly invading sounds, like horse snickers, cattle wheezes, pig whines, and goat trills, punctuated by a caw, some coos, and a squawk, all percolating amid the all too familiar baas, barks, and an almost expected bray (at least in these parts), donkey shrills, they were called. Then they were followed by a discontented series of oinks, topped off with a few distantly familiar yips and yaps. The impromptu concert was brought to a close by the totally, out of place, dawn-is-rising cry of a rooster. Wait! It is not morning. Why that? Perhaps he had the difference between sunset and sunrise confused?

Each sound was clearly distinct, somehow forming a docile, welcoming, and deeply stirring symphony that was seemingly coordinated on celebrating that my very arrival through the wide-open spiritual door of ciudad Santo Domingo de la Calzada had happened. This place, would undoubtedly be my home for the night. I was being bombarded with God's grace, within God's ordained natural habitat, and his symphony, practically singing a welcome hymn to me.

Seriously and profoundly grateful that this cozy tiny town providentially appeared to be my next overnight stop brought an air of peaceful comfort to my wholly provoked and excessively excited soul. I continued making my way along the seemingly deserted main road by following the ever-present, painted yellow arrows, pointing out the direction to Santiago de Compostela, still three weeks journey away. But I would, indeed, stay here tonight.

(The foot-long arrows are used to mark the entire way of the Camino along with images of conch shells—the pilgrimage route's universal symbol—dispersed every hundred meters or so. The directional arrows are affixed along the stone walkways, the sides of poles or trees, and even sometimes audaciously painted on buildings and other prominent structures.)

The Camino route pulsed right through the spirited heart of Santo Domingo which had two auberges—the specialized hostel-like lodges expressly equipped to accommodate pilgrims passing through and always willing to pay near poverty rates for a minimally basic night's stay. Most of the "bunk-houses" evolved from converted older buildings, some even multiple centuries old, having large open halls with efficient rows of minimally invasive bunk beds for pilgrims to crash on. The monkish sleeping "chambers" (often being comprised of nothing more than a backache-inducing narrow sleeping mattress, and in the better places, optionally clad with a clean set of sheets and a blanket), have the sole function of furnishing a place for a traversing pilgrim who is done-in to turn-in for a few hours before forging onward.

Most of the large sleeping areas that are found in an auberge are characteristically European in nature, which means that they are co-ed in the sleeping quarters with adjacent shower rooms and WCs which, thankfully, are typically not co-ed. ("WC" is the European equivalent of restroom/shower room derived from "Water Closet".) Pilgrims utilizing auberges are assumed to have overtly demure attitudes regarding both their own overall demeanor and especially expressed in the modest way in which they dress for sleep—characteristic of an unspoken general respect and supportive regard for one another's personal spiritual quest.

Some auberges would also offer an optional, generously portioned, nightly homestyle meal. These are comprised typically of half a roasted chicken, along with some sort of pasta with tomato sauce, and a garden salad, and most are complete with a requisite bottle of the region's most popular wine. A few even include a simple send-off continental breakfast. The inclusion of meals being more of a way to foster community among the diversity of pilgrims than to provide actual nourishment. For all of these illustrious accommodations a pilgrim could expect to be set back anywhere between three to five euros (equal to four to six dollars U.S.) which comprises the typical suggested "donation". Of course, most pilgrims being penitential in their dispositions contribute much more.

The two auberges in Santo Domingo maintained a total of sixty beds between them according to the official *Pilgrim's Guide* stowed in the easy access flap of my backpack, always at the ready, which was my second go-to "bible" (after the actual Bible, of course). Being that it was late in the travel day, that is, well after six o'clock, there was a very good chance that all the beds would be already taken. I felt a sudden selfish pang of anxiety at the thought that I might have no choice but to camp outside under the stars for the night. Again.

Then I saw it.

The town church's engrossing entrance thoroughly engaged me with its ornate, carved wooden, arched double doors as it came fully into sight just ahead of me on the right side of the road. Almost simultaneously, I noticed that directly facing the church on the opposite side of the street, was a large, antiquated, multi-family, house-like building, dwarfing all the others nearby. A large, rustic, wooden sign mounted onto the facade, having stylishly shaded, baby blue, capital letters against a flush white background proclaimed the place to be: "AVE MARIA AUBERGE."

Really. God?

Already feeling a rising sensation of joy well up inside just upon reading the sign, my heart raced furiously. The most perfect spot to sojourn for the night suddenly became visible before me.

Yes!

At once, I felt compelled to rush into the auberge in order to secure a bed for the night.

But wait. Suddenly, the consummate pilgrim lack of ego welled up inside.

It was then that I suddenly paused and thought that I should go into the church first, in order to give thanks for God's gift of the day's journey and the enchantingly profound experience I had while traversing the majestic Spanish countryside. My mind engaged in an internal tennis match over what I should do first. I stood there, stupidly immobile in the middle of the road, turning my head from left to right, repeatedly looking with longing at each beckoning entrance: the door to the auberge, humbly offering a warm invitation to come, comfortably rest. Then the door to the church's tantalizing enigmatical interior summoning from just beyond its arched gateway calling me to take refuge in the comforting spiritual, and deeply mysterious, realm within.

Back and forth. Back and forth. My head turned. The curious duel in my mind led only to a stubborn impasse between two conflicting internal voices demanding equal compliance.

Which do I do first?

"Get a bed reserved at the auberge first. It's getting late and you might not get one if you wait," said one voice in my head.

"Remember to give thanks to God before anything else! If you truly trust in God and if there is a bed meant for you, it will still be there after all. Go to the church first," the other voice intoned.

"God showed you the auberge too, probably for a good reason, so go in there first!" The seemingly logical point reverted.

It was promptly countered with, *'Recall Luke's gospel, where in chapter nine, verse fifty-eight, Jesus says, 'Foxes have dens and birds of the air have nests, but the Son of Man has nowhere to rest his head.' So, go into the church first. Don't worry about resting!"*

My ridiculously overinflated, obviously quasi-moral, internal dilemma was abruptly settled when I was snapped back to the present reality by a young woman who suddenly materialized in my line of vision, having just bolted out of the church herself, and resolutely was headed across the street while coming right toward me. She was strikingly graceful in both her outward appearance and the manner in which she carried herself. Her silky, flowing, knee-length dress, having a light violet flowered print, aptly accentuated her shapely, firm and fit athletic build. Quite attractive in all regards.

She radiated her womanly physique with a captivating, yet modest appeal in stature. Her shiny polished, black, low-heeled shoes with white bobbysocks even belied any anti-femininity in spite of being chosen for their walking-on-cobblestone practicality and church-bound appropriateness. Her long, thick, jet-black, tightly undulated mane was pulled back from her face and smartly splayed into a manifest ponytail, fixed firmly by a soft, puff cotton, dress-matching bow. Her pure and smooth olive color complexion was freely expressed beyond an intense angelic glow in the carroty diffused luminosity being imposed due to the setting of the late afternoon sun. Even her exquisite innate, unpretentious and guileless female facial features were all made to look much more stunning by the congealed lighting's histrionic effect.

My heart jumped. Such breathless beauty to stop my incessant mind game and take pause in beholding the nature of God's exquisite creation expressed in the woman before me. There was much more than just the visual appreciation that this distant sister in Christ evoked, she had an enrapturing, sylphlike, holy presence about her as well. She seemed not to be a stranger at all, but much more like an intimate close family member who could be completely trusted. Or, maybe, just maybe she was, an actual angel. To this day I do not conclusively know.

Stopping straightaway in front of me, we stood there, in the middle of the road face to face. Her inscrutable, chestnut brown, almond shaped eyes, hooded with prolonged deep dark lashes, peered directly into mine, even as her perfectly white teeth, surrounded by her pink accented glistening full lips, slowly revealed a heart-warming smile.

Then she spoke.

In a pleasantly gratifying tone of voice came a chorus of alto-level, staccato queries, "Bom Camino, Señor! Ingles? American? Estados Unidos? U.S.A.? Si? Yes? You are American. Am I right? You are?"

Completely stupefied, I muttered back, "Si, yes! I mean, yes I am!" At the same time, I wondered, *How did you know? Is it that obvious?* I was completely oblivious to the obvious, forgetting that I had sewn a rather gaudy American flag patch on my backpack before beginning the pilgrimage which she had undoubtedly noticed in spite of my own blatant sudden lack of self-awareness. The red, white, and blue of Old Glory was brilliantly trimmed with a shimmering gold boarder so that it contrasted starkly against the deep navy-blue hue of my pack. It practically screamed "I'm a proud American!" or, probably more apropos, "I am an American tourist!"

Then she completely stunned me with the next bit of information to come singing out of her demure smiling lips in a most perfect Oxford English voice. "If you need a place for the night, I am the hospitaler, or, perhaps as you would say, manager of the auberge across the street. Sir, I could reserve you an accommodation if you wish. Top or bottom bunk. Your choice. It is only five euros and unlike many places, that includes dinner at twenty, or, I mean, sorry, for you as an American, would be eight o'clock. But you obviously would like to go into the church now, first, I guess. Yes?"

What words do I possibly use to describe what came over me in that moment?

Seriously, this really did, actually happen.

Snapping to, after noticing that I was repeatedly standing there in the middle of the road, nodding like a bobblehead idiot, my suddenly realized random good fortune expressed itself through my own ears-wide grin and was accentuated by a resounding school-girl-like, screech-voiced, affirmation that even shocked me as I spewed it. "Yes! Yes, and yes, I would!" Then, stammering (while trying to get back under adult control and lowering the tone of voice, realizing the ridiculous spectacle I was actually creating) I continued, "Oh, and yes, I would like very much to stay at your Ave Maria Auberge, as you call it. I am very fond of the name alone. Oh, and yes, also the church. It is indeed my next desire to do, like you said, I do want to go into the church, to give thanks. Thanks to God, of course. As I have had a very blessed journey this entire day and all the prior days that led me here. I would like to go in there now."

I must have amused her more than any average hapless American pilgrim as she suddenly giggled out loud at my fumbling words, which I also animated with a rapid succession of pointing and waving arms back and forth between the auberge, myself, and the church; gesticulating as if my body language was somehow helping with a totally unnecessary need for a better translation. Her obvious amusement under control, she spoke up, "Hello, I am Carla. I will mark you in the register for tonight. Do you prefer a top or bottom bunk?"

"I'd be happy with either. Thank you. Oh, and I'm Michael. Do you need my passport to reserve the bed?"

"When you come in, after visiting the church, that will be fine. I will reserve you a comfortable place. No worry. It is nice to meet you Michael. You seem like a nice man. All the way from U.S.A.!"

Her smile melted what was left of any pretense that I might have had being in control of myself, in that moment. Then she turned nimbly, at once, with an ears-wide grin and continued her way spryly across the street toward the auberge, shouting over her shoulder, "Oh! Just walk in and find me. I'll be cooking in the kitchen. For the pilgrim's dinner tonight. Just follow your nose! You will find me."

I stood dumbfounded (and probably gaping) in the middle of the road watching her walk away toward the entrance of the auberge. Her hips swayed, tossing about the ruffled edge of her dress, declaring a distinctive purpose and audacious prominence with her every step— her swinging ponytail keeping time like a metronome—until she faded to black while passing through the open doorway of the Ave Maria Auberge.

My definite place for resurgence for the next night.

What just happened?

Then I spun around and strode decisively into the church which was consecrated to the benevolent guidance and protection of "Santo Isadore" as indicated by the tempered brass plaque at the pinnacle of the decoratively incised, hardwood trimmed, arched double doors. Passing through the entryway was like crossing the threshold of a portal into an alternate universe, a common feeling I've experienced innumerable times upon entering a Catholic or Orthodox church, especially along the Camino or in other pilgrimage sites, like Fátima.

Perhaps it is due to the interplay that all the externalities have on influencing the senses: the divergent illumination cast capriciously about by the sun's inexorable beams streaming through stained glass windows, the magnanimous statue renderings of revered angels and saints keeping their silent watch, the iconic works of sacred art adorning the walls, the tiny beeswax votive candles with their delicate flickering flame reflections pulsing off the blood-red glass of their cylindric enclosures, or that impeccably distinctive "church smell"—an amalgamation of the indolently melting bee's wax wafting about with the lingering remnant scent of burnt incense meted out of a thurible during the most recent liturgical celebration. And the quiet; the unequivocal deafening quiet, fortified within the sacred space, safely enclosed and shielded by the church's embracing, muscular, marble-clad walls. All of these vivid expressions of deep spiritual comfort were once again immediately apparent to me, and as experience has proven time and again, they are seemingly omnipresent in any Roman Catholic church, anywhere in the world. A sentiment and an entirely comforting refuge in and of itself, in the universal Church. It is the definition of the late Latin word, "Catholicus" after all.

Universal. A church for all.

There are all the captivating sensory allures, which include each of the expected specific familiarities reticent to change in the Church's tradition—universal in consistency, yet uniquely and culturally manifested by each individual parish community in their locale's contextual expression. As a patent example, there was the unpretentious wooden altar with its intricate hand carvings that reaffirmed the simple beauty and effectual toil embodied in the prevalent lifestyle of the local peasantry. It stood stoic and solidly gallant on its gated, raised marble rostrum as both the focal point and consummate purpose for the existence of this particular place of worship. The communion table, the altar, in the center of the church, a place of familial grace, cleaved to its ultimate efficacy as the most sacred place for the supreme sacrificial mercy offering. It is the exact spot where the consecration of the bread and wine into the living Body, Blood, Soul, and Divinity of Christ by dying on the cross, actually took place during every Mass.

Another invariable element of expressed Catholic devotion, were the fourteen Stations of the Cross, which were piously posted along the nave walls beginning at the cross-point of the south transept on my left, traversing back to the Port of Paradise (or main entryway), then returning back along the right-side wall. These stations are present in every Catholic church anywhere in the world. It is actually a good indicator (in case you are unsure) that you have found your way into a genuine Roman Catholic Church. The distinctively familiar thick white candle, known as the "altar light", another sure and prominently unique Catholic sign, was also evidently aflame. Quite easily seen through its clean, transparent, crystal glass tube holder.

The altar light stood, as a beacon, proclaiming the real presence of Christ, in the consecrated Eucharist steadfastly reserved inside the opulent golden tabernacle. Which, surrounded by throngs of fresh cut flower bouquets, sat ensconced upon its own smaller marble altar table positioned to the left of the main altar. With two rows of devoutly, almost worn-out kneelers purposefully arrayed before the shrine, it was obviously an oft frequented place of individual petitioned prayers by parishioners and pilgrims alike. Each of these tangible, profound expressions of faith were saliently and silently preserved inside the simple, serene, country church entrusted to Santo Isadore in the center of Santo Domingo de la Calzada. All of the intended externalities seemed to almost royally decree a liege call for my undivided attention, especially being a wayward pilgrim who was "just visiting." This particular welcoming house of faith, profoundly appealing with the unashamedly modest vassal art forms within, had a deeply spiritual invitation, which I felt was a personal call spoken here to me alone, in this place. A call to a life of humble obedience to God's providence.

"Jesus is here. Worship him now." My heart spoke.

A precariously compelling expression of the local Catholic culture was the stunningly realistic look of the (again, required) compulsory crucifix located in its typical place, conspicuously prominent, and directly adjacent to the altar. An intricately detailed, carved corpus, presenting the body of the crucified Christ, was postured atop a long, reed-like, crossed staff that resembled a shepherd's crook or bishop's crosier. It stood out precariously dauntless, due in part to the backdrop of the meekly whitewashed walls, which were predominantly bare, having only the aforementioned Stations of the Cross delineated in rudimentary symbolic representations aligned at eye-level between the long, arch-topped, stained-glass, external windows along the sides of the church. What was intriguing was that each glistening pane portrayed a different mystery of the Holy Rosary. They were especially accentuated with the sun's rays, either when rising in the east or while setting in the west, and thereby ruminated through the mosaic-clad stained-glass tincture cuts of the specialized windows which were composed of mostly reds and blues.

The permeating beams of lingering sunlight that I experienced this late in the day, coming in from the westward bank of glass, projected the amalgamated colors in precise beams seemingly afloat in the airborne dust motes before me. They resembled dancing holographic swirls of whirligigs extending down to the excessively trodden light oak floor and shiny white, caramel-swirled, marble surface ordered to surround the holy altar. A unique spectacle for anyone to behold, yet one that only I was made purvey to witness, at this precise moment in time, at this exact place of pilgrimage. Alone.

Overall, the interior was much brighter than what would be expected, mostly due to the immense, smoked-beige, glass, and somewhat provoking, onion dome span that dominated the towering steeple rise located directly above the altar. The sun was still high enough in the firmament to vibrantly shine through it and cast a spotlight effect on the altar proper. Its radiance, then normally white-light brilliance, changed abruptly, because of the glass quality, and diffused into only the first few rows of the polished smooth, dark-wooden, utilitarian pews. It created an eerie, yet enrapturing, calloused luminous effect. It almost alerted one to sit in the first few, illuminated pews just to appreciate the very conspicuous, rainbow-like, transitional light show currently being displayed, entirely without the need for any electronic, artificial, special effects. It was a totally natural, light-emphasized, call from God.

Hello.

Complying to an invigorating, innate sense of suddenly realized inspiration, I perceptually made my way down the center aisle, that led to the low altar rail. It too, highlighted by the rays, led to the naturally provided guarded circumference along the main altar rise, complete with its traditional narrow line of kneelers. I realized that this very place is where the faithful would reverently position themselves to receive Holy Communion during Mass. I noticed that there were only a few conventional overhead lights turned on along the stout transepts, due probably to the day's prevailing sunlight. These were obviously quite modern with their space capsule-like conical shapes, and precisely pointed beams. Perhaps they were a reticent improvement along with the obviously miniature, and overtly modern, Bose brand speaker sticks, inconspicuously and strategically deployed throughout the church—both renovations disturbingly anachronistic in the centuries-old, stalwart house of worship. Yet, somehow, they were pleasantly welcome by the modern pilgrim—like me.

When my slow, staggered, sauntering survey of the sacred surroundings eventually led me to the front-most pew before the altar, I acquiesced to tradition, turning timorously toward the relic, blessed sacrament tabernacle that towered to the left, and genuflected— gesturing my obsequious reverential and conscious acknowledgement, as well as my servile devotion, to the Real Presence of Jesus Christ in the Most Holy Eucharist. I, as a Catholic, believe that Jesus Himself, was then and there dwelling within the hallowed rampart.

There I was. Alone in this magnificent church. Somewhere in the middle of Spain. On Pilgrimage. Alone with Jesus Christ himself. Imagine that.

I slid my waning backpack off my shoulder onto the pew beside me as I sat there and began to thoroughly appreciate the holy presence that was so engulfing and evident in every inch of space around and within me. Including the air. Yes, even my breathing, each breath, felt holy here.

After fully enjoying a few meditative moments of the complete silence, I began to scan the walls around me, starting just left of the tabernacle, and settling on the first few Stations of the Cross. They were simple, intentionally abstruse and symbolic, ovately shaped, overly common, two-toned painted, hand-carved plaster pieces. Lofty simple works of sacred art.

A conch shell, with water pouring from it onto a pair of cupped hands, had only the Roman numeral "I" under it denoting the first station where "Pilate Condemns Jesus." Next, along the wall to the left, was the likeness of a hand gripping the junction of a cross with the Roman numeral "II," the second station where "Jesus Receives His Cross." Then a bent knee, "Jesus Falls the First Time," the third station denoted by "III." And on they went. I advanced my gaze upon each station, stopping briefly to consider the relationship of Christ's sacrificial plight to my own current journey in life, my pilgrimage, progressively traversing visually along the entire left wall and returning back down the wall to my right. Each stop delineated a simple somber exemplification of Christ's impassioned suffering on the way to Calvary, leading to His crucifixion and death. All of which led me finally to the focus of the last image. A large circular stone with the Roman numeral "XIV" beneath signified the fourteenth and final station where "Jesus is Laid in the Tomb."

Jesus Christ's passion along with the exquisite and artistically displayed *Way of the Cross* leading to His death and eventual resurrection was made obviously and immediately prevalent before me. That prominent depiction, in this humble little church, was entirely, in essence, my sole reason for existence. I spontaneously wept with both incursions of joy and remorse.

Really. (I was also very glad that I was still alone.)

Having regained composure and reconnoitered the circumfluent walls of the church, my gaze reached the right side of the main altar where stood another small shrine to complement the Eucharistic adoration tabernacle on the left. This one also had a small marble altar table, but was accentuated with a candle encased in a royal blue glass cylinder hovering over it. It was suspended by a shiny brass chain, looped along an extension arm and linked to the top of the elaborate latticework behind. The reredos supported numerous flower-filled decorative vases seeming to float on indiscernible glass shelves.

On a Doric pillar stand, positioned next to the mini-altar, was an exquisite statue of the Blessed Virgin Mary. She was dramatically portrayed as Our Lady of Fátima wontedly distinguished by her pure white robe trimmed in gold, while wearing a bulbous, cross-topped crown, sprinkled with jewels. A glistening pearl rosary and the brown scapular of Our Lady of Mount Carmel was draped all along the front of her robe. The beads were laced between her thumbs and the tender fingers within her hands, enjoined together in a steepled praying gesture demurely positioned over her heart. There could be no doubt. This church was duly dedicated to the benevolence of Our Lady of Fátima.

The providential collision of circumstances that had guided me to now behold my personal favorite of myriad depictions of the Holy Virgin Mother, located in such a remote and random happenstance, created an overwhelming burst of joy in my heart. Immediately, I felt compelled to express my grateful appreciation by devoutly and elatedly invoking the Ave Maria aloud: "Hail Mary full of grace, the Lord is with Thee. Blessed are you among women, and blessed is the fruit of your womb, Jesus. Holy Mary, Mother of God, pray for us sinners, now and at the hour of our death. Amen."

After the prayer, and once again taking in all of the church's walled surfaces and prominent constructs, my eyes finally settled on the most intriguing walled altar piece of artwork that I have ever seen. The colossal painting had me at once fascinated and mesmerized by both its peculiar portrayal and strikingly captivating subjects. I rose from my seat and slowly walked trance-like onto the altar until I was a mere two meters away—all the while my gaze firmly affixed to it, completely powerless to look away.

The meticulously detailed, expertly brushed, predominantly earthen-toned, oil painting depicted an aging farmer as he was driving a plow. The scuffing effect of many monotonous years of relentless hard labor were evident by both his over-worn togs of turbid, traditional, black woolen peasant garb and the calloused accents on his forlorn body, particularly noticeable on his distended, thick hands. His tattered leather vest was securely holstering a long pair of support beams linking him harmoniously to a compound yoke that harnessed four brawny, brown oxen as they doggedly teamed along with their tenaciously toiling task. Five beasts of burden synchronized as one metamorphic, mechanized cultivator—fully engaged in their charge.

All the facial expressions of both the man and the beasts revealed only placid determination as they navigated the rusty tempered steel blade of the tiller as it carved a long, plumb, furrowed channel in the fertile earth. Like the ocean surface being cut by the bow of an overtly seaworthy ship, it left two opposing waves of dirt in its wake, all the while creating a miniature valley of a moist soil darkness between. I recalled in Saint Luke's gospel, chapter eight, the parable told by Jesus, of the sower, comparing the moist, good soil awaiting the seeds of the crop, as the most perfect disposition of faith. The farmer was preparing the soil for seeding. The abundantly new planting of life about to be sown into the face of spring.

The stunning, solitary work of art on the time-worn wall behind the altar was entitled: "Santo Isadore Grunjero" (Saint Isadore the Farmer) and was deftly indicated by the imperfect, freehand, scripted words written on a placard set just below the iconic image. It also stated: "Artisto Desconocido" (Artist Unknown). Obviously, the altar piece was positioned where it was to honor the venerable image and likeness of the consecrated church's namesake.

The custom sized, tubular, honey-yellow diffused up-light positioned just under the bottom of the frame, always aflame, imparted a surreal glowing aura to the farmland pictured under the farmer Isadore's feet. The burnt sienna effect manifestly highlighted the working crew encompassing the right two-thirds of the piece. Compellingly, my eyes were initially drawn to that impoverished ensemble as the main subject, and was keenly focused on the man (Saint Isadore) in particular.

Then, almost simultaneously, I became captivated by the startling image filling the left third of the painting. There was, equally astounding, a second plowing gang, leading the main subject positioned ahead, and slightly up to the left. That team was juxtaposed as a stark contrast. Like an inverse pervasive shadow. Their impressive group slogged a complimentary team of four oxen, gleaming immaculately white—pristine, in spite of the grimy task in which they were engaged. Behind them was not one, but instead two drivers, working side-by-side. They were without cumbersome vests or heavy wooden poles lashed to a yoke. Instead, they clasped austere, thin, loosely bound leather reins, both having considerable slack, and each driver was using only one of their velvety soft, smooth-skinned, slender hands to administer control.

It was as if the gesture of cowing their snowy, sanguine, servile brutes were a meager formality. Completely devoid of any concerted effort. The need to somehow bridal the beasts, was entirely unnecessary. The twin drivers were obviously angels, classically depicted with pious facial expressions, flowing white robes, with long, wavy blonde locks, and mighty majestic wings. For the unknown artist to have included halos would have been overkill.

At last, I noticed that yet still, each of the angels held a mattock along their respective extended arms, clasped in the right hand. Their rust-colored blades mockingly dragged behind, gently caressing the soil into two troughs that were precisely identical to Isadore's, so that their combination of tills equaled a total of three undulated channels being carved into God's good green earth. While Isadore painstakingly worked in the field by the sweat of his brow (as the Genesis cure deemed necessary), the angels were assisting him effortlessly, accomplishing two-fold his results due to their allied, divine, holy oxen provided, assistance. Understanding the angels and their team to actually be invisible (though palpably apparent in the painting), they elucidated the saint's renowned ability to produce three times a much harvest bounty than any other "normal" mortal could—an overt Trinitarian association alluding to God's loving presence and blessing upon Isadore for his steadfast humble labor offered as his daily personal prayer in faithful loving service.

I would later learn that the curious painting precisely portrayed what tradition had already recanted numerous times through the ages regarding a certain Isadore the Farmer and his seemingly miraculous level of production in the fields throughout the rich agricultural La Rioja region of Spain at the turn of the twelfth century. Indeed, it was historically and biographically most commonly said of him, "It is as if he does the work of three instead of just one." Again, a trinitarian reference to Isadore's insipid divine assistance. He became increasingly well-known and revered, throughout Spain especially, and was canonized a saint in 1622—the patron of Madrid and, of course, farmers.

The sudden shattering echo of the church's bells abruptly startled me back from my comforting contemplative posture. The eight universally familiar tones signaled the bottom of the hour as they droned their punctual watch over time's passing. Fully aware and that it was time to move on after just one more prayer, I was also inspired to offer the prayer of Saint Gertrude the Great for the souls in Purgatory. It would be the best way to conclude my visit. Saint Gertrude the Great was a medieval nun who lived at the turn of the fourteenth century and who also was a renowned mystic. She had a vision of the Lord Jesus who showed her that a particular prayer (which has since become known as the prayer of Saint Gertrude the Great) would release a vast number of souls from Purgatory, each time that it was reverently recited.

Dropping to my knees, I recollected the prayer entrusted to us from Christ through Saint Gertrude: *Eternal Father, I offer Thee the most Precious Blood of Thy Divine Son, Jesus, in union with all the Masses said throughout the world today for all the Holy Souls in Purgatory, and also for all the sinners within my own household and among my own family.*

It was the most appropriate way to end my day of traveling the Camino before my evening stay at the Ave Maria Auberge. As I was about to grab my backpack to leave, I suddenly felt compelled to take out my copy of *The Spiritual Exercises of Saint Ignatius Loyola* that I had used to start my day. I turned to the last page in the book where Ignatius wrote what has become the Jesuit motto and took the words to be my final farewell, saying aloud such that my voice echoed off the church walls: "Ad Majorem Dei Gloriam." All for the greater glory of God.

Acknowledgements

This is a collection of fictional short stories. Some may even have an autobiographical nature. The goal has been to seamlessly merge the autobiographical and fictive elements of some of the short stories to interest any reader. The characters and circumstances are fictional but may still illustrate interactions with people and events that have been encountered in the abounding actual experiences of the author's life. One example of this is the emphasis on Polish heritage which figures prominently throughout several stories in the book. Another is using locations and settings that are notably familiar such as Manchester, Connecticut, Cape Cod, San Diego, and La Jolla.

This is ultimately a work of fiction, so names, characters, businesses, places, events, locales, and incidents are either the products of the author's imagination or are used in a fictitious manner. Any resemblance to actual persons, living or dead, or actual events is purely coincidental.

In a project such as this, there are certain specific people to thank for their input and critical contributions whether it be through proof editing, sampling chapters or simply moral support. Some need to be named explicitly.

A deep heartfelt thank you goes to my amazing wife Shea Lynn. For her undying support on all fronts over these past months of editing and reediting and for putting up with me as I have isolated to complete the work. She is first and foremost my true impetus in bringing this project to fruition.

Special thanks to Diane Malloy and all the members of the Pen to Paper writing group in La Jolla who have met with me on a weekly basis to share your writing abilities, creativity, and captivating stories over the past three years. It is with your group that the vast majority of the prompts and writing of these stories originated. You have aided in sharpening my skills and been a true inspiration to forge ahead. I have been honored to write along-side all of you.

To all the folks at Workbook Press who have diligently guided and supported my efforts to bring this work to publication. For all your attention to the finer details in getting me through the process especially, I am grateful.

Finally, and most importantly, thanks be to God. It is through God's grace that I have been blessed with the opportunity and the faculties to author and complete this work at all.